"Talk to me, Marina,"

he said forcefully. "I need to know."

She nodded, still not meeting his eyes.

"I don't know what to tell you," she said at last. "I don't know what I'm afraid of," she whispered suddenly. "I only know that lately, it's felt like someone's been watching me. Except when I turn around, no one's there."

Cagney's frown deepened. "Did you feel this 'sensation' on the night of the murder?" he asked sharply.

She nodded her head.

"Out here in the lot?"

Once again she nodded.

"Then why are you here now, Marina?"

She hesitated. "Because it's worse at home," she said simply.

Dear Reader,

Once again, we've got an irresistible month of reading coming your way. One look at our lead title will be all you need to know what I'm talking about. Of course I'm referring to *The Heart of Devin MacKade,* by award-winning, *New York Times* bestselling author Nora Roberts. This is the third installment of her family-oriented miniseries, "The MacKade Brothers," which moves back and forth between Silhouette Intimate Moments and Silhouette Special Edition. Enjoy every word of it!

Next up, begin a new miniseries from another award winner, Justine Davis. "Trinity Street West" leads off with the story of Quisto Romero in *Lover Under Cover.* You'll remember Quisto from *One Last Chance,* and you'll be glad to know that not only does he find a love of his own this time around, he introduces you to a whole cast of characters to follow through the rest of this terrific series. Two more miniseries are represented this month, as well: *The Quiet One* is the latest in Alicia Scott's "The Guiness Gang," while Cathryn Clare's "Assignment: Romance" begins with *The Wedding Assignment.* And don't forget Lee Magner's *Dangerous* and Sally Tyler Hayes' *Homecoming,* which round out the month with more of the compellingly emotional stories you've come to expect from us.

Enjoy them all—and come back next month for more excitingly romantic reading, here at Silhouette Intimate Moments.

Yours,

Leslie Wainger
Senior Editor and Editorial Coordinator

Please address questions and book requests to:
Silhouette Reader Service
U.S.: 3010 Walden Ave., P.O. Box 1325, Buffalo, NY 14269
Canadian: P.O. Box 609, Fort Erie, Ont. L2A 5X3

THE QUIET ONE

ALICIA SCOTT

Published by Silhouette Books

America's Publisher of Contemporary Romance

SILHOUETTE BOOKS

ISBN 0-373-07701-7

THE QUIET ONE

Books by Alicia Scott

Silhouette Intimate Moments

Walking After Midnight #466
Shadow's Flame #546
Waking Nightmare #586
*At the Midnight Hour #658
*Hiding Jessica #668
*The Quiet One #701

*The Guiness Gang

ALICIA SCOTT

recently escaped the corporate world to pursue her writing full-time. According to the former consultant, "I've been a writer for as long as I can remember. For me, it's the perfect job and you can't beat the dress code." Born in Hawaii, she grew up in Oregon before moving to Massachusetts. Now an avid traveler, she spends her time chasing after two feisty felines, watching Val Kilmer movies and eating chocolate when she's not running around the globe.

She is currently at work on her latest project in Boston, where she awaits the discovery of true love or ownership of a chocolate shop—whichever comes first.

To my agent, Damaris Rowland. First, because her insightful comments truly improved this book, and second, because she's a fabulous agent. Here's to the start of a beautiful relationship.

Prologue

Maddensfield, North Carolina
1971

They found the dog first.

Years later, both men would talk about the dog—if they talked about that day at all. The dog was horrible enough. What had happened to the woman was beyond comprehension.

"Sweet Jesus," Roy breathed when the German shepherd came into sight. He pushed back the cowboy hat on his head, his hand automatically coming to rest on his left shoulder and covering the dull sheriff's badge on his chest. Mike Johnson, his deputy of two years, didn't say anything. Instead the twenty-three-year-old crossed himself.

"We best go inside," Roy said at last, half nodding toward the house. He couldn't quite take his eyes off the German shepherd, though.

Good old Lobo. Hell, Roy remembered when Sarita had first gotten the shepherd as a pup from Lloyd. She'd said the dog made her feel better, living alone the way she did. Grew into a big dog, too. One hundred fifty pounds of well-toned muscle and purebred flesh. Lloyd bought only the best.

'Course, you couldn't tell to look at the dog now.

Roy forced his eyes back to the house. Sarita... And what about little Kristi?

Beads of sweat popped out on his brow as he stared at the mangled screen on the sliding-glass door. No sound came from the tiny two-room rancher, just the faint drone of flies.

"We best get to the house," he said again.

Mike nodded, but didn't meet Roy's eyes.

When Big Gloria had called the sheriff's office thirty minutes ago, Roy had been concerned but not worried. Sarita hadn't shown up for her waitressing shift at Gloria's Diner—which was unusual, given her reliable nature and the fact that she needed the money. That Gloria could only get a busy signal at Sarita's home was also strange. But this was Maddensfield. Other than the occasional bar fight and mill accident, nothing much happened here.

Roy and Mike had come out expecting to find Sarita home with a sick baby, maybe even Sarita down with the flu. Roy figured it would be more like a neighborly call, folks looking after folks. And he liked Sarita. She always had a smile and she'd even invited him over for dinner a few times. People talked about her, having a kid out of wedlock like that. But Roy didn't think she was fast or loose. She struck him as a serious girl, a good mother.

Someone who deserved more than she'd gotten.

He glanced back at the ripped screen door and shook his head.

"Sweet Jesus," he whispered.

They walked slowly, Roy's hand on the gun he already knew he wouldn't need. He peeled back the flapping screen gingerly, moving aside until the hot June sun could flood the tiny house with light.

"My God."

Roy had to look away this time. The sweat rolling down his shirt had nothing to do with the North Carolina heat and humidity. It had nothing to do with the buzzing of the flies or the insistent hum of the mosquitoes. He had to look away, and even then he thought he might be sick.

Mike couldn't move at all. He stood there rigid, his eyes glued to the scene as they turned desperate with the horror.

"We've got a job to do, boy," Roy reminded him at last. "She was a good woman. Remember that."

Slowly Mike nodded, his brown eyes still agonized.

They moved into the house.

They had to walk carefully, not wanting to disturb the chaos that told the story. They avoided the body at first—there was no need to check for a pulse. Instead they followed the trail of destruction back to the bedroom.

"He found her here," Roy said. "Seems she put up a good fight, though."

With a light touch, he picked up the worn white cotton sheet, the only cover that would be necessary in this heat. It was sliced to ribbons.

"She threw it over him," he guessed out loud. Good girl, Sarita. "Must have taken him a bit to hack clear of it. In the meantime, she ran around the bed to the doorway."

They stepped out of the tiny bedroom into the hall. The bloodstain on the wall revealed where the intruder had caught her the first time.

"Stabbed her once," Roy said, "but she got away."

Left, down the hall, toward the living room, where they had entered. She'd made it to the phone in the kitchen, immediately to the right. The receiver dangled limply from its cord on the wall.

In the kitchen a drawer had been pulled halfway out. Roy peered in to see a collection of silverware, including knives. Another bloodstain indicated the intruder had stabbed her again before she'd had a chance to access the possible weapons.

But Sarita hadn't gone down in the kitchen, either. Somehow she'd still managed to get away.

Into the living room.

Broken china now crunched at their feet, a mangled glass buffet revealing where Sarita had found her ammunition. Roy knew the china. She'd inherited it from her mother when the woman had died of cancer a year before. It had been her only inheritance—china passed down for four generations from mother to daughter, a living memory of the days when the Bastíno name bespoke Spanish wealth. Until last night.

A glass decanter had shattered against one wall. Then a lamp. Even sofa pillows had been thrown. She'd been running and fighting, heading toward the screen door and the relative security of the night.

Maddensfield wasn't that big. Maybe if she'd made it outside, maybe if she'd screamed loud enough, Sarita would have survived the night.

Instead she'd died in her living room, overcome once more by the intruder and his brutal knife. Roy had to look away again, but that didn't keep the image from his mind.

Sarita Davis, the quiet twenty-two-year-old waitress who'd borne a child out of wedlock just a year and a half ago. Folks had been shocked, shunning the girl. But she'd kept her head up and her shoulders straight, a true tribute to her Spanish heritage. She'd done what she could to eke out a living for herself and her daughter. In time, with her quiet persistence—not to mention Lloyd's endorsement— she'd begun to make progress.

Roy had always liked Sarita. He still remembered eating apple pie and drinking black coffee from her delicate white china.

"There's just one thing I don't understand," Mike said at last, his voice thick as his young Adam's apple bobbed. "Why did she try for the screen door so far away? What not go out the back door? It was so much closer." He paused, swallowing heavily as his head came down. "Panic, I suppose."

Roy shook his head. "No, son," he said quietly, his voice suddenly hoarse. "Sarita had her reasons, all right."

He turned on his heels and headed back down the dark hall. After a moment, Mike followed.

At the end of the hall, the back door beckoned, small streams of light threading through the blinds. For the first time, Mike saw the door on the right-hand side.

As he watched, Roy took a deep breath and opened it.

Roy had expected to see more chaos. He'd expected blood and ravages and sights a man should never have to see.

He hadn't expected to see the eighteen-month-old child standing in her crib, wide eyed and silent. "Kristi," he whispered. At his side, Mike once more crossed himself.

She had to hold on to the rails to keep standing, but she didn't make a sound as the two men entered the room. Her large eyes, just beginning to darken from a baby's natural blue, followed their progression. And Roy saw that part of her hair, the black tousled silk so much like her mother's, had gone gray. He reached down for her, and without even a whimper, she let him pick her up.

"It's all right, Kristi," Roy said, soothing her thick black-and-gray hair. "Hush, sweetheart. It's all right now."

But there was no need for the reassurance. The baby Sarita had been protecting until her last breath didn't cry. Instead it was Roy who felt his throat tighten, Roy who felt the tears prickle his wrinkled eyes.

He hugged the baby tighter than necessary, but even then she didn't whimper. He turned and carried her out the back door into the sun. At the car, Mike picked up the radio and called for the State Bureau of Investigations (SBI). Roy simply stood there under the bright June sky, holding the baby in his arms.

For a long time, he looked at her and he thought he could see the whole thing. Sarita abruptly awakened by the stranger in her room. Her first thought, after the panic jumped into her throat, being for her child. Her desperate race to the living room, trying to lead the beast away. Side-tracking him with her quiet fight, hoping beyond hope that Kristi wouldn't waken, that Kristi wouldn't cry.

Until she'd gone down in the living room, fighting for her life and her baby's.

Roy felt the tears stream down his dry, leathery cheeks; he didn't even try to wipe them away. Instead he met the silent gaze of the baby, who looked at him with emptiness in her eyes.

She'd left them, he realized suddenly. Retreated to some inner place where there wasn't the desperate sound of heirloom china crashing to the floor or the dull thud of a serrated blade hitting home. Little Kristi had left it all behind. Seeing her dull gaze, Roy felt the tears stream a little harder.

The distant sound of sirens filled the air. He turned back to the cruiser and noticed Mike sitting like a drugged man in the front seat.

"They'll be here soon," Roy said to no one in particular. "They'll take care of everything."

Neither Mike nor Kristi replied.

The State police, however, never did figure out what had happened to Sarita Davis that last dark night. Kristi was adopted and spirited away to another state. The manhunts droned on. The years came and went, season rolled into season, and eventually folks stopped locking their doors again and daughters were allowed back out on dates.

Slowly but surely, Maddensfield returned to normal. Roy retired as sheriff, and spent his days taking long hikes in the cool hills. Mike Johnson married, and over time learned how to keep from jolting awake with a scream on his lips.

And the baby, Kristi, was never seen nor heard from again.

Until twenty-five years later, when death came to Maddensfield once more.

Chapter 1

"Damn."

He muttered the word gravely, but that didn't stop the phone's insistent ringing. With a sigh of frustration, Cagney rolled over in his narrow, lumpy bed. The phone *would* ring during his one rare night of dreamless slumber. He picked up the receiver with barely restrained frustration.

"What?" he barked, staring up at the dark ceiling.

"Sheriff, sir?" came Andersen's voice, young and eager. Cagney felt the frustration increase tenfold. Andersen. He should have known. The new nineteen-year-old deputy had enrolled the day he'd received his GED in the mail, and was as green as a sapling.

Cage's voice was much sharper than necessary. His leg was bothering him again, and the hot, humid June weather made sleep challenging enough already.

"Look, son," he found himself saying, "I told you not to bother me unless it was important. Now, if Mrs. Browning called about her cat again, I'm telling you, you just go to the tree, open a can of tuna, and Lester will climb right down to you. Hell, the cat trees himself now 'cause he likes the food. Which you might want to mention to Mrs. Browning again, though God knows the woman hasn't listened to any of us for the past fifty years.''

"It's not Lester, sir," Andersen assured him. "I remember what you said about how to handle him."

For the first time, Cage frowned. He looked at his watch, seeing the glowing dial of 3:42 a.m. Maddensfield wasn't that exciting a place, which was exactly why he'd agreed to take over the position of Maddensfield County sheriff one year ago. He oversaw the towns of Maddensfield, Marion and Maynerd, and the three of them combined generally saw twenty-one domestic disputes, fifteen drunken brawls, two mill-related injuries and one hunting accident a year. That was it.

The one exception had been four years ago, when Cagney's own brother-in-law had been caught in the cross fire of a bank robbery shoot-out. Nick had died in Liz's arms outside the Main Street matinee. But even then, the criminals had been caught and nothing like it had happened since. In short, there was very little to wake up a man at nearly four in the morning.

"What is it?" Cage said, his voice suddenly alert, the North Carolina accent fading until he almost sounded like the D.C. detective he'd been just thirteen months earlier. Then he'd gotten lots of calls at four in the morning.

"A code—" Cagney could hear the sound of flipping paper "—a code 187, sir!" Andersen declared triumphantly. "At least, I think so!"

"Code 187?" Cagney repeated dumbly, even as his mind automatically filled in the blanks of the Maddensfield County code.

"A homicide, sir. At, least we think it's a homicide. It sounds like a homicide."

For one moment, Cage felt his body go rigid as something deep and inarticulate shuddered through him. Time seemed to slip out of synch, and eight years of D.C. cop instinct took over. He found himself automatically reaching for his gun and a pair of slacks, before he remembered he didn't wear either anymore.

"Where?" he asked softly, balancing the phone between his chin and his shoulder while his hands found the worn fabric of his jeans on the floor.

"East side," Andersen replied eagerly. "After the railroad tracks by the old general station. Someone said they found a woman's body, knifed. Can I go, too?"

In the darkness, Cagney winced at the eagerness in the boy's voice. In a nineteen-year-old's world, murder seemed an exciting prospect. As a man, he would realize the true toll. The way Cagney did. Still, the Maddensfield sheriff's office didn't have the resources for a homicide. He would need all the help he could get.

"All right," he said into the phone, already tugging on his boots. "Call Davey, too, and bring the patrol car. If you get there first, secure the area with crime tape and don't touch anything. And I mean that, Andersen. Don't touch one damn thing."

"Right, sir. Got it. Andersen out."

The boy hung up with a sudden burst of seriousness, but Cage put down the receiver much slower, his gray eyes suddenly bleak and uncertain in the darkness. He rose, bare chested and sweaty in the humid night. For one moment, his gaze turned to the locked trunk at the foot of the bed. The .357 Magnum still resided there, along with a badge he hadn't looked at since he'd returned to Maddensfield. With a sudden darkening of his eyes, he turned away and reached for his shirt, instead.

His shoulders squared, he set his hat on his head. He wouldn't take the gun. The sheriff's star on his shirt was mockery enough.

She whirled around for the third time, her dark eyes searching the night hovering just beyond the light of her strategically placed lanterns. Once more, she saw nothing. She bit off the low curse of frustration that rose to her lips, and turned back to the wall.

It was the heat, she told herself. The mid-June scorcher was killing them all. She could feel the humidity in the heavy pull of her long, tumbling hair and the clinging feel of her light T-shirt. She half expected the paint to sizzle as she stroked it across the huge cement wall of the abandoned building.

But even as she focused once again on the golden stirrups of the rearing destrier, she could feel the darkness creeping up her spine.

Marina forced her shoulders straight and concentrated on the brilliant colors and vibrant life of her mural. There was nothing dark about the painting. It celebrated life and fantasy and romance. It blazed out like a spark of vitality in a poor, rundown neighborhood that needed the injection of color. She'd been working on it for a month now, practically splattering the paint across the wall in her thirst for zest and vivacity. After five years of limiting her artistic talent to computer graphics and trifold brochures, the challenge and scope thrilled her.

So far, she was happy with her progress. In the middle of the emerging market scene, a splashing fountain burst to life, the water so blue and bubbly it made her thirsty just to look at it. Red and yellow tulips bordered the cobblestone floor of the market, and bit by bit, exotic animals and vendors were beginning to appear. To the left, an Indian hawked fine woven rugs from Mexico. Behind the Indian, a Gypsy read the palm of a beautiful, blond princess.

And now, a white-blazed stallion reared to glorious life in the right-hand corner. She was putting on the finishing touches to the intricate gold-and-jeweled stirrups. Tomorrow night, she thought she might do a full-blown peacock strutting under the horse's hooves.

Tomorrow night. She shivered once more, then cursed herself for her weakness.

This wasn't New York anymore, dammit. This was Maddensfield, North Carolina, and the real-estate agent had assured her just two months ago that bad things didn't happen here. At the time the move had seemed the perfect solution for her. She'd wanted to escape the concrete prison of Manhattan. She'd wanted to live someplace where her nocturnal habits weren't limited by the crime statistics she saw every night in the newspaper. She wanted to live someplace simple and warm, where the darkness would seem even farther away. And she'd never have to recall that last look on Bradley's face.

But now, for the past week, she'd felt the dread creep up. First, just a strange nervousness as she set up her ladder for the night's work. Then, the creepy sensation that she was no longer alone. Even tonight she'd whirled around three times, only to see the darkness of the hot June night.

The brush in her hand trembled slightly, and she cursed herself once more. She'd come too far, fought too long, to jump at shadows now. She knew who she was, and she knew her limits. She'd stuck to her routine and the strange sleeping schedule that had brought her peace for the past thirteen years. She refused to fall back into the paralyzing fear. She refused to have the nightmares, and she refused to doubt her own mind.

There was nothing out there in the darkness. Nothing at all. Her eyes told her so, and she would believe them.

"Ma'am?"

Her hand jerked, a golden line of paint smearing into the rich brown of the stallion. For one long minute she stilled and fought to keep her heart from leaping out of her chest. But when she finally turned, each and every muscle rigid, she knew the fear was still visible in her eyes.

"Sorry to startle you," the low, deep voice said again.

As she watched, the stranger stepped forward until the golden glow of his sheriff's star winked in the lantern light.

"Sheriff Guiness," he said by way of introduction.

Relief hit her with such intensity she almost sagged against the freshly painted wall.

"Oh, shoot!" she suddenly exclaimed. With the relief also came the realization that she'd just smeared her horse. She whirled back around just as quickly and dabbed earnestly at the damage.

From across the lot, Cage watched the frenzy of activity and frowned.

From his vantage point he could make out the shiny mane of black hair tumbling down her back as she rushed to repair the paint streak. She wore a white T-shirt, tied just below her breasts to leave her back bare and vulnerable every time her hair swayed with her movements. Her faded blue skirt hung low at her hips and was splattered with so many shades of bright colors it appeared an art work in and of itself. Under the swaying folds of the skirt, brown legs curved to delicate ankles and bare feet.

She looked wild and graceful and much too slender to have created such power as the horse plunging above her head.

So this was the "paint lady." A local at the crime scene had said they should go talk to her, describing her as a bright-colored fairy, but she struck Cage as more of a witch. She had thickly lashed eyes that revealed a sultry darkness when they'd swept up to meet his gaze. And her bare arms were lean and strong, the kind that could pull down a man's head and show him a thing or two about good loving.

If a man was looking for that kind of thing.

His eyes carefully dispassionate, Cage took a step toward her. He'd walked the four blocks from the crime scene just to find her. The few residents who'd appeared at the scene claimed not to have seen anything. Finally, one man had pointed down the street.

"The paint lady," he'd said.

"The paint lady?"

"Sí. She works on the wall. All night, she paints."

Even having seen the wall himself just two weeks ago, Cage had a hard time believing the man. Who painted all night long? But now, gazing at the woman before him, it did indeed appear true. The real question was, what did she know about the murder just four blocks from here?

"Ma'am," he said again, keeping his voice steady. Her relentless movement slowed a fraction. She appeared to have repaired most of the damage. "I need to ask you a few questions," he said levelly.

Marina half nodded, pulling herself back around until she faced him once more. Given how jittery she'd been lately, maybe she should be glad the sheriff had come to check up on her. Even from across the lot, he seemed like a capable man. He had that lean, rangy build of a cowboy, and that soft Southern drawl she still found so intriguing. And his eyes—deep, steady eyes. You could tell a lot about a person from his eyes. If she'd trusted that observation sooner, she might have saved herself a lot of grief with Bradley.

"Is, is everything all right?" she asked finally. He was eyeing her with a steady gray gaze that didn't give anything away.

"No, ma'am," he said finally, his voice grave.

For the first time, her brief euphoria faded. The man before her wasn't smiling; nor was he looking at her in a hospitable way. No, he appeared grim and serious, one hundred percent business.

Slowly but surely, she felt the dread wrap itself around her spine. She took a deep breath and forced herself to keep her head up. She wasn't a scared child anymore. She was a strong woman who'd fought long and hard to be standing here in an abandoned lot at five a.m. Her hand trembled only slightly when she brought the brush down to her side.

"You've been here all night?" he asked quietly.

"Since twelve."

"Do you always paint?" he asked slowly, watching her relax by degrees. She wasn't from around here; he could tell by the flat, northern tones of her voice. Beneath that sultry beauty, she appeared intelligent and composed.

"Yes. Every night."

He walked toward her, and for the first time, she noticed his limp. Her gaze went to his leg, and when it came back up, she saw the knowing look in his eyes. He kept walking, his legs long and muscular as he covered the distance between them. When he finally stopped before her,

she could see the true breadth of his shoulders and the
corded strength of his exposed forearms.

Something low and hot uncurled in her stomach, catching her by surprise. The heat spell, she told herself vaguely.
Damn if this June didn't kill them all.

"You being paid for this?"

She shook her head. "I just like to paint—" she shrugged
"—and no one else seemed to be using the wall for anything constructive."

"It certainly brightens up the neighborhood."

She acknowledged the compliment with a small nod, the
slightest flush of color coming to her cheeks. "Everyone's
entitled to color and beauty. Regardless of income."

"Where are you from, Miss—"

"Walden. Marina Walden."

He continued to watch her until she answered the rest of
the question in a rush.

"New York. I'm from New York."

"Been living here long?"

"Two months."

"Maddensfield is quite a change from New York."

"Yes, it is."

"Did you paint walls in New York, too?"

"What is it you want?" The question was softly challenging, and she enforced it with an upward tilt of her chin,
a darkening of her eyes. She knew his presence had little to
do with polite chit-chat, and in a matter of time, the true
questions would come.

Like what was out there in the darkness?

"Did you hear anything tonight?" he asked her with
measuring eyes. "A car? The sounds of a struggle? A
scream?"

She stiffened, feeling the fear strike low. A shadow
moved in the back of her mind, the faint feeling of terror
pressing against her subconscious. She steeled herself
against it, but all of a sudden, she was grateful for this
man's steady presence.

Slowly she shook her head.

Cage watched the movement, noted the way her hair tumbled wild around her face when she did it. For the first time, he noticed the thin streak of gray hair tracing the left side of her face. It looked like a white ribbon tossed amid a stormy sea. And it highlighted the shadow of fear passing through her dark-violet eyes.

He leaned slightly closer, refusing to relent. "Not even the sound of footsteps?"

"What happened?" she said suddenly. "Just tell me what happened." There was an urgency in her voice she hadn't intended. A need to know, when somehow she thought she might already have the information. And when he finally told her what dark thing had brought a sheriff out in Maddensfield at five in the morning, she wouldn't feel surprise, but only a strange sense of déjà vu.

"There's been a murder."

Her eyes grew round. She'd been wrong; the shock was genuine.

"But this is Maddensfield!" she exclaimed.

He almost smiled, a crooked, knowing smile. Hadn't that been his reaction just over an hour ago?

"I know," Cage said levelly. "But I'm afraid it's true. Just four blocks from here. And you're telling me you didn't see or hear anything? You want to try this again?"

For one small moment she actually hesitated, then realized he noted it as reluctance. What in the world was she thinking? She hadn't seen anything; she hadn't heard anything. It was just that the past few nights...

The thought that she wasn't alone. The thought that something else was out there in the darkness. Something thick and something evil. Something she knew...

She pushed the thoughts away, barely restraining the desire to wrap her arms protectively around her middle. She took a deep breath and forced herself to think of colors and lights and life. She hadn't seen anything; she hadn't heard anything. Her five senses told her nothing existed beyond her and this man in this night, and that's what was important. She certainly wasn't going to tell him about her fickle mind. What if he ever learned about her past? What would he say then?

Loony tune, crazy, bats in the belfry, lights on but nobody home...

Unconsciously her lips curved up into a wry smile. Bradley had been more instructive than she'd ever imagined.

"I didn't see anything," she told him clearly, punctuating the words with a slight nod.

Cage, however, had been watching her face too closely.

"Liar," he challenged softly.

She stiffened immediately, her violet eyes growing dark and serious. She stood slightly straighter, her lean, sensuous build nearly meeting his shoulder.

"I don't lie," she countered steadily. "You can ask anyone to verify that."

His steady gaze refused to relent, however. "You're afraid," he told her quietly. "What are you afraid of, Marina Walden? If you saw something, if someone said something to you, you should tell me. I'm the sheriff. I can help you."

Her hand fidgeting in her skirt suddenly stilled. She gave him a long, searching look, taking in the deep steadiness of his gaze.

"Some of the biggest terrors we face, Sheriff, aren't of people."

For one moment, she thought she might have seen a shadow flicker across those gray eyes. But then the steely depths were back, boring patiently into her own. They were hard eyes to resist.

"I'm sorry, Sheriff," she said briskly, bringing up her chin. "But I honestly can't help you."

"'Cagney,'" he said. "You can call me 'Cagney.' Or 'Cage,' if you'd like."

"Cagney," she repeated.

He offered her a small, faint smile in return, and her lips instantly curved. The movement accentuated her high cheekbones and he could see the smudge of blue paint across her right cheek. It suited her.

She looked wild, the kind of woman who could seduce a man with her eyes alone. When she smiled, it seemed at once genuine and secretive. How many men had succumbed to that look? Standing alone with her in the intimate circle of the lanterns' glow, it wasn't hard to understand. But Cage Guiness didn't feel such things anymore. Only the ache in his leg and the memory of the day he'd shot a fourteen-year-old kid.

He didn't want wild or sensual or sultry. He just wanted to know what this one woman had to do with the body the lab men from the State Bureau of Investigations were bagging four blocks away. He wanted to know who had stabbed Cecille Manning so many times it had taken him a full two minutes to identify the body—and he'd gone to school with her. Hell, he'd watched her, along with the rest of the female population, pursue his older brother Garret. He even remembered her screaming at the top of her lungs at Suzanne Montgomery after finding out that Garret had walked Suzanne home.

And now she'd been tossed out along the side of the road like yesterday's garbage.

His gray gaze bore into this woman once more. She met his gaze straight on, her chin set, her back trembling only slightly.

"You must be tired," he said abruptly, "considering you started at midnight."

Her eyes went to the lightening sky, and then almost on cue she yawned. She started to stretch out her arms above her head, then caught herself. "It must be nearing six," she said.

"And what happens then? If the sunlight touches you, do you suddenly turn to dust?"

She flushed a little, then shrugged self-consciously. "I keep unusual hours. I work six hours, then sleep two. Then work six hours and sleep two. Meaning I'm due to sleep from six to eight." Once more, her shoulders curved in an elegant little shrug. "I've always been like that."

He nodded, filing the information away in the back of his mind.

"You've been painting on this schedule for over a month?"

"Yes."

"This wall, just this wall, every night from twelve to six in the morning?"

Again she nodded.

"And have you ever noticed anything strange at all? Someone watching, someone constantly passing through? A car slowing down, anything?"

The intensity of his voice was compelling, the pull of his eyes powerful. But she hadn't actually seen or heard anything. She only knew the night didn't feel the same anymore, and that his words were once more filling her with fear.

"Honest," she said, her eyes half pleading. "I didn't see anything. I didn't hear anything. Don't you think I would tell you if I had? For goodness' sakes, I moved here because everyone told me there wasn't any crime. How else could I justify spending strange hours of the night painting alone in an abandoned lot?"

He frowned, registering the logic of her words. But the instinct in his gut refused to relent. Maddensfield was witnessing its first murder in decades, and he was coming face-to-face with a woman who looked like a gypsy, smelled like warm spiced cider and literally painted all night long.

He didn't like any of it.

He glanced at his watch and she followed the movement with her gaze.

"The time?" she asked.

"Five forty-five."

She nodded, the news no surprise. After all these years, she could tell the hour by the simple alarm of exhaustion. Her six hours were up. She needed to sleep now. The deep, dreamless slumber that had never failed her since she'd adopted this strange, grueling schedule thirteen years before.

"Did you drive here?" Cagney asked quietly, easily following her train of thought.

She shook her head. "I don't drive."

He filed away that bit of information, as well. "You don't own a car?" he pressed carefully.

She shook her head again. "I don't even know how to drive." She offered him another small smile. "Welcome to the side effect of living in downtown Manhattan."

"But Maddensfield doesn't have a subway."

"But I bought a bike." She smiled at him and tapped a foot impatiently at his insistent questions.

He crossed his arms in front of him. "And the paints?"

"I don't take them with me. I just line it all up against the wall. No one disturbs anything. I don't think there's a good blackmarket for oil paints."

"I suppose you're right." He looked at her a minute longer. "Can I offer you a ride home?" he asked quietly.

She hesitated, surprised but recovering. She was tired. Her arms hurt and a dull ache had settled in her shoulders. And the thought of being suddenly alone in this lot... She looked back at the man before her. Cagney Guiness, he said. The Guiness name sounded familiar, though she couldn't quite pinpoint from where. He was the sheriff, though. Certainly a girl ought to be able to accept a ride home from the sheriff.

Abruptly she agreed. "That would be very nice, thank you, if it's not any trouble."

His gaze told her it wouldn't be.

"Where do you live?"

"Addleson and Rain," she replied. She finally moved away, walking to the small pail filled with paint thinner. She placed her brush inside, then set about sealing all the cans of paint. She could feel his eyes on her as she moved, and it made her fingers tremble.

"Husband? Roommates?"

"Alone." She pounded down the first lid, then was shocked to notice him following her lead.

"That's not the best area for a woman to live in alone," he said levelly, bending down and hammering on a lid despite the protests of his leg.

"Just needs paint and a little construction," she countered.

She rose, carrying the paint cans over to the base of the ladder. She turned, and he was standing right behind her, holding four pails. For one moment, she sucked in her breath with the shock. This close, she could see the dark shadow of a near-twenty-four-hour beard. Coal-black hair rimmed his black cowboy hat and accentuated the darkest gray eyes she'd ever seen. Those eyes were watching her now, the slate depths steady and not giving away anything.

Her gaze drifted down to his lips. She noted the full shape, the sensuous cut. Slowly her eyes came back up to find his. He returned her gaze without blinking.

She flushed with embarrassment and quickly turned before she made a total fool of herself. She scurried away to find her sandals.

He watched her go, his gaze still locked on the wild disarray of her hair as he forcefully expelled the breath he'd been holding. He could still smell her scent on the air around him, something warm and spicy and mysterious. He could see the faint sheen of sweat across her chest, the full heaving of her rounded breasts. She definitely wasn't from around here.

As he watched, she bent to slide the first sandal on her foot, wrapping the straps carefully around her ankle. His eyes went to the curve of her hips, then the exposed skin of her midriff, smooth and dusky by the lantern light. He could see the light splatters of paint on her arms and stomach, the hot summer sheen of sweat. His eyes grew a shade darker, the long-unknown tenseness seizing his stomach.

With savage curtness, he swiped the sensation away. He didn't feel such things anymore, dammit. He just knew the ache in his leg and the heat of a too-damn-hot summer.

He wanted nothing to do with anything else at all.

"I'm ready."

Her voice was still slightly breathless, but they both ignored it. Instead they kept a couple of feet between them, and a civil silence. They walked the first block easily, Marina adapting quickly to his light limp. She didn't try to rush him, nor did she slow down to an artificial speed. If he appreciated the deference, he didn't say anything.

At the end of the block, he cut over to where his truck was parked, two blocks away. From there, it was just possible to make out the yellow tape of the crime scene and the blue and red lights of the two state police cars. For one moment, Marina looked over and hesitated.

Then she turned and climbed into his truck.

"So what do you do when you get up at eight?" Cage finally asked to break the silence as they drove the ten blocks to her house.

"I go to work."

He gave her a sideways glance. "More painting?"

"No. I'm really a graphics artist. These days, most of that's done on a computer, with a bit of sketching on the draft board."

"Graphics artist?"

"Yes. Or I was. Now I'm actually the full art director for an ad agency downtown."

He pulled up before her porch, killing the engine as he eyed her with an intense look on his face.

"Which agency, Marina?"

"Manning and Harding. Have you heard of it?"

Slowly he nodded. "Known it all my life. I grew up with Cecille Manning. Tonight, I identified her body."

For one long moment, she stared at him in confusion.

Chapter 2

"Don't you find it strange that the dead woman should turn up just four blocks from one of her employees?"

Cage nodded slowly, watching the special agent from the SBI pace the tiny sheriff's office with unrestrained intensity.

"Don't you find it even stranger that this woman supposedly paints all night and by her own admission, rarely sleeps?"

Once again, Cage nodded at the burly, impatient man treading before him. Special Agent Daniels had arrived just after Cage had dropped Marina off. He would officially be coordinating the efforts and resources of the state, including its crime lab, with Cagney's own. So far, the special agent appeared tough, blunt and crass—not necessarily in that order.

"Does she have an alibi?"

Cage shook his head.

"Come on. Five seven, long black hair and violet eyes? The woman sounds like a real looker. Betcha anything she was doing a hell of lot more than painting at two in the morning. Ask around. We'll find a name."

"She doesn't drive."

For a moment Daniels stopped pacing. His heavy features pulled into a frown. "Doesn't drive or doesn't have a car?"

"Either."

"License check?"

"North Carolina and New York motor vehicle divisions. Nothing appears."

Daniels's bushy eyebrows arched and he acknowledged for one moment that he was impressed by Cage's thoroughness. Cage merely returned the look with a steely gaze; he really didn't give a damn what this man thought of him one way or another.

"They told me you were good," Daniels said after a minute, rocking back on his heels as he contemplated the younger man in front of him. "Tough break about the kid."

Cage still didn't say anything; he never did on that subject.

"So if she doesn't drive or have a car, she couldn't have transported the body," Daniels mumbled. "What did the victim's house show?"

"Preliminary reports indicate nothing—certainly it doesn't appear to be the murder scene. They took a bunch of evidence bags back to the lab, though. Maybe something will turn up."

Daniels nodded. "Meaning, we don't even know where this woman was killed. Maybe in the car. Maybe in the murderer's house. Did you see Marina Walden's house?"

"Only the outside."

"Anything interesting?"

"It looked like the outside of a house."

"Maybe we should poke around."

"Coincidence doesn't equal probable cause," Cage said levelly.

Daniels pivoted sharply and pinned Cagney with impatient brown eyes. "Okay, boy wonder, what do you think happened?"

"I don't know," Cage said without a trace of defensiveness. "I know Cecille Manning wasn't the type to hang out in the east side of town, and she was too much of a snob to hook up with strangers. I think Marina Walden is scared. Maybe she saw something. She says she didn't. Maybe I believe her—maybe I don't. We have no motive and no crime scene."

"Purse?"

"Gone."

"Hmmm. Robbery?"

"Could be. Cecille was an uptown sort of woman. Drove a Mustang convertible but was waiting for the day she could buy a Mercedes."

"Rape?"

"Don't know, yet. You're the state man, so you'll hear before I do."

Daniels didn't say anything, just grunted and paused in front of the window. Cagney could already see the sweat stains on the heavy man's shirt from the heat. He'd bet money the tie would off by noon, and Daniels would be parading around in his T-shirt by four. That was about the only way a man could survive this weather.

"You really like it here?" Daniels asked suddenly.

Cagney stiffened only slightly in his wooden chair. "I grew up here," he said neutrally.

Daniels turned, looking at him with squinted brown eyes. "I saw your file. You had a damn fine record as a homicide detective in D.C. More like you, and maybe the city wouldn't in the top three for homicides per capita."

Cagney didn't say anything. He just returned Daniels's scrutiny with his dispassionate gaze. Daniels was beginning to think that gaze could stare down the devil himself. The silence dragged on, and it became blatantly apparent that Cagney wasn't going to respond to that statement one way or the other.

"It's your town," Daniels said finally. "You're the big fish in the little pond. What the hell do you want to do?"

"Investigate," Cagney said simply. "I want to know everything about Cecille's last twenty-four hours. What she did, who she was with, what appointments she may have had. Davey says her car is still in the parking lot of Manning and Harding. We can start there."

Daniels grinned at him while he fought with his suffocating tie. "Hell, you got an extra shirt I can borrow?"

Cagney stared pointedly at the other man's thick build. "I'm sure Davey does—that is, if you don't mind looking like a small-pond deputy."

"Damn if it doesn't always come down to that. Comfort or pride, comfort or pride. When does it cool down in this godforsaken town?"

"October."

"Damn. Give me the shirt. No one can have pride sweating like a pig anyway."

"Whatever you say."

Cagney rose, walking the two steps to throw open the door of his closetlike office. He called to Davey, and the young deputy promptly produced the extra tan deputy's shirt from his desk drawer. Cagney handed the shirt to Daniels who could only shake his head.

"Ten years of service and I'm about to dress like a deputy. What a crying shame," the man mumbled. He uttered a melodramatic sigh, then headed for the door. "Fifteen minutes and we leave, right?"

Cagney nodded, watching the state agent exit. At the last moment, Daniels stopped and popped his head back through the doorway.

"Tell me, Cagney, do you ever swear? Beside a 'damn' here or there."

Slowly Cagney shook his head.

"Drink to excess? Chase wild women?"

Cage merely arched an eyebrow.

"Wasted potential, if you ask me," Daniels said. "You're too young to have thrown it all away because of some gang scumball who'd already killed three people."

If his barb struck home, nothing showed on Cage's face. After a moment, Daniels gave one last sigh.

"Let me guess—you don't get mad, either."

"Never have," Cage drawled. He looked at Daniels dispassionately. "Never will."

Daniels didn't say anything more, just ducked out and headed away in pursuit of cooler air and greater comfort.

Cage closed the door behind the man and sat down hard on the wooden chair, stretching his left leg up onto the desk while he stared out the window through the cracks in the blind.

The office was hot. The air conditioner had given out just last week and they hadn't quite gotten around to replacing it. Given the intensity of the heat wave, Cage had never thought the air conditioner provided much relief anyway. Let alone what it did to the electric bill of this low-budget, three-man operation.

He was a long way from D.C.

In the beginning, people had asked a lot of questions. Quickly enough, however, they had learned that they could ask all they wanted—Cagney wouldn't answer.

He'd killed the fourteen-year-old homicide suspect in the line of duty and in self-defense. That was the only thing they needed to know. That he sometimes still dreamed of that last moment—QVee's bullet entering his leg, his own gun returning fire while his partner screamed her too-late warning—was no one's business but his own.

He'd once thought he could change the streets. That afternoon, he'd watch a young gang member fulfill his statistical destiny, and had understood that far from making a difference, he'd been the one to pull the trigger.

A lot more than QVee's life had been lost that day.

But again, it was no one's business except Cagney's.

In the aftermath, his family had offered him their comfort and he had listened, searching for answers to questions he didn't know how to ask. His oldest brother Mitch had told him that a man's job came with no guarantee of ease. You did what was necessary, and at the end of the day, you went home to live with your conscience. No one could ever tell you how to face yourself in the mirror; each man had to learn how to do that on his own.

His brother Garret had called from God-knows-where at two a.m. with a more oblique message: in today's world, the darkness grew stronger and increasingly subtle, until danger could be everywhere—in the heart of your neighbor and in the eyes of a child. Today's warrior no longer charged down a black-clad knight, but instead challenged the damsel in distress, the steed on which he rode and the friend at his back. But the wars still had to be fought, even if victory was no longer clear.

His brother Jake, the Harvard man, had argued statistics: according to FBI records, the number of juveniles committing homicide had increased by sixty percent in the past decade. Cage couldn't hold himself responsible for the growing influence of gangs, the declining stability of the family unit and the increasing availability of guns.

His sister, Liz, had simply said she loved him and believed in him, and would be there for him always.

Liz always had known just what to say.

Cage placed his left leg back on the floor, then rose to walk over to the window again. With dark-gray eyes he peered out at the lush crop of trees growing in the bright June sun. Maddensfield was a beautiful town, a quiet town. A man could do a lot worse than serve as county sheriff here.

Except that now he was back in the business of homicide.

He looked down at his watch. Five more minutes and then they'd leave. He wondered what Marina Walden was up to right now....

She seemed a strong woman. And her painting revealed an appreciation for color and vitality. So what could bring fear to her eyes? And why wouldn't she tell him?

He narrowed his gaze, the summer scene before him disappearing until he saw only the mane of thick black hair, the dusky smile and the lean, sensual body. For a moment, he could almost see the smudge of paint on her cheek again, smell her perfume.

He abruptly shook his head, clearing the images from his mind.

She was a potential suspect, he reminded himself firmly. And found himself remembering her thickly lashed eyes once more.

"How well do you know Marina Walden?"

Daniels was leaning against the wall, practically pinning the young mailroom clerk with his squinted brown eyes. The eighteen-year-old's eyes went from Cagney to Daniels to Cagney again.

"It's okay, Larry," Cage drawled. "Special Agent Daniels here is really with the North Carolina State Bureau of Investigations. He just likes to play dress-up as a deputy."

"Is Miss Walden a suspect?" Larry blurted out, blue eyes wide.

"Not at all, son. We're just trying to talk to everyone involved. Now, she told me she's been working here for the past two months."

Larry nodded. "She's the best, sir. She's been helping me learn the computer and all—and I'm just the mail clerk! Once she even let me take a shot at designing a brochure for Mac's Hardware. And when I brought it back to her, she looked at it for just an instant and told me it was good, but slightly crooked. Now, I didn't think it was crooked, but I want back to the drafting board, and damn if she wasn't right. I was off by one-sixteenth of an inch. Can you imagine being able to see that? And then she showed me how to adjust the tracking and the leading, and boy did it make a difference. She's just . . . just incredible, sir."

To his right, Cage could see Daniels roll his eyes at the young man's exuberance.

"I take it you know Miss Walden rather well," Daniels stated baldly.

Larry blushed only slightly. "She lets me do work for her every now and then. If that's what you mean."

"Do you know her friends, her family? Who does she socialize with?" Daniels pressed.

For a moment, Larry appeared startled. "Well, I don't know, sir. I mean, she's very nice and always smiling and all. I heard she's from New York and used to work for some big-time agency there. But she doesn't really talk about her personal life much. And well, I know a lot of the guys are interested in her. Shoot, haven't you seen her? But I don't think she's ever said yes. At least, I never heard so."

"Keeps to herself?" Cagney said.

"In a pleasant sort of way, sir."

Cagney nodded, not surprised. From what he'd observed just eight hours ago, Marina Walden was a carefully constructed mix of lush vitality and guarded secrets.

Daniels spoke up. "And her relationship with Ms. Manning? How was it?"

Now Larry looked openly uncomfortable. "They had their differences," he said at last.

Cagney and Daniels exchanged glances.

"And what might those differences be?" Cage asked slowly.

"The tobacco contract," Larry finally said after a few moments. He didn't appear happy to be speaking on this subject. "Cecille just landed it two months ago, a good-sized job. I . . . I overheard a thing or two, that the company was willing to go with a smaller agency like ours because of Miss Walden's reputation. Cecille was handling the account personally, of course, and she wanted all these bright neon colors and some computer animation. Real cutting-edge stuff. She kept going on and on about how this was going to launch Manning and Harding into the big leagues, you know?"

"And?" Daniels prodded, clearly impatient with the long-winded explanation.

"Well. Basically, Miss Walden refused to do it. Said the ads were geared too much toward attracting kids and it wouldn't be right. She's pretty strongly opposed, and well, sir—" Larry shrugged and looked at Cagney. "You know how Cecille is—was."

Cage nodded. He could imagine just how Cecille would have handled such opposition. The strong-willed woman didn't believe in obstacles, and definitely didn't believe in not getting her way. Since inheriting the agency two years ago from her father, she'd adopted an aggressive strategy for shooting it toward major contracts. People had begun grumbling that Cecille Manning was getting too big for her britches. He was surprised she hadn't just fired Marina. Then again, it appeared that if she lost Marina, she might have lost the account, as well. He would have loved to see her face when she figured that all out.

"Thank you, Larry," Cage told the boy. He turned to Daniels. "We have some more investigating to do now."

Cage rose from the chair as Daniels pushed away from the wall. But just as they were about to walk through the doorway, Larry stopped them with one last, anxious look.

"I...I didn't get her in trouble or anything, did I?" Larry said.

Daniels opened his mouth, but Cage cut him off cleanly. "You did just fine," he told Larry. "I'm sure Miss Walden would want you to be honest with the police."

Larry nodded, not entirely convinced, but at least returning to his work.

They'd barely gotten into the hall of the agency, when Daniels let out a low whistle. "Hell, you'd think she was a candidate for sainthood to listen to that kid. I betcha he dreams of her every night. Really good dreams, if you know what I mean."

For a moment, Cagney felt a sudden flash of anger at the crude insinuation. The sharp emotion startled him, and he immediately pushed it away. Daniels was just Daniels, he reminded himself.

"We should find out more about Cecille's schedule," he said, his voice carefully neutral as they approached the receptionist. "You want to do some checking around?"

"Sure," Daniels said, then his eyes suddenly narrowed. "And what might you be doing?"

"I think I'm going to go call upon Marina Walden," Cage said levelly.

Daniels came to an abrupt halt in his tracks, grabbing Cagney's arm. Cage's slate gaze slipped to the hand on his arm, then came back up to stare at Daniels with steely intensity. With an exasperated look, the burly criminalist dropped his grip, but didn't hide his anger.

"What do you mean, going to question her without me? I'm not your deputy, despite the fact that I'm wearing his shirt."

"That's not it at all," Cagney corrected calmly. "We've got a lot of ground to cover and we'd cover it faster if we split up. Besides," he drawled smoothly, "I've already met Marina Walden, and I know one thing about her. You start drilling her with your bad-cop routine, and she'll button up as tight as a clam on the beach."

Daniels's eyes narrowed. "I'm part of this case," he warned.

"Daniels," Cagney said slowly, "I'd deal with the devil himself if he'd help me find who killed Cecille. I'm just a small-town sheriff, and I don't have time for politics or egos or turfs. I'm not trying to do anything other than what's best for this case."

There was tense silence. Then gradually the tension in Daniels's shoulders abated. "I'll give you fifteen minutes," he said gruffly. "Then I'm coming upstairs to find you. I won't ask questions if you think it's best, but two viewpoints are better then one."

"Sounds reasonable," Cage concurred.

He left Daniels with the receptionist and headed to the second floor, where the creative department sat. He didn't need to see the nameplate to know when he'd found her office; he could tell it was hers simply by looking.

It was a large office, befitting a New York hotshot. A huge glass window had been left curtainless to draw in the bright sun and blue sky. Everywhere plants jumped out at him. The file tops were covered by the trailing green vines, while trees rose from pots all over the floor. The only surface she'd left clear was the drafting board against the right-hand wall, as well as a small perimeter around the computer and color monitor on her desk. The office had originally been painted a tasteful eggshell blue, but she'd covered the walls with large canvases of blazing colors. Even the cream love seat facing the desk had a pink-and-purple afghan thrown over the back, while dark-green pillows sat in each corner.

After the sterility of his cramped quarters, the office seemed almost insanely alive. He could even smell the whisper of her deep, spicy perfume.

"Shocking, isn't it?"

He turned a shade too fast, cramping his leg until he nearly fell. In a flash, he felt warm hands on his shoulders, steadying him even as the contact sent a jolt through him. He looked up to find himself staring once more into deep-violet eyes.

"I'm sorry," she said softly. "I didn't mean to startle you."

She didn't pull back right away, nor did he immediately move. Instead his eyes roamed over the creature in front of him. Her wild hair was pulled sleekly back, the narrow gray streak striking against the black depths. Her cheekbones were exposed, as well as her finely arched eyebrows and perfect nose. Mostly, however, he just noticed her eyes. They were huge and dark and beguiling in the dusky contours of her face.

"Are you all right?" she asked, the concern in her gaze genuine.

All of a sudden he became aware of the fact that he was still half leaning on her. He straightened instantly, the slightest hint of color rising to his cheeks.

"Sorry," he said tightly. "Sometimes I forget."

She nodded, watching him step hastily back with open curiosity. He didn't say anything more, however, and the shuttered look in his eyes betrayed nothing. The Maddensfield sheriff didn't seem to like people getting too close.

She moved quietly around him to her desk chair, then pointed to the sofa.

"You can sit if you like," she said casually. "I'm afraid I don't have too much time, though. Given Cecille's.. passing, it's been a hectic day."

He didn't say anything but didn't sit, either. He looked at her a bit longer, his black hat in his hands, and a small frown furrowed his brow. She appeared very different than she had last night. Her sleek, dark-purple suit was expertly tailored and one hundred percent professional. Discreet black lace peeked above the edges of the double-breasted jacket, adding a sophisticated touch. Her legs, encased in black hose and set off by black suede heels, struck him as trim and untouchable.

"You rode your bike here in that?" he said at last, arching a fine brow.

She gave him a small smile that revealed dimples. "No. Actually I changed here this time. Normal dress around here is much more casual, but given the circumstances and the emergency board meeting . . ."

He looked at her sharply. "You sit on the board?"

She nodded, toying with a pencil on her desk.

"Isn't that unusual for an employee of two months?"

She gave him a guarded look. "You didn't question me enough last night, Sheriff?"

"Just doing my job," he countered.

The pencil stilled for a moment on the desk, then dropped as she sighed. "All right then, Cage. Yes, I am on the board. Yes, that might be unusual, except I was hired to be in charge of the creative department, which include art development, layout and design, as well as writing. And given where I came from, I made sitting on the board a condition of my employment."

"Where did you come from?"

"Sampson and Sampson," she said simply.

Cage's eyebrows rose slightly. Even he recognized the name of one of the top advertising agencies in the nation.

"You're a long way from home," he drawled softly. "Did you really move all the way down here just to paint a wall at night?"

She smiled, that full vibrant smile he recognized from last night.

"I think maybe I did," she said.

"And now?"

The smile faltered, and for one moment, he saw the uneasiness in her eyes. Her gaze shifted to the far wall, and he could see her abruptly focusing on the colors there. It seemed to him that she drew strength from those colors.

"I don't know what's going to happen anymore," she said at last. "Cecille's death is most tragic."

"What will happen with the tobacco account?" Cage asked quietly.

Her eyes opened wide with shock. She looked at him a minute longer, then shook her head. "My, my, Sheriff. You really have done your homework."

He didn't say anything, just watched her with his gray eyes. She remembered those eyes from last night, how strong and steady his gaze had seemed. And now those eyes were back, staring into her own, looking for answers she couldn't give him.

If he knew more about her, he would know she almost never wore suits. And he would know that when she did, it was because she was trying to hide the doubts inside herself with the polished exterior.

Maybe he would even know that for the first time in thirteen years, her two-hour sleep had not been dreamless.

She rose abruptly, trying to appear casual as she crossed to the warm light of the window. His gaze followed her.

"The tobacco account will survive," she said at last. "At five hundred thousand dollars, it's worth too much money for the board not to scramble to save it."

"And the ad?"

"We were only in the concept stage anyway," she said with a shrug. She gazed at him clear eyed. "Look, it's no secret that Cecille and I fought over the approach. I don't know what you think, but I certainly have no intention of creating something that will attract kids to smoking. If the tobacco company can't accept that, it's their problem, not mine. I've never made any secret of that."

Cage nodded, watching her carefully. She spoke with conviction, appearing to relax in the glow of the sun. Her shoulders had come down slightly, though one arm was still wrapped protectively around her waist. He wondered if she was aware of that posture and what it told him about her. He walked toward her with his eyes never leaving her face.

She stiffened but didn't move away as he neared. If anything, her chin came up slightly, even as the wariness entered her eyes.

"You're still afraid," he whispered. He was so close he could smell the rich scent of her warm cinnamon perfume. And he could feel the slight trembles of her body.

"Don't you have anyone else to intimidate today, Sheriff?"

Slowly the man in front of her shook his head.

"I told you before I didn't see anything," she said. "Sooner or later, you'll have to believe me."

"Then why are you afraid?"

His gray gaze swept across her face, lingering on her hair, her neck, her lips, until she felt it as a physical touch.

For one moment, she actually leaned forward. He stood quiet and steady, his eyes like the Rock of Gibraltar, and after last night, she needed a rock to lean against. She'd never met anyone with his kind of presence before, anyone so...solid.

Her mouth opened, her eyes darkened and the words welled in her throat. Maybe he would understand. Maybe a man with such gray eyes would actually understand.

But then abruptly she saw Bradley's face in her mind, his limpid mouth opened with horror.

She turned her face away, but not before Cage saw the flash of pain through her eyes. Unconsciously he frowned.

"I don't have anything more to say," she told him quietly.

She glanced back over at him, and just for a moment, her gaze seemed defiant.

"You sure about that, ma'am?" he persisted softly.

She nodded.

"I wouldn't like to think you're holding anything back," he continued levelly, "obstructing justice—"

"Am I a suspect?" she interrupted evenly.

"Should you be?" he countered.

She smiled at him knowingly, and her eyes grew hard. "Don't play mind games with me, Sheriff. I come from tougher stock than that. I'm telling you honestly—I know nothing about Cecille's death. Now, whether you choose to believe that or not is your business."

He nodded, but his gray eyes were shrewd. "So you wouldn't be holding anything back?" he repeated.

"Nothing you need to know."

"Now, I'd think it would be my job to make that call."

"Sheriff, you're beating a dead horse. It's almost two o'clock now. I'm afraid I'll have to ask you to leave."

"Time to sleep?" he asked, recalling last night's conversation. He looked at the couch quizzically and she nodded. "I wouldn't think you'd get much rest."

"People know better than to disturb me by now."

He raised a brow skeptically, and a faint smile relaxed her lips. "It's the advantage of working with artists," she told him. "They expect you to be eccentric." She glanced at her watch and immediately yawned. "Please, Sheriff? Unless you're telling bedtime stories, I'm not interested."

His eyes rounded slightly as the comment put several unexpected ideas into his head, but she was herding him toward the door before he could think of a suitable reply.

"You won't be leaving town anytime soon?" he remembered to ask.

"Of course not, Cage. At this point, I'm simply getting some sleep."

She maneuvered him into the hallway, taking refuge behind her door. "Good luck with your investigation," she told him, then added without a hint of irony, "please let me know if there's anything else I can do to help."

He nodded, his gaze intent on her face. "Sweet dreams," he told her.

She gave him a smile, but this time it was twisted. "No, Sheriff. No dreams. That's the whole point of the schedule."

She closed the door before he could question that last comment.

Chapter 3

"So what do you know about a Bennett Jensen?"

Daniels and Cagney were just leaving the ad agency, the hot June air hitting them like a furnace as the doors closed on the air-conditioned building behind them. Daniels muttered something graphic as the wave of heat hit them both.

"Bennett owns Jensen Textiles," Cagney replied, seemingly unperturbed by the boiling temperature as he headed them toward his sheriff's Ranger. "The textile mill was started by his great-grandfather in '25, and employs a good quarter of Maddensfield people. Smaller sewing facilities exist in Marion and Maynerd. Why?"

Daniels was nodding shrewdly, as he squinted against the bright glare of the sun. They came to the Ranger and he swung himself in while reaching for the air-conditioning buttons.

"The receptionist, Martha, seemed to think there was something between Cecille and Bennett. He took her out to dinner a lot, that kind of thing." He swung his piercing gaze over to Cagney, who was starting the vehicle. "Martha says Cecille dated you a couple of times, as well."

"'Dated' would be a strong word," Cage replied neutrally.

Daniels regarded him with keen interest, clearly waiting for an explanation. After a moment, Cagney complied with a small shrug.

"She saw a picture of my older brother Jake in the society pages of a New York paper. Jake went to Harvard and he's done rather well for himself. Moves in some interesting circles these days. She wanted to know when he would be back in town."

"And?"

Cagney merely shook his head. "I didn't have a whole lot to say on the subject one way or another. Jake keeps his own schedule. Once I made that clear, the dinners stopped. I can assure you, Cecille had set her sights much higher than a small-town sheriff."

"Like a wealthy mill owner?"

Slowly Cagney nodded. "God," he drawled softly, "what a combination."

"What do you mean?"

Cagney downshifted the clutch to make a sharp turn, his eyes narrowing as he tried to put into words the feeling in his gut. "Bennett's smart," he said at last, "in a ruthless sort of way. He's been running that mill since, oh, '86, I suppose. It's done all right, but I can tell you people miss his daddy, Lloyd. Lloyd was tough, but he was a fair man. Bennett...Bennett maybe likes the power a little too much. He's got a wife, you know, one of the meekest women you'll ever meet. I think she might have been something once, but four miscarriages and twenty years of marriage to Bennett pretty much took all the life out of her. Now she's just this brown shadow that jumps every time Bennett raises his voice. And then you got Cecille—ambitious, power hungry and selfish." He shook his head.

Daniels chuckled. "Between the two of them, you gotta wonder who got to be on top."

Cagney didn't say anything, but gave Daniels a long, serious stare.

"Oh, lighten up," Daniels said. Still, he shifted slightly under the impact of that gaze.

"So we got Cecille and Bennett," Cagney restated. "Maybe Cecille had her eyes on him, but I can't imagine Bennett ever leaving Evie. If for no other reason than a divorce could jeopardize the textile operations—split things in half, maybe forcing him to sell off the mills altogether."

"What if Evie found out about Cecille and Bennett?"

"Evie?" Cagney couldn't quite keep the doubt out of his voice, but then he shrugged, his eyes glued to the road. "Stranger things have happened, I suppose. Do we know anything else?"

"Only that Cecille had a dinner date with Bennett at seven. Martha saw them meet in the lobby at six-thirty. But then, Cecille called Martha from the office a little after ten, looking for some files on the Reynolds accounts. Martha told her where to find them, and that's the last she heard from Cecille. According to Martha, it wasn't unusual for Cecille to sometimes work until two or three in the morning."

"Maybe someone grabbed her in the parking lot," Cagney mused. "There's no security guard or anyone else to notice. We could ask around, see if anyone might have been in the area to hear something."

Daniels shrugged, looking at Cagney with sharp eyes. "Assuming there was something to hear. Maybe she didn't struggle. Maybe she knew the person who approached her in the parking lot. Speaking of which, what did you learn from the beautiful Miss Walden?"

Cagney tightened his grip a fraction on the steering wheel, then he forced himself to relax. "She's nervous about something," he said at last. "'Afraid' is a better word. But she still says she didn't see anything. Also, she sits on the board of directors."

Daniels nodded. "I learned the same from Martha," he said. "Not to mention the fact that those weren't minor arguments Cecille and Marina had over the Reynolds account. According to Martha, you could hear Cecille yelling clear across the lobby. But even then Marina wouldn't back down. Must be pretty convenient for her now, I suppose. Cecille's gone, and as a board member, she can ensure that she gets control over the account.''

Cagney felt a muscle slowly clench in his jaw. He forced it to relax, keeping his gray eyes on the city streets before him. He was in no position one way or another to argue Marina's innocence. People had killed for a lot less than a five-hundred-thousand-dollar business deal. His gut just told him the fear in Marina's eyes was real, and it wasn't fear of discovery. She was scared of something or someone.

But then, why wouldn't she tell him?

He had no answers.

He pulled at last into the parking lot of the tiny sheriff's office, turning off the engine as he looked over at Daniels. "I say it's time to pay Mr. Jensen a visit," he said quietly.

Daniels nodded but glanced down at his watch. "It's a little after two now, and God knows we have a bit of paperwork to file. Maybe we can catch up with Mr. Jensen on Monday.''

"I'll look into it.''

"In the meantime," Daniels continued with a tired sigh, "I'll check in with the lab and find out if all those evidence bags amounted to squat. I thought I oughtta run the crime descript through the computer and see if anything pops up. Maybe we got a sicko passing through towns and stabbing women to death. In this day and age, anything's possible.''

"Davey's checking around to see what strangers we had passing through last night," Cagney said.

"Sounds good." Daniels opened his door, wincing as the heat rolled in. "God almighty," he said with a sigh. He leaped out, then turned around to face Cagney as one last thought jumped into his mind.

"Since you've established the connection," he drawled, "maybe you ought to be the one to keep an eye on Marina Walden. I know she doesn't have a car, but I think we can both agree something's up with her. If not as a suspect, then as a witness who still isn't talking. Spending a weekend with a beautiful woman can't be that big of a hardship.''

Slowly Cage nodded. Daniel's suggestion made perfect sense and certainly shouldn't cause this sudden tightness in his stomach.

"Well, then," Daniels was saying. "Get some rest. I'll give you a ring if I learn anything new from the lab." Then Daniels turned and walked to his unmarked police car.

Cage watched the man for a minute longer. Daniels might be rough around the edges, but Cage respected his police skills. He did good work and he seemed sharp. Together they ought to be able to get to the bottom of this murder once and for all.

So why then was his stomach still tight? And why on this hot June day did he suddenly feel a chill?

"Hello?"

The voice was throaty, and Cagney felt its impact in the sudden small tremor that raced down his spine. His grip on the phone tightened unnecessarily.

"Marina?" he confirmed. "This is Cagney Guiness."

There was a small pause, and he could almost feel her wariness over the phone lines.

"Yes?" she said finally.

The word was unquestioningly formal and distant. His task was going to be harder than expected. "I wanted to see how you were doing," he said finally, keeping his voice carefully neutral and firm. "Given what has happened, I hope you aren't planning on painting tonight."

She sighed, a small wistful sound of regret. "No. I suppose I can't. And the wall was coming along so well."

The disappointment was genuine, but she hadn't counted on the relief, also. No more standing in the circle of lights, wondering what was just beyond the edges. The murder was horribly real, not some shadowy fear. Staying in simply meant she was prudent, not cowardly.

"What will you do, instead?" came Cagney's voice, low and reassuring in her ear. She liked his voice. It reminded her of his eyes, deep and steady. For one moment, she found herself wishing he were nearby.

She shook the sensation away. "I think I'll work on my house," she replied. "Only the downstairs has been finished, so there's plenty to keep me occupied."

"You sure about that?" he drawled.

She could hear the underlying concern in his voice. "Sheriff, my house is perfectly safe. I had a bolt lock installed."

"It's not the best area."

"Now, now, some of my neighbors are very nice people. And frankly, after a lifetime in Manhattan this block seems as safe as a chapel."

"So you have nothing to be afraid of?" he quizzed dryly.

At her end of the phone, she blushed, seeing too late how easily he'd led her down the primrose path. She was about to protest, when he spoke again.

"Perhaps I could come over and help you," he suggested casually. "I think I could manage to pound a nail or two."

She didn't reply immediately, the suggestion catching her off guard. She was even more surprised by the magnitude of its appeal. Sheriff Guiness, with his lean build and steady eyes, helping her out. Cage, standing in her living room and chasing the shadows away.

Marina, shadows can't hurt you, anyway.

"That's very nice of you to offer," she said at last. "But surely you must be tired after last night."

"I had an afternoon nap."

"I don't know." she said, the indecision real in her voice. Her old house still had creaks and groans she found unsettling, and somehow, after the past twenty-four hours, the thought of a long night alone made her uneasy.

But she didn't want to find strength in Cagney's presence—or anyone else's, for that matter. She wanted to find strength in herself. Sometimes she could still recall those two years of terror. How the fear had bubbled up from inside until she couldn't move, could only curl up in a ball and tremble from a horror she could never name.

Two years of her life, lost to the darkness no one had ever been able to understand, least of all her. But she wasn't twelve or thirteen anymore. She was a twenty-seven-year-old woman who'd gone off to college, worked in Manhattan and once even had the misfortune of thinking she'd fallen in love. And now she'd moved here, far from the protective shield of her two overly loving parents, because she'd known she could make it on her own.

She wasn't going to give up on that now.

"It's all right," she said, forcing her voice to sound bright. "I'll be all right."

"You're sure?" Cagney drawled.

"Of course," Marina said cheerily, hoping it didn't sound as overdone as it felt.

"Well, if you need anything," Cagney said, "you call the sheriff's office, you hear?"

"All right, Cage."

"Oh, and Marina? Tomorrow is the big baseball game. The Maddensfield Mad Hatters face the Winston-Salem Spirits. It's only Single A ball, but it's the big rivalry, so most of the town will be there. Don't suppose you want to go?"

"Oh!" she said in surprise. "I've never been to a baseball game before." Nor had she ever expected it to appeal to her as much as it appealed to her right now.

"Pick you up at five?"

"That sounds wonderful. I'll see you then."

"All right, then. Have a good night, Marina." For one moment he hesitated. "And take care."

She nodded, already hearing the small click as he hung up. Much more slowly, she set down the phone. Strange that she should feel so suddenly lost now. She didn't even really know anything about this man except that he wore a star on his chest and possessed the world's steadiest pair of eyes.

He was simply Sheriff Guiness, a man who treated her as a murder suspect, and right now she would give anything to pick up the phone again and call him right over to keep the darkness away.

She looked at the tool kit at her feet with grim determination. She'd already changed into a pair of cut-off jeans and a tank top that left her lean arms bare for the long night ahead. She scanned the living room around her.

Like her office, plants flourished in every nook and cranny. A curved blue couch sat before huge bay windows, liberally decorated with bright pillows of green and purple. Brilliant artwork decorated the walls, and a good six hundred watts' worth of lights blazed from lamps and chandeliers and wall units.

For a moment, she saw it all for what it was: a one-woman war against the darkness.

Then she picked up her tool kit and her lanterns and headed upstairs. She started to work, and for the next six hours did her best to pretend that she didn't feel the sensation of someone watching her.

Not at all.

So it was a good thing she didn't head downstairs, or she would have seen the face pressed against her sliding-glass door with unrestrained satisfaction. And she would have seen the twenty-five years' worth of hatred burning once more.

Cagney awoke the next morning with a strange, unfamiliar feeling in his stomach. He lay in his narrow bed for a full two minutes, already too damn hot, as he stared at the ceiling. And then it came to him: anticipation. He was feeling anticipation.

He frowned and rolled out of bed.

He didn't like the feeling, especially because he knew it was associated with a slender, dark-haired woman with violet eyes. He was just the sheriff doing his job, and he had every intention of keeping it that way.

So why was he suddenly going to a baseball game that just twenty-four hours ago he'd had no intention of attending? Hell, he'd only been to one game since he'd returned to Maddensfield, and that was back in the beginning, when he'd still been trying to pretend nothing had changed.

The seats were too uncomfortable, he reminded himself. They bothered his leg. So he didn't go, just as he didn't do lots of things he once did.

He shouldn't be changing that for one woman he barely knew. Even if she was beautiful, even if she was sensual.

Those things didn't affect him, at least not these days. Now he was just a burned-out cop who'd shot and killed a kid. He would have most likely lived out his days calling Mrs. Browning's cat down from the tree except for this murder.

He limped to the shower and turned on a sharp blast of cold spray. Showering was about the only time a man felt cool in this heat. The radio had promised last night that the heat wave might break around midweek. He sure as hell hoped so. The rise in temperature also led to a rise in temperaments. Hell, as edgy as people were becoming, he'd soon have more than Cecille's death to investigate.

He found himself suddenly wondering how Marina was doing, and on the heels of that thought came the strong urge to call. Had she gotten much done last night? Would the wariness still be in her voice? Why wouldn't she tell him about the fear in her eyes?

He slammed off the water with a burst of impatience. He wasn't going to think about her anymore. He would pick her up at five for the game, learn more about her over baseball, and that would be that. Just his job. That's all.

He could drop her off after the game, then attend the traditional barbecue his parents held each year after the rivalry. He could kiss his mom on the cheek, assure her he was doing fine, then take off after an hour without anyone making a fuss. They knew him well enough by now not to expect him to be social. Cagney was the quiet one. Everyone knew that.

He limped back into his bedroom and pulled on a fresh pair of jeans, then a plain black T-shirt. He should be doing his stretches. The doctors had told him he could probably walk without a limp at all if he took proper care of the leg. But he didn't feel like playing ballerina in this heat. He just wanted to get in his truck and head for the office. He had reports to look at, new angles to figure out.

He had a dark-haired woman to forget.

He frowned at himself once more, grabbed his hat and headed for the door.

She had tried on three outfits; that was always a bad sign. Two outfits could simply mean you had a poor idea the first time around. Three outfits, though, three outfits meant you were trying. She shouldn't be trying, she reminded herself for the fourth time as she examined the fuchsia tank top and black denim shorts with a critical eye. He was just taking her to a baseball game, and not even real baseball at that. He probably figured he could pick her brain under the guise of socializing and she wouldn't even notice.

But somehow, that didn't dampen her mood. Last night had been long and tense, but the day was bright and sunny and she was going to spend her evening in the company of a good-looking man. She found herself wondering idly what his hands were like. He probably had large hands, the kind that were hard and callused from work. She could see him chopping wood or hammering a "nail or two." For that matter, she could see him without a shirt, sitting in his truck.

She blushed in front of her mirror, and let out a low, self-conscious laugh. The man wasn't even interested in her, and she'd already mentally undressed him. What in the world had gotten into her?

She pulled her long, thick hair through the back of a navy blue baseball cap, and heard the sound of a truck pulling up her driveway. She couldn't help herself. She blushed once more and felt the quiver go all the way up her spine.

Enough, she told herself firmly. He was doing his job, and she was going to enjoy her first baseball game. And after the strain of the past couple days, she had every intention of having a wonderful time.

The doorbell rang, and with one last critical glance, she grabbed her sunglasses and scrambled to answer it.

Cagney had unconsciously braced himself when the door first swung open, but that wasn't quite enough to stop his mouth from going dry. His first impression was of long, lean legs that went on forever. Then he became aware of slender hips, rounded breasts and graceful arms. Not to mention the thousand-watt smile that threatened to burn a hole through his chest.

Today the violet eyes held no fear. Instead they gleamed merrily beneath the flirty jaunt of a crooked baseball cap.

"So?" she questioned throatily. "Am I the reluctant witness or the evil suspect this afternoon?"

Cage blinked, searching for a retort, while she winked at him with genuine amusement.

"You tell me," he drawled at last.

"I'll take option C," she declared firmly.

"Which is?"

"The overworked art director who needs to get out more."

She smiled at him again and held out her arm. Long, tan, bare. He had no choice but to place his hand on the warm, soft skin and guide her to his truck. She felt strong beneath his touch. Firm and vivacious and vital. He thought his fingers might burn from the heat alone, and his jaw clenched in response.

Just out of the starting gate and he was already infused with unprofessional thoughts. He shook his head at himself.

He let go to allow her to climb into the truck, turning away before he had to suffer through the long, limber flash of her legs. He didn't like it, he thought again. He shook his head and climbed into the driver's seat.

"Are you a big baseball fan?" Marina asked as he started the truck. She felt lightly breathless, as if she'd climbed onto some big fairground ride and didn't know where the end was yet. In just a pair of jeans and a T-shirt, Cagney looked solid and strong. He wore his black cowboy hat again, and she found herself thinking cowboy hats were much sexier than she'd ever realized. Her gaze fell to the whipcord muscles of his arms as he turned the wheel, and indeed his hands appeared large and capable. She could almost feel them again on her arm.

"I like baseball," Cagney answered, keeping his eyes on the road and far away from finely shaped legs hovering in his peripheral vision.

"Did you ever play?"

"In high school," he said shortly.

"Position?"

"Pitcher."

She eyed him curiously. "Is that how you hurt your leg?"

She saw his hands tighten for just one moment on the wheel, then forcibly relax.

"No," he said.

She waited for a moment, but it became clear he had no intention of volunteering anything else. She nodded, more to herself than him, and tried to tell herself his reticence wasn't important.

Silence filled the cab.

"You're from New York, right?" he asked presently, his gaze sliding over.

"That's right," she said, her eyes brightening again at his overture. She flashed him a warm, friendly smile.

"You never watched the Yankees?" he asked, quickly returning his eyes to the road.

She shook her head, the tinkling of her earrings filling the cab. "My parents were more ballet and museum kind of people."

"Maddensfield doesn't exactly offer that," he said quietly.

"Oh, I wanted the change of pace," she assured him. "New York has its opportunities, but after a lifetime of roaring concrete, I wanted something new. Something small and quaint where people really get to know each other."

"How did you hear of Maddensfield?"

He was basically interviewing her again, but she decided she didn't mind. She hadn't done anything, and she had little to hide. If it made him feel better and entitled her to one early-summer evening out, it seemed a small price to pay. Besides, after all these years, she knew exactly which details to omit.

She shrugged, that careless, elegant gesture that automatically drew his eyes to her shoulders and breasts.

"It was kind of a fluke, really," she said. "In the spring, I took two weeks off with a girlfriend just to drive along the coast. We went down to Florida, then took a rather scenic route back up. I think we actually stopped here for lunch. But we walked around some and, I don't know, it just felt right. Then I found out about the opening with Manning and Harding, and everything kind of fell into place. So here I am, about to go to my first small-town baseball game."

The way she said it, he would have thought he was taking her for an eight-course French dinner. "Single A ball isn't exactly the world's best baseball," he warned.

"I know," she assured him. "I grew up in America. I understand the difference between Single A, Double A, Triple A and the Majors. Ballet isn't that stifling."

He turned to apologize but found she was grinning at him with such easy amusement that he lost his train of thought. He returned his eyes belatedly to the road, only to find himself driving past the stadium. He slammed on the brakes, barely making the turn-in.

"Cagney," Marina announced as she looked up, "this is perfect."

It was, from the milling crowds of Boy Scouts and grandparents to the lukewarm hot dogs piled high with mustard and relish. Maddensfield Ballpark looked like everything American to her. Rock-and-roll filled the stadium, while cups of flat beer filled the spectators' hands. She could smell the salty tang of popcorn in the warm evening air, and practically taste fresh roasted peanuts on her tongue.

When she'd dreamed of leaving behind New York high rises, this is exactly what she had had in mind. No frantic pace, no high pressure. Just a low-key evening of community fun with freshly mowed grass and mid-June heat.

She could barely contain herself as Cagney led them to their seats.

"I want to know everything," she announced as they plopped down into the wooden fold-down chairs. She was trying to take a bite of her hot dog at the same time, and some relish promptly squished out the back to land on her leg. Unperturbed, she scooped up the relish with her index finger and popped it into her mouth. She looked up to find Cagney watching her with a strange tightness to his normally calm gaze.

"Everything?" he replied somewhat hoarsely.

He shifted, and for the first time, she could see how much the cramped seats would bother his leg. Immediately her eyes darkened with concern.

"Maybe this isn't such a good idea," she said.

Cagney just looked at her with his gray eyes. After a moment, she realized that this was his way of telling her he had no intention of referencing his leg at all. Men really could be so stubborn, she thought. But then she frowned and once more found herself wondering how he'd hurt himself.

And if he might ever tell her.

The announcer's voice suddenly filled the speakers, and she turned her attention to the field. The first inning went rather quickly, and true to Cagney's assessment, the players weren't that great. Still, they tried hard, and the crowd's enthusiasm more than compensated for their lack of skill.

"So you can overrun first but not second?" Marina quizzed halfway through the second inning. She sat forward on the edge of her seat, her fuchsia tank top silky and flowing against her skin.

"That's right," Cagney said. He could smell the deep, spicy scent of her perfume when she leaned forward like that. He also received tantalizing glimpses of other things. He shifted slightly, doing his best to accommodate his leg and pretend he truly didn't care.

But that didn't quite stop his eyes from drifting back.

"Did you come to the park a lot as a child?" Marina asked, her violet eyes bright with frank curiosity.

He nodded. "My parents are real baseball fans. They brought all five of us every Saturday there was a home game, and some weeknights, too. They have a box down front."

Marina looked at him, her brow crinkling into a small frown. "If they have a box, why do you sit back here?"

There was suspicion in that voice, and he heard and understood it. The need to reassure her was much stronger than it should have been.

"I was away for a long time," he said at last. "My parents fell into their own habits. They have a group of friends who almost always sit with them in the box. When I came back, I didn't want to disturb those arrangements."

It had hurt his parents in the beginning. They'd wanted him to disturb them—that's what family was all about. But they'd also always known that Cagney was slightly different. More than anyone in the family, he kept to himself. And part of being family was accepting those differences.

"What did you do?" Marina asked, her eyes growing intense as she watched his face.

"I lived in D.C. for a bit," he said in passing.

"Were you a sheriff?"

His jaw grew a bit tighter. "No, I worked as a Detective, actually. Homicide."

"Oh," she said, eyes widening.

He smiled dryly, not meeting her gaze. "I guess the experience is about to come in handy," he commented.

"I guess so," she said.

Chapter 4

"Nice double play," he said after a bit, his gaze back on the field.

She had to smile. "The most beautiful I've ever seen," she commented dryly. It was obvious he wanted to change the topic. But then, she'd been well versed in small talk and she had no business prying into his life anyway. The inning ended, Billy Joel music filling the stands as the players jogged off the field. "Good song," she commented politely, better at music than baseball.

"Reminds me of high school," he said.

She flashed him a more enthusiastic smile. "We used to listen to this every day during gym class. It was even the theme for our high-school prom."

He turned, his gaze unconsciously sweeping over her face. "So who was the lucky man? High-school sweetheart?"

She shook her head. "No high-school sweetheart. No prom."

He raised a surprised brow. She was a vibrant, intelligent woman. He would have thought she'd have more than her pick of dates.

As if reading his look, she simply smiled. "I just wasn't the prom type of person," she said.

But he thought he heard something wistful in her voice. "Kinda hard to go out all night when you have to sleep by ten, isn't it?" he guessed shrewdly.

"Very good, Sheriff," she told him. "Those detective instincts are still sharp."

"So why the schedule?" he persisted.

She shrugged, nearly flippant, but a faint wariness shadowed her eyes. "I'm an eccentric," she declared.

"You just like your secrets," he corrected.

This time, she arched a knowing brow. "Isn't that a little like the pot calling the kettle black, Sheriff?"

He found himself smiling reluctantly. "Score one," he drawled, his eyes lingering on her face, narrowing slightly. She was very astute. Very intelligent. And still very secretive.

They both drifted back into silence, staring once more at the field.

"So what about your brothers and sisters?" Marina asked after a bit, selecting a neutral topic as she moved forward to stretch out her back. "Are they still in the area?"

Cage swung his gaze around, slightly startled to find her leaning so close. He could see the sheen of sweat on her face from the heat and a few stray strands of hair curled damply around her cheeks. She stretched, her tank top rippling with her, and he felt it in his stomach.

This time, he had to force his gaze back to the field.

"My oldest brother, Mitch, lives in D.C. with his wife, Jessica," he replied at last. "They're expecting now. Then there's Garret, who's a Navy SEAL. We never know where he is. Jake was in Poland last I heard, investigating ceramics. And my sister, Liz, and her husband, Richard, live in

Connecticut. They just had a daughter, plus Richard has an eight-year-old son.'' He shrugged. ''And I live here.''

She nodded, twisting to the left and finding herself sitting even closer to him. He had the beginnings of a shadow on his cheeks. Dark, rasping whiskers. ''I don't have any brothers or sisters,'' she said after a moment. ''My parents adopted me when I was a baby but never adopted anyone else. And they couldn't have children of their own.''

She hadn't meant to, but for one moment, she sounded wistful. Cagney returned his gaze to her, drinking in her clear eyes, her graceful features. More of her hair was beginning to escape from her cap, falling in wispy disarray around her face. He liked how the strands framed her face.

His eyes settled on her lips. They were soft and full, and even as he watched, they parted slightly in a gasp of anticipation.

For one long moment, he didn't hear the crack of the bat or the roar of the crowd. He didn't feel the heat of the waning sun, or see the masses of people around them. He just heard her quick intake of breath, felt the responding tightness of his stomach and saw the lush promise of her lips.

And he felt something tear inside himself, a fierce pang of need knifing through the numbness that had been his existence for the past thirteen months. Until he was torn between the urgent desire to pull her into his arms and the overpowering need to simply fold up inside himself with eyes so gray and muscles so tense he wasn't a man but only unfeeling stone.

''Sheriff?''

The voice penetrated like a splash of cold water, breaking the spell and saving the dilemma. But when Cagney looked down at his hand, he could see it shaking with the strain. And for one long moment, he wondered which action he would have pursued.

He sat back sharply, his gray eyes harsh as they peered up from beneath his cowboy hat. ''Bennett,'' he said, his gaze flickering from the older man to the small woman standing quietly beside him. He touched his hat, nodding in greeting. "Evie."

Two pairs of eyes swiveled toward Marina, and belatedly Cagney remembered his manners.

"It's okay," she said, as he went to introduce her. "We've already met."

Something in her tone made him turn, and before his eyes he saw her shoulders go rigid. It appeared that Marina not only knew Bennett, but, judging by the sudden layer of frost in her eyes, she didn't like the man, either.

"It's okay, Sheriff," Bennett was saying, his gaze clearly flickering between Marina and Cagney with open speculation. "It's good to finally see you catching a game once more, so we'll only take a minute of your time. I just wanted to know how the murder investigation was coming. Things like that aren't supposed to happen around here. Why, I'm getting worried about the safety of my Evie."

Bennett put a solid arm around his shrinking wife as a protective gesture; she managed to flinch only a little at the contact. Cagney watched Evie silently for a moment, taking in her petite build and the simple flowered cotton dress that made her appear countrified and young. In contrast, her husband wore tan slacks and an open dress shirt that played up his wealth and power. His solid build and graying temples only added to the picture.

Cagney could see Cecille's interest in Bennett; Bennett appeared powerful and attractive at forty-one. Had Evie known of Cecille's interest, too? And even then, could this tiny shell of a woman really be capable of something so drastic as a vicious murder? He watched her for a moment longer, and saw her squirm under the intensity of his gaze. Interesting.

"Well, Sheriff?" Bennett prodded in a booming voice.

Cagney turned his steady gaze up to Bennett's sharp eyes. "It's coming along," he said levelly. "I imagine you'll be hearing something soon."

Marina's interest level seemed to perk at his words, something that wasn't lost on him.

"Good, good," Bennett said. "The sooner this whole business is behind us, the better." He nodded once more to Cagney, then gave a curt nod to Marina. "Shame about Cecille." Marina merely nodded back, her shoulders stiff. Bennett appeared to notice the tension, and the smile he gave her was openly amused. "Ma'am," he said by way of parting, flashing one last wolfish smile. Then he turned, and with his arm still tight around his wife's shoulders led Evie away.

"I don't like him," Marina whispered.

Cagney nodded. The last sixty seconds hadn't done a lot of improve his opinion of the older man, either. His speculative gaze remained on the disappearing couple, his mind still considering the possibilities. And he wondered if he shouldn't pay a visit to Evie Jensen some near afternoon.

Marina looked from the somber-faced man beside her to the retreating couple and uttered a small, internal sigh. She seemed to have lost her companion for the evening. It was just as well, Marina decided. The moment was lost already.

For some reason, that filled her with greater disappointment than it should have. So one moment she'd thought he might kiss her. So one moment, she'd wanted that kiss with every fiber of her being. Fool. He was the sheriff, and there were things she simply didn't want his eyes to see.

Bradley really had taught her a lot.

Cagney turned around and, as if he'd read her mind, pinned her with his dispassionate stare.

"So how long have you known Bennett?" he asked quietly.

She looked at him for a long moment and battled the desire to hit him. Damn him for interrogating her again. Damn him for being so completely determined he might as well have been carved from stone. To see him now, you never would have guessed he'd almost kissed her.

"Since I started work at Manning and Harding," she said finally, her voice purposefully cool and professional. Cagney wasn't the only one who could play this game. She crossed her legs smoothly, turning away from him to stare at the field with feigned interest. Some young player was coming up to bat.

"Seems he and Cecille were tight."

"So it seems," she said vaguely. She could feel his eyes on her, but she didn't turn.

"That's Tracy Coal coming up to bat," he remarked casually at last, following her gaze. "He's had a great year, hitting .343. He keeps that up he won't have to play Single A very long. Just look at that swing."

Tracy Coal's powerful arms swung the bat around solidly to connect with the ball in a ear-splitting crack. As Marina watched, the ball arched up and over the ad-covered fence. The young kid dropped his bat and began his jog around the bases to the swelling roar of the crowd.

"I thought Bennett just said you didn't come to the games," she said suddenly, swinging her head around to pin Cagney with her dark eyes. "So how do you know so much about this player?"

Cagney shrugged, calm and steady in spite of her intensity. "I have a radio," he said.

"Why don't you just come?" she persisted, her eyes unwavering. "You said you use to come as a child—sounds like you certainly love the game. So why not come to the park?"

For the first time, she had the satisfaction of watching his gray eyes darken.

"I don't like the seats," he said vaguely.

She leaned a little closer, her eyes unrelenting. "You could always sit down in the box with your parents."

"I suppose I could."

"It's about your leg, isn't it," she said suddenly, her intense gaze searching his expressionless face. She willed him to look at her, but his slate eyes gazed blandly out at the field.

"It's my leg that bothers me," he agreed, the wariness only faintly edging his voice.

Marina shook her head. "I don't mean physically," she said. "You don't limp that badly, and except for a little shifting here and there, you're doing fine now. It has to do with how you injured it, doesn't it? Why don't you talk about your leg, Cagney?"

"It's no one's business but my own," he said evenly. He finally turned, forcing himself to meet her gaze with his traditional dispassionate stare. It was hard, though. He could feel the intensity of those beautiful eyes boring into his, shifting through the shadows, determined to find the man underneath.

She leaned over even more, the warm spicy scent of her perfume teasing his senses, and his stomach tightened.

"Is the interrogation over?" he asked tersely.

"All right," she said immediately. "If you'll return the favor."

Slowly, reluctantly, he had to smile. He nodded at her point. "Score two," he acknowledged.

She arched a brow and nodded in satisfaction. "You know, not all of us eccentric types are flakes."

"I never would've dreamed of calling you a flake," he assured her. "Truce? I won't ask you and you don't ask me and we'll enjoy the rest of this fine ball game."

"Deal. Wanna seal it with a beer?"

"I suppose I can do that much."

She tilted her head playfully. "And peanuts?"

"And peanuts."

They managed to enjoy the rest of the game a great deal. When Tracy Coal came up to bat again, bottom of the ninth, 2–2 score, they held their breath together to see if the young power hitter would deliver. And when he struck out, they groaned with the rest of the fans. Then cheered as the next batter knocked one out of the park.

Maddensfield was redeemed, and everyone looked at each other with all-around goodwill. Even Cage found himself relaxed, with light crinkles around his eyes. The thrill of the game returned to him, the situation with Marina was back under control.

Until he looked over and saw her gaze on the darkening sky, and watched her shoulders slowly set with the tension. The game was ending, night descending, and he could almost feel the fear creeping up her spine.

His eyes darkened with the impact.

"Nice sunset," he remarked casually.

She nodded, not taking her eyes away from the sky. Then slowly, she turned back to him.

"I suppose we should be going," she said quietly.

He nodded, watching her look at the emptying stands with wistful eyes. "What will you do tonight?" he asked.

She shrugged. "Work upstairs, I guess." She could remember the tension of last night, the persistent feeling of another presence that had lasted well into the morning hours. Her shoulders tightened a notch more. "I miss my painting," she found herself saying softly. And at that moment she did. She missed the bright colors, the flowing magic. And somehow, it seemed more natural to jump at shifting shadows in a deserted lot than in the privacy of her own, supposedly safe, house.

Cage stood, stretching out his leg as he silently contemplated the situation. He should take her home—he was due to pay a visit to his parents now. But looking at her, seeing the shadows creep around her eyes, he couldn't quite imagine just leaving her at her doorstep.

Once more, she was scared. And once more, she didn't seem inclined to tell him why. But one thing was clear: the fear was genuine, and her house didn't seem to offer her any comfort.

"Want to go to a barbecue?" he found himself asking.

Almost immediately she perked up, her eyes growing bright with a vibrant enthusiasm that made his stomach clench and unclench.

"A barbecue?" she echoed. "That would be wonderful!"

Oh, he was going to pay for this. He hadn't brought a girl over to his mother's since he was sixteen; he'd never hear the end of it. But seeing Marina's glowing smile, he didn't feel bad about it. Hell, a man would sell his soul for a girl to smile at him so brightly.

He held out his arm and she took it with her strong, dusky fingers. He led her to his truck, and neither of them commented on the falling night.

At his mother's, it was easy to forget the darkness. Already the backyard of the six-bedroom rancher glowed with a bonfire and brightly hanging latterns. The smell of sizzling hamburgers filled the air, while the sound of laughter drifted through the warm, smoky night. The neighborhood always came to the barbecue, and now a good forty people ambled about the property, drinking beers, telling jokes and spinning gossip.

Cage led Marina around back to the yard he'd grown up playing in, searching with keen eyes for his parents. He might as well get this over with quickly.

Henry was manning the grill, complete in a red-checked apron and white chef's hat. He was also armed with a flipper, and waving it through the air as he talked.

"Cagney," he called out as he saw his youngest son approach. "'Bout time you showed up!" Then Henry noticed the young woman at his son's side, and his face broke into a patented Guiness grin. "Now I understand completely," he said.

"Dad," Cage acknowledged. "This is Marina—she's the new artist in town, working for Manning and Harding. Marina, this is my father, Henry. He's a nice enough man, but don't believe any of the stories he tells. He lies."

"I don't lie," Henry protested. "I spin yarns, a time-honored Southern art form. Now, tell me young lady, would you like your hamburger dead or still kicking?"

Marina grinned back at the man in front of her. He looked just like a sixty-year-old version of Cage, right down to the lean build and gray eyes. Except his hair was no longer full or jet black, and his eyes had a warm, mellow glow. "It's nice to meet you," she said. "And I'd like my hamburger still kicking, if it's not a problem."

"It's never a problem to serve a beautiful lady," Henry assured her. "'Bout time Cage brought one home. Are you keeping him out of trouble?" he quizzed.

Marina smiled, and deftly shook her head.

"Perfect," Henry informed her. "Someone has to kick a little life into that boy. A man could die from such seriousness. Don't know where he gets it. Must be a throwback to his mother's side."

Cage shot his father a level stare but, after years of experience, knew better than to launch a verbal protest. His father was a genuinely happy man who reveled in good stories and great jokes and wanted more grandkids. By those standards, Cage wasn't acting according to plan. But then, he never had.

"Cagney!"

Cage turned to see his mother bearing down on them, her brown eyes sparkling with affection. Then, of course, her gaze found Marina.

"And who do we have here?" Dotti exclaimed with a warm smile of welcome.

"This is Cagney's friend," Henry interjected with just the right amount of innuendo. "She's that new artist in town, Marina." He turned abruptly back to Marina. "Hey, aren't you doing that wall over there on the east side? Why, we just went to see it the other day, we'd heard so much. It's some piece of work. You did that all by yourself?"

"Yes, thank you."

He looked up and down at her slender build, then shook his head.

"Now, Henry," Dotti scolded. "Don't make her feel self-conscious. That's what we have Cagney for." She granted her son another smile, the mischievous gleam in her eyes unmistakable.

"They're always like this," Cagney said in answer to Marina's bemused gaze.

But when he looked back at his parents, she could see the affection in his eyes, and it tugged at her. In this bright circle of fire and family warmth, the darkness seemed to recede so far away it was only an echo of a shadow.

On instinct, she picked up his hand and squeezed it in silent gratitude before letting it go again. Henry and Dotti both noted the gesture, and exchanged glances. It was about time, their looks said. Cagney needed more happiness in his life.

Henry and Dotti would never tell their son the nights they spent worrying about him. Cagney, the quiet one. Cagney, the loner. And then after the shooting, Cagney, the empty one.

"Henry," Dottie said, keeping her voice bright, even as her heart contracted, "those patties are burning."

Henry jumped back to attention, rescuing the hamburgers from the flames just in time. With forty-years of practice, he neatly flipped the hamburgers onto paper plates, then handed them out to Marina and Cagney.

Marina closed her eyes and inhaled the mixing scents of seared beef and blazing charcoal in the warm summer air. She was quite sure nothing in Manhattan had ever smelled like this—though to be fair, her parents threw the best cocktail parties.

"Thank you." She half sighed, the obvious pleasure in her face enough to still even Henry's long-stolen heart.

"Thanks, Dad," Cage also replied. Having braved enough of his parents' speculative glances, he pulled Marina off to a more distant corner of the yard where they could eat in peace.

"Your parents are wonderful people," Marina said as they sat down on the grass.

"Wouldn't trade them for the world," Cagney agreed. He was silent for a moment, then carefully queried, "Are you close to your own?"

"Oh, yes," she assured him, eyeing the hamburger before her. She'd already eaten at the game, so she wasn't too hungry. Still, it smelled so good. "We talk at least once a week," she continued. "And, at times, I still really miss them. But somehow, being here makes Manhattan seem worlds away. The pace, the people, the sights and smells. Everything here is so different, and after twenty-seven years exactly what I've been looking for."

Except, of course, for the long nights when the shadows pushed in from every corner.

Cagney nodded, understanding better than she realized. He might have returned home for all the wrong reasons, but having come back, it was hard to believe that he would ever want to live anyplace else.

"Did you grow up here?" Marina asked, gesturing to the yard and the house.

"Yep," Cagney confirmed. "All five of us used to tear around this yard. It's a miracle any of the grass survived."

"Do you miss your brothers and sisters?"

Cagney nodded, considering the matter for the first time in a while. "Yeah, I suppose. Seems lately everyone's scattered about and we don't get together as often as we did. But you know, family's family. You hear their voice on the other end of the phone, and it's as if you're ten years old and hiding out in the tree house again."

"Tell me more about them," she urged, her eyes earnest. She'd always wanted siblings.

Cage just shrugged. "I don't know what to say. Let's see, Mitch is the oldest, the responsible one who kept us out of trouble. Then there's Garret, who got us all in trouble. Wild one," he said with a shake of his head, his eyes perturbed. "Jake's definitely the smart one—he went off to Harvard and runs his own company now. And Liz kept up with us all and kept us sane."

"So you were the youngest son?"

He nodded.

"Wow, I bet you got teased a lot." She seemed to sigh. "I always wanted brothers and sisters. I bet it was wonderful."

"Well," he said, and a smile tickled his lips, "I got teased a lot."

She laughed, a wonderful, rich sound like warm whiskey. He looked at her, enraptured by the expression on her face, the sound of her voice; he felt slightly dazed.

"I like your family," she told him. "I do miss my parents."

He leaned forward, not quite able to help himself, and wiped a bit of ketchup from her cheek. "I'll share," he said, his voice huskier than he'd intended.

Her eyes darkened a fraction, her lashes sweeping down. "Share what?"

"My family. You've already met my folks and they'd love the excuse to set one more plate at dinner. Anytime you want, you can just come right over. And next time Liz is in town, I'll introduce you. You'd really like Liz."

She nodded breathlessly, intrigued by his nearness, touched by his offer. "That's very kind of you."

"Just neighborly."

"Cagney!" a female voice exclaimed out of the darkness. "There's where you've been hiding."

Marina glanced up to see a pleasant-looking woman walking toward them. She had fine brown hair that had been pulled up onto a knot on the top of her head, but now strands were escaping to frame a soft, rounded face. With her lacy top and flowing skirt, she reminded Marina of a cameo portrait. She also came to an abrupt stop when she noticed Marina next to Cagney.

"I'm sorry," the woman said. "I didn't mean to interrupt."

"It's okay," Marina assured her. She automatically held out her hand. "I'm Marina Walden."

The woman immediately nodded, shaking her hand while she smiled with friendly Southern charm. "Of course," the woman drawled. "I'm Suzanne Montgomery, the kindergarten teacher in Maddensfield. It's so nice to finally meet the artist of that gorgeous wall. Cagney, you ought to be ashamed of yourself, hogging her all to yourself like this!"

Cagney just smiled, a slow, lazy grin that Marina had never before seen on his face. It reminded her at once of his father, while sending a strange pang through her chest. Why hadn't he smiled like that for her?

"Suzanne," he drawled comfortably. "Figured I might see you here. How's everything?"

Suzanne remained standing, her gaze going between the two with open curiosity. "I don't want to take up too much of your time," she declared. "I just have a quick question for Cagney and then I'll leave you two on your own."

She turned to Cagney, and Marina could see the sudden softening of the woman's face. She recognized the look: it was compassion.

"Now, Cagney dear, you know I wouldn't ask this of you if I didn't have to, but we really are in dire straits. We have fifteen kids with mitts and bats and who are so very eager to play. We just need a coach, that's all, and why, with your experience and the fact that you coached before..."

Suzanne's voice drifted off, and Marina couldn't blame her. Beside her, Cagney had gone rigid in the warm night and his gaze was positively steely.

"No," he said flatly.

To her credit, Suzanne gave a valiant try. "Cagney," she said firmly. "I've known you for thirty years now and that gives me the right to speak my mind. You can't hide forever, Cagney. You can't keep avoiding kids and you can't keep pretending you don't care about anything. I remember you coaching that team back in high school. You did such a great job, and the kids really loved you."

If possible, Cagney's gaze grew even chillier. "Suzanne," he said levelly. "Given the condition of my leg, I have no business coaching. Let alone what parents might say. I gave you my answer. Don't abuse our friendship by asking again. Now, if you'll excuse me," he said curtly, "I'm going to go dispose of my plate."

He rose abruptly, as if it suddenly pained him to sit. And it seemed to Marina that he limped more than usual as he hobbled off into the night. Beside her, Suzanne Montgomery watched him go with a shake of her head.

"He always was too stubborn." Suzanne sighed out loud. "I believe it's a Guiness trait." She turned back to give Marina a speculative glance. "A girl could do a lot worse than Cage Guiness," she said.

Marina looked at her with shock, though the thought had been echoing in her head not too long ago. "We're just friends," she managed to protest.

Suzanne digested this for a moment. "You be careful with him," she said at last. "Cage is one the best men Maddensfield ever produced. And he's suffered enough already."

"What do you mean by that?" Marina pressed. "And what do you mean about hiding from kids and baseball and everything? I thought he'd love to coach. He seems to love the game."

Suzanne looked slightly surpised. "He hasn't told you about D.C.?"

Marina shook her head, the need to know burning in her throat. But the woman before her merely shook her head.

"It's not my place to tell you," Suzanne said at last. "It's up to Cagney. Just remember, no matter what he says, Cagney always was too hard on himself. Did you know the doctors said he would be able to walk without a limp given enough time and proper care? But over a year later, he still limps. I'm telling you, he needs the pain, the penance." She shook her head with a soft sigh. "Make him smile, Marina. The man needs to learn to live again."

Marina could only sit there, a strange mixture of compassion and uncertainty twisting in her chest. She did want to make him smile, but then, she'd just met him twenty-four hours ago, and not exactly under the best of circumstances.

"Why... why are you telling me this?" she forced herself to ask.

Suzanne appeared genuinely surprised. "Why, he brought you here, didn't he? Cage Guiness hasn't brought a date home since high school. I figured it must be something serious. Besides, I've seen your work. You're perfect for him.''

Marina shook her head. "He's just—'' she searched for a word "—just helping me out, that's all.''

"Oh, a girl can change that quickly enough,'' Suzanne said firmly. "Just give him a little push.''

Marina looked at her with an uncomfortable, puzzled expression, and after a moment, Suzanne understood. She held up a hand in the air, smiling broadly. "Oh, no,'' she said. "Cagney and I are just best friends. Goodness, we've been friends forever now. That's it. You take care now. And remember, all Guiness males are stubborn and all Guiness males think they're right. That's exactly why they need a good woman to set 'em straight.''

Marina opened her mouth to protest, but it was too late; Suzanne was already turning and walking back to the glow of the fire. Thirty seconds later, Cagney was back at her side, his eyes expressionless once more.

"You didn't eat your burger,'' he said.

She glanced down at the hamburger, marveling at the sheer simplicity of the comment when there were so many questions she suddenly wanted to ask him. And she hadn't the right to utter a single one of them.

"I wasn't hungry,'' she said, instead. "Would you like it?''

"I'm fine.''

"My mother used to say I had to eat things because somewhere in the world another little girl was starving.''

"My mom had similar lines.''

"What should I do?''

"We're not children anymore, Marina.''

She nodded, feeling her throat grow unaccountably tight. She wasn't a child anymore. She understood that what she ate didn't make a difference on whether or not someone else went hungry. And she understood that the shadows under her bed weren't really monsters, nor were her tennis shoes glowing fangs in the dark. She'd grown into a logical, rational woman, well versed in the ways of the world. There was no reason to be afraid of things she couldn't see.

No reason to worry about the unknown shadows.

But still, her eyes went to the dark sky, and she shivered. And the exhaustion that filled her was nearly complete.

"It's nine forty-five," Cage said quietly, his ability to follow her thoughts uncanny. He took the plate from her, offering her his hand to help her up. "We should be getting you home now."

She nodded, the sudden tiredness genuine. She was due to sleep in fifteen minutes, and her biological clock, long ignored, was now insistent. She should be happy to be so tired. It meant she would fall asleep immediately.

It meant she wouldn't dream.

But somehow, as she fell into step with the quiet man beside her, she wasn't sure anymore. Cage would take her home, drop her off and then leave.

She'd be alone in her house.

For no good reason, that scared her to death.

Chapter 5

They drove with all the windows rolled down, the warm night air whipping through the truck's cab to mix with the sound of Clint Black and the smell of honeysuckle. Marina took off her baseball cap, and the heavy Southern wind tangled sweetly through her long, dark hair.

For a minute, it was easy to think they were simply on a late-night drive, relishing the warm June night and soft, moonstruck sky. It was beautiful and perfect and semiwild with the power of the truck around them.

Except when they crossed the railroad tracks and Marina could see the remains of the yellow crime tape still circling the side of the road. And even as they passed the brilliant promise of her unfinished mural, each block brought them closer and closer to her house.

The smell of honeysuckle faded, to be replaced by the dusty residue of the nearby textile mill. Cage pulled into her driveway, shutting off the truck, and the night grew silent.

For a long moment she just looked at her house, looming before her. Funny how when she'd first seen it, the peeling paint and sagging front porch had seemed merely superficial problems that could be easily remedied. She'd been caught up in the large bay windows that welcomed the North Carolina sun; the warm, redbrick chimney that contributed a solid, cozy feel. She'd seen the dismally small second-floor rooms as one huge art studio, and envisioned a remodeled dining room with glowing hardwood floors.

Now she just saw a rundown pseudo-Victorian home, way past its prime and easy to break into.

"I could stick around if you'd like," came Cagney's low voice. Could that man read everyone's mind, or was the fear written so clearly across her face?

Slowly, not looking at him, she shook her head. It was her house, dammit. She'd been proud to find it two months ago, the first thing she'd ever really owned. She'd even planted a tiny sapling in the front yard, eagerly anticipating the years she would watch it grow.

She wasn't going to give in to some irrational thirteen-year-old fear now. She'd *earned* the right to sleep at night. She'd earned the right to live alone in her own house. She squared her shoulders, set her jaw and opened the truck door.

Watching her from across the cab, Cagney thought she looked more like a woman preparing for war than a woman returning to her home. He followed her out into the warm, lush night.

"You should have left the porch light on," he said as she fumbled with her keys in the dark.

"I thought I did," she replied with a small shrug. "But I still have a habit of forgetting."

Next to her, Cagney frowned. "Maybe I ought to come in with you," he said levelly. "Just to look around."

Her hand stilled on the knob for a moment, then she resolutely pushed the key into the lock. She nodded, wondering if it was right to feel so relieved that this man was beside her.

She opened the door, but before she could step in, Cage grabbed her arm. She turned, startled, but he silently shook

his head at her. With steely, careful eyes, he stepped ahead
of her into the darkened entryway.

He remained still, letting his eyes adjust to the lack of
light. Slowly he could make out the rise of a staircase immediately in front of him. To his left, an arched doorway
yawned like a black, gaping mouth. To his right the bay
windows let in enough light to reveal the soft forms of a
couch and love seat positioned in a living room.

He reached along the wall to find the light switch. His
muscles were bunched and tight, ready for anything as he
abruptly snapped on the light.

Two hundred watts of electricity flooded the entryway,
momentarily blinding him with the intensity. He had to
swallow back the curt words that rose to his lips.

But as a long moment passed, nothing moved or stirred.
Behind him, he could hear the soft sigh of Marina's relief,
and it seemed to echo all the way down to his toes.

"You must pay a fortune in electricity bills," he drawled,
moving out of the entryway to snap on the other lights. He
could hear Marina's small, nervous laugh as she switched
on the lights in the left room to reveal the dining room.

"I've always liked bright things," she half muttered.

Standing now in the living room, Cagney nodded. From
what he could tell, the rooms were consistent with her wall,
her office and, for that matter, her. Lush plants and bright
colors flooded every nook and cranny. The living room was
a dazzling array of dark green, deep purple and bright
fuchsia. The furniture consisted of white-and-eggshell-
painted pine, lending a country comfort to the blazing light
and colors. As he moved back through the entryway into
the dining room, he could see a similar motif.

A light-blue-and-taupe Oriental rug covered the scruffed-
up hardwood floor. The dining-room table was also pine,
covered with a clear glaze and marked with enough
scratches and bangs to have a lived-in feel. The chairs
sported mint-green slips over the back, while the cushions
were white with rose-colored specks. The brass chandelier
threw hundreds of watts of electricity over a huge, vibrant

flower arrangement and the hutch was covered with lavender violets and pink impatiens.

He journeyed through the dining room into the kitchen. Here the floor creaked under his footsteps and he could see the telltale signs of water rot in the corners. The old enamel sink was cracked, the countertops scarred and stained. What concerned him most, however, was the sliding-glass door that led to the backyard. A preliminary check revealed old doors with loose hinges. At least Marina had had the good sense to stick half a broomstick along the track.

Even then, a determined four-year-old could probably break into her kitchen. He rose from his inspection, shaking his head, to find Marina watching him.

In the bright light of the kitchen, he could see the exhaustion clearly around her eyes. He could also see the tight strain of barely checked fear.

"The place needs a lot of work," she said quietly. "I've only lived here two months."

"You shouldn't have moved here," he told her levelly. "This isn't a good neighborhood for a woman alone."

He recognized by now the stubborn tilt of her chin.

"I wanted to live here," she replied evenly, a glint of spirit replacing the exhaustion in her eyes. "This used to be a beautiful neighborhood, and it could be again if people cared enough to try. It's just that everyone walks away from old things once they've lost their beauty. People would rather just throw them away and buy something new."

Cagney shook his head, though her words triggered something inside him. "You've got a lot of interesting notions for a Manhattan Yankee," he told her. "Mind if I check the upstairs?"

She shook her head, letting him brush by her in the tiny eating nook to pass into the living room. For a long moment, her gaze rested on the sliding-glass door. She felt something slow and sinister shiver down her spine.

Abruptly, she whirled and followed Cage upstairs. She caught up with him on the landing, perusing the construction zone upstairs with a critical eye.

"At least the floor's solid," he muttered.

She'd pretty much gutted the upstairs from what he could tell. One wall was already half knocked down to turn two small rooms into one big one. After just a moment, he could see her vision. Rather than being eaten up by an attic, the upstairs ceiling towered above them in a magnificent arch, complete with an old ceiling fan and unfinished pine boards. Once the rooms were completely joined, the area would be a large and expansive. He could already see her filling it with leafy palms and exotic paintings.

And for one moment, he understood why she bought the house. But then the vision faded, he was back to staring at a gaping wall and construction dust. He remembered the old front door, the huge bay windows and the sliding-glass door, and his city-cop instincts registered a whopping red alert.

"The bedroom?" he asked curtly.

She gestured to his right and together they walked into a tiny room that barely held the queen-size bed and an overflowing dresser. Compared with the rest of the house, the room was noticeably devoid of personality or care. No pictures, no pillows. Just an unmade bed with rose-colored sheets and a mint-and-pink-flowered bedspread. Shirts, shorts and a few lacy garments hung loosely out of the dresser. The rest of the house had been clean and organized in comparison.

But it was suitable, Cage registered after a minute, for a woman who only slept in two-hour intervals three times a day. Of all the rooms, this was the one in which she never lingered.

He looked over at Marina and found her gazing at the bed with a strange mixture of longing and despair. Then slowly, her gaze slid over to meet his, and he saw a starkness there that shook him.

For one minute, he remained riveted by those violet eyes. And at once he was aware of the tiny quarters and how close to him she stood. He could smell her perfume tangled with the rumpled sheets, and with only the tiniest stretch of imagination, he could see her long black hair tumbled over the flowered bedspread.

"Everything seems to be all right," he said, his voice hoarser than intended.

She nodded, a minute motion that was nearly lost by the impact of her gaze dropping to his lips, then flickering back up to find his eyes.

"All seems well," she agreed, her voice a husky whisper as her eyes lashes suddenly swept down to cover the longing she knew must be in her eyes.

She had to clench her hand into a fist to keep from reaching out to him. She abruptly wanted this man, was attracted to his steady presence and quiet strength.

What it would be like to feel his strength all around her, his lean, muscular build laboring above her, his level eyes boring into her? What would it be like to hear her name torn from his lips, to feel herself shattering into a million pieces with his lips hot and hungry upon hers?

To wake up with his arms around her, the sound of his heartbeat a reassuring rhythm in her ear?

She thought he could probably hold the shadows at bay. Maybe in his arms, the inexplicable fear would leave her altogether.

In the small confines of her bedroom, she turned away from him so he could not see the emotions stinging her eyes. She wouldn't ask him to stay.

She fought her own battles.

"Well," she said at last with sudden and artificial brightness, "I guess that takes care of everything." She turned and hoped her face appeared casual.

Before her, Cage nodded with dark, unreadable eyes.

"I imagine you're very tired," he drawled.

She nodded, her smile only faltering a bit. "Yes," she declared. "It is way past my bedtime."

"Why are you so afraid, Marina?"

This time her smile faltered blatantly, and another pang of longing seized her chest. For one moment she wavered, her mouth opening with words she had never said and fears she had never acknowledged out loud. Then abruptly, she forced the picture of Bradley in front of her eyes, his jaw slack with dawning horror.

Her shoulders went straight, her chin came up and her eyes set with the resolution of a soldier.

"I'm just tired," she said evenly. "I apologize for taking up so much of your time."

Cage waited another long moment, not saying anything, not moving. But she didn't relent, and after a minute, he was the one who gave in with a small nod. He allowed her to lead him back down the stairs and onto the porch. This time the porch light shone in the darkness.

On the porch, however, he hesitated once more.

He didn't like the idea of leaving her alone in this house. He didn't like the grimness he now saw in her face, as if she were preparing for something unpleasant but that had to be done.

He stalled on the porch, not comfortable with leaving.

She looked too damn alone. And too damn resigned to it.

"Good night, Cagney," she said quietly. "And thank you for the evening. It...it was lovely."

He nodded, turning back to look at his truck, gleaming blue in the darkness, waiting for him. He took two steps toward it, feeling her stoic gaze on his back. He took another few steps.

"Cage?" she whispered.

He pivoted sharply, finding her needy gaze in the night, and in three long strides he was before her, dragging her close as his lips thundered down onto her own. It was nothing soft or gentle or reassuring. It was dark and hungry and demanding, and she surrendered to it instantly, her strong painter's arms wrapping around his neck with equal fierceness.

She welcomed his tongue into her mouth, welcomed the long, hard feel of his body pressed almost savagely against her own. Fill her, take her, possess her—she wanted it all.

Consume her in worlds where fear did not exist and the shadows weren't real.

His hands plowed through the thick mass of her hair, arching her head to deepen the kiss. She responded with equal fervor, feeling the rasp of his sixteen-hour-old beard against her tender skin, tasting the rich, male heat of his mouth, the salty tang of sweat. Her hands gripped his shoulders, outlining rippling muscles as his hips pressed intimately against her own. She could feel the hard length of him through his jeans, and groaned.

He jerked his hips closer, and she accommodated by wrapping one long, tanned leg around his waist. This time, he was the one who uttered a primal growl.

Like a drugged man, he raised his head to look at her with glittering gray eyes. "We shouldn't be doing this," he told her, his voice low. His entire body was on fire, roaring with the flames of hell as long-suppressed passion raged with equally suppressed anger and guilt. He didn't know whether he wanted to run away or plunge into her lithe body with the fury of a condemned man.

"Take me anyway," she said.

And in her violet eyes he saw a burning intensity equal to his own. He succumbed to those eyes and his passion, his lips slanting across hers once more. He unwrapped her leg briefly, feeling her shudder with the loss. But it was only temporary, as he backed her up against the house wall, wrapping both her legs around his waist and pulling himself tight against the warm welcome of her body. She moved her hips in helpless rhythm, straining against the rigid outline of his desire as her tongue dueled with his.

Savagely, his hands found and caressed the long, hot silk of her bare legs. He could feel the supple outline of conditioned muscles and slender curves. He could feel her shiver and groan against his lips, wanting him, needing him.

And beneath all the passion and fury, he felt the first sliver of pain.

Oh, God, what was he doing, to himself, to her?

He'd come back to Maddensfield seeking isolation, probably even penance. But not this. He had nothing to give a woman, only brittle memories of one afternoon he still couldn't get out of his mind.

Marina felt the change, felt the sudden darkness descend upon the passion. And she felt the long, black shudder that moved through his lean frame with unimaginable force. Until suddenly her lips were no longer hungry upon his but had softened to the gentle caress of a woman's unerring instinct.

He pulled his lips away from hers, cursing himself and the weakness that had led him to touch her in the first place. But even as the self-loathing coursed through him, he couldn't quite step back. Instead he buried his face in the soft silk of her hair and cursed himself some more.

She didn't say anything, but her hands soothed down his back as the untapped passion gripped her in a long, deep shudder. She could feel his heartbeat thundering against her chest, and a sudden burning stung her eyes. She hadn't expected the passion, and she didn't understand his sudden pain. But she thought that if he left her now, she would shatter into a million pieces.'

The thought didn't do her any good.

He pulled away from her with such suddenness she could barely get her feet beneath her in time. She would have blushed in mortification at her boldness of just a few minutes ago, but the harshness in his gray eyes made her want to cry out, instead.

"Forgive me, ma'am," he said, his voice sounded at once level and strained. He bent over and picked up his black hat, which had fallen off in the heat of the moment.

This time, she did blush, a creep of color that caused her to turn away. "It...it was my fault," she said quietly, compelling her mouth to work, even if the rest of her still reeled with the shock. "There's no need to apologize."

"It won't happen again," he answered remotely.

She looked at him a moment, struggling to say something to make things right. But with the passion fled the boldness, and now she was just a lonely woman who knew too much about fear and how to stand alone.

"I'm not normally like that," she whispered. She forced her eyes up. "Honest."

Standing on her porch with the light behind her, she'd appeared at once lonely and proud. The image tugged at him. It hadn't been her fault, after all. He'd been the one to turn around; he'd been the one pulling her lips beneath his. She didn't know what had made him draw away and he wouldn't explain it to her. But he could at least make the effort to salvage her pride. He owed her that much.

He took a deep breath, searching for something witty and casual to break the tension. Something light and clever like his brother Jake would say. He finally settled for a faint, apologetic smile.

"Well," he drawled, meeting her eyes with a steady gaze. "This weather does crazy things to people. Nothing quite like a North Carolina heat spell."

Her shoulders relaxed a fraction. "And I thought it was the Southern hospitality," she said dryly.

"I think I was more than a bit neighborly," he acknowledged, and they both shared a self-conscious laugh. "You understand we can't do this again?" he said at last.

"So you've said."

He nodded turning his hat in his hand and still feeling restless at the sight of her long, limber legs and bare, supple arms. He'd never been good at these things. Garret and Jake had always been the ones with the women.

"Cagney?"

He looked up to find her smiling faintly, her gaze soft. She gave a little shrug, leaning against her porch railing.

"Thank you for coming in," she told him levelly. "Thank you for checking out my house. That was kind of you."

"Just doing my job."

"I suppose."

"You really should get a new sliding-glass door, something stronger with roller locks so it can't be popped off the tracks. I could check into it for you if you'd like."

"Thanks, but I can take care of it."

"All right." He put his hat back on his head, setting it firmly in place. Time to go. But he still found himself lingering, the restlessness still gnawing at his belly.

On the porch, she yawned.

"Past your bedtime," he commented.

She nodded wryly. "I'm going to turn into a pumpkin anytime now."

"Good night, Marina."

"Good night, Cage."

He walked to his truck, and minutes later he roared away into the hot June night, leaving her alone on the rundown porch of her first house.

She lowered her head for one moment, and allowed herself to miss him, and allowed herself to curse her inexplicable passion. She'd never responded to anyone the way she'd just responded to Cage. She wasn't a woman who dated much, and her own sexual experience had been mediocre encounters with Bradley.

Maybe it was the heat or the scent of honeysuckle in the air. Or maybe it was the steadiness she'd seen in Cage's eyes. Certainly Bradley had never looked at her so calmly and clearly.

She forced her head up and her shoulders back, taking a last deep breath as she composed herself. She was a strong woman, stronger than Cagney Guiness would ever know. She'd fought wars on battlegrounds other people never even saw, and she'd gained ground inch by painstaking inch. And no one had ever understood or appreciated her victory but her and her parents.

She didn't need Cage to keep the demons at bay, she told herself vehemently. She'd learned the hard way how to do that for herself.

She made herself go back inside as the exhaustion hit sharply. She was off her sleep schedule and that never boded well.

She took a quick, cool shower, then tumbled at last into bed. The clocked glowed 10:45 p.m.

And it glowed 12:15 a.m. when she jerked awake with a scream in her throat and terror in her eyes.

He sat on the drab, olive-colored carpet of his one-bedroon apartment, a fan blowing against his bare, sweat-slicked chest, as he looked at the scrapbook in his hand. With unfocused eyes, he turned page after page of newspaper clippings.

He'd started compiling the scrapbook the week right after the shooting. At first he'd just put the articles in a file. But as weeks turned into months without the hard knot of guilt leaving his stomach, he'd collected more and more of the articles, combing more and more newspapers. It became his obsession. Now he had the *Washington Post,* the *New York Times* and the local paper all delivered daily. So he could go through searching for the answers that still eluded him.

The pages offered grim headlines. Youth violence on the rise. Kids killing kids. Research findings of dispassion and insensitivity in a new generation who murdered for high tops and gold hoop earrings. An overwhelmed juvenile system that processed fourteen-year-old killers and released them at eighteen. Or tried them as adults, locked them up with older, even more hardened, criminals, to spit them back out a thirty.

So many articles, and none of them gave him the answers he was looking for, only more questions to ponder on the dark nights when he couldn't sleep.

QVee might as well have stepped out of the pages of the newspapers; his life had been so clichéd it could have been the case study for any of the special reports. He'd grown up in the projects, his mother a prostitute and cocaine addict who'd had four children by three different men, and none of the men had stuck around. QVee's older brother was an Original Gangster—(O.G.)—who'd been convicted of murder at sixteen. His elder sister had been stabbed to death by a jealous boyfriend. According to rumors on the streets, the cops never would find the boyfriend's body—QVee had been that thorough in his revenge. QVee's five-year-old brother now lived and raised himself on the same streets where he could see his future on every face around him. He would most likely be jumped into the gang at age eight. Maybe he could even break QVee's family record of first homicide by age eleven. His options didn't look that great.

And that's what Cagney couldn't bear. He'd become a cop naively, believing he could make the world a better place. Over time, he'd come to understand that life wasn't that simple. But still, he remembered the thrill of coaching Little League, the satisfaction that came from working with a kid, helping a kid and then watching the first time that kid nailed one out of the park. You gave. You helped. You had at least a small impact.

Cage hadn't helped QVee. Cage and his partner, Melissa, had walked down the streets of QVee's life carrying his statistical destiny in the holsters at their waist.

And over and over again, Cagney wondered if there was anything he could have done differently. Maybe he should have aimed at the kid's leg, instead. Maybe they never should have interviewed him on his front porch but taken him in the patrol car down to the controlled environment of the police station. Maybe they should have researched things ahead of time so that they would have understood QVee was too angry, too bitter, to fear death. In fact, he'd deliberately sought it out.

Cagney hadn't stopped him. Cagney hadn't helped him. QV had raised and fired his gun thirteen months ago, and Cage had been forced to do the same. He'd become a participant in the cycle of violence. Part of the problem, not the solution.

That's not why he'd become a cop. That's not who he wanted to be. But in this new era of thirteen-year-olds carrying and using guns, none of the ''special reports'' could tell him what his role was supposed to be. No one knew how to handle children who, in their simple worlds, shot and killed the random stranger for money, then went home to watch cartoons.

Cagney had thought he'd known once what being a cop was all about. But in the space of fifteen seconds, he'd learned he was wrong.

Now he no longer knew what his duty was supposed to be.

And he wondered what his tall, strong older brothers would think to know that Cagney Guiness could no longer stand to hold a gun.

The phone rang shrilly, cutting through the hot, humid night. Instantly his gaze went to the digital clock: two a.m.

Marina. Her image leaped into his mind and immediately the anticipation tightened his stomach. He closed the collection of newspaper articles with a snap, frowning disapprovingly at his sharp reaction.

He rose, wincing a little at the pinprick of pain in his left leg, and picked up the phone.

''Hello?''

''Guiness?''

Cage recognized Daniels's gruff voice immediately. ''It took you damn long enough to answer the phone.''

''What happened?'' Cage demanded clearly, all muscles tensed for action.

''We found the car, Guiness. 'Least we're pretty sure. A car-rental agency in the Piedmont Triad International Airport called about a recent return that had blood all over the trunk. The lab boys went to investigate the scene, and one of them pulled out a couple of coarse strands of brown hair. He doesn't have the reports back yet with a match, but he was at the Manning scene. He's ninety-eight percent sure it's the same victim.''

"The Piedmont Triad Airport is only an hour from here. That could be," Cagney agreed with a quick nod in the darkness. "What else do we know?"

"Oh, you're going to like this, Guiness. The car was checked out at ten-thirty p.m. on June 5, same night of the murder. It was returned at seven a.m. June 6. The name they have is a Kristi Davis, but I'm willing to bet the driver's license was a fake. What's important is that the clerk remembers the woman as having long, black hair with a gray streak. Now, does that remind you of anyone, Cagney?"

On the bed, Cagney felt his stomach lurch, and for a long moment he didn't say anything. His grip on the phone tightened, but he forced his voice to remain level.

"It obviously sounds like Marina Walden," he said quietly. "Any other evidence?"

"Sure. I just got done calling all the cab companies. One of them has logged a trip from Maddensfield to the airport, nine-thirty pickup, for one Marina Walden at the Manning and Harding Ad Agency. We haven't gotten to the driver yet, but the dispatcher did remember that the woman paid in cash."

"Does that sound strange to you?" Cagney said suddenly. "That she'd be smart enough to use a fake license but not cover up something as distinguishing as a gray streak in her black hair? Or, for that matter, that she called the cab in her own name but had ID for an alias?"

"Come on. Of course she made mistakes. All criminals make mistakes. That's how we catch them."

"I don't like it," Cagney said simply. "It's too pat, too easy."

"Guiness, a simple answer ain't necessarily wrong. Let's not make this more complicated than it has to be."

"When will you have confirmation from the lab?" Cage asked quietly. His stomach felt abruptly hollow.

"Hopefully first thing in the morning. You bring her in. I'll meet you at the office. Hell, have you gotten that air conditioner fixed yet? Oh, doesn't matter. Maybe the heat will make her talk faster. And let me tell you, she's got a lot of explaining to do!''

"She won't have answers," Cagney said suddenly, and at that moment, the niggling on his instincts fired home. "Of course she can't have answers."

"What the hell are you talking about?"

"It's the times," Cage replied tersely, his eyes narrowing in the darkness. "She has to account for where she was from nine-thirty to eleven-thirty, right—the time it would take to get to the airport, pick up the car and drive back. Now, we know Cecille was alive at ten-thirty because she called her secretary, but dead by four a.m. So the second time frame would be twelve to four a.m. Finally, she'd have to leave around six to get the car back to the airport by seven, returning to Maddensfield by eight. But Marina keeps this schedule where she sleeps from ten to midnight, works from midnight to six on the wall, then sleeps from six to eight. So she can't have an alibi, because she would normally be sleeping or painting alone at those times."

"There you go," Daniels stated firmly. "She had ample opportunity to kill Cecille."

"Or ample opportunity to be framed," Cagney retaliated. "Don't you see, everyone knows that schedule. According to her, she's been on it forever. And if she really was the killer, don't you think she'd make some effort to have an alibi?"

"She can argue her schedule. Maybe she thinks that's good enough."

"But I saw her that night, Daniels, and she didn't look like a woman who'd been up all night, driven one hundred twenty miles and committed a murder. Not to mention that I took her home and there wasn't any car parked around her house."

"She hid it," Daniels replied evenly.

This time Cage couldn't completely hide his impatience. "So according to your theory, she has enough intelligence to get a fake license and hide the rental car, but not enough to camouflage a distinguishing gray streak, use a fake name with a cab company or stage an alibi. I'm telling you, Daniels, none of this is right."

"And I'm telling you," Daniels replied angrily, "that you're too close to know. Come on, Guiness, if you were still in D.C. you'd have that woman down to the station and printed by now. We have motive, we have opportunity and we have circumstantial evidence. Maybe you've stopped being a cop, but I haven't."

For one fraction of a moment, Cage couldn't even speak. He could just see fourteen-year-old QVee falling down on his front porch, the look of surprise etched across his face. He could remember the sound of the gun, the smell of the gunpowder, the feel of QVee's shot beginning to register in his leg.

He forced himself to sit up straight. He forced himself to sound calm.

"I'll go watch her," he heard himself say, each word enunciated low and even. "But I won't book her yet, Daniels. And you can call me anything you want, but I'm still sheriff here. You think we have answers. I say we have more questions, and I want each and every one of them answered to my satisfaction. In the meantime, we'll keep her under surveillance so tight she won't be able to sneeze without a witness. I believe that's fair."

On the other end of the phone, Daniels supplied him with a long, rich string of interesting words. Finally the fluent cursing ground to a mumbled halt. "Fine," Daniels rasped. "But if she kills anyone else, it's on your head."

Cagney nodded, well aware of the responsibility. "Find the taxi driver," Cagney instructed. "See if he knows what she was wearing, maybe something like the scent of her perfume. He had an hour to talk to her—what did she say? And figure out how she got back to Maddensfield after dropping off the rental car. There had to be either a return taxi or maybe an accomplice."

"And what about you, boy wonder?"

"I'll speak to her," he said. "And I want to get my hands on Bennett and Evie Jensen. Maybe another chat with

Martha would be good. Trust me, I'll keep in touch. Let me know about the lab reports.''

"Fine. But you'd better keep your eye on her. I don't know about you, but I still remember how Cecille Manning looked.''

Cagney nodded and hung up the phone. He allowed himself one moment of self-doubt, sitting in the dark isolation of his sparse bedroom. Maybe he *was* too close to Marina. Maybe he wasn't ready to be a cop again. Maybe Daniels was right.

He stood and pulled on his jeans in the darkness.

He wasn't a D.C. detective anymore; he was just a small-town sheriff with more guilt than bravado. But he was still an intelligent man, and he still stood by the star he'd pinned on his chest.

What happened to Cecille Manning went beyond all definitions of savagery, and he had every intention of getting to the bottom of it. He would keep his eye on Marina Walden, and he would get those answers from her lips.

But he also recognized the fear in her eyes, and his instincts told him that while the murder had everything to do with her, she was still another victim, not the killer.

He pulled on a clean shirt and grabbed his hat, setting it on his head as he strode for the door.

If the time came, he told himself grimly, he would arrest Marina. Because he did remember Cecille's body, and he would do her justice. He was the sheriff, and he took his responsibilities seriously.

As Mitch had said, a man did his job, then found a way to live with himself on his own.

He started his pickup and drove off through the thick June night to Marina's house.

Chapter 6

He saw the distant glow of the lantern lights as he first crossed over the railroad tracks, and his hands tightened instantly on the wheel. She was at the wall, dammit. Painting alone in the middle of an abandoned lot at 2:45 in the morning just four blocks from a two-day-old murder scene. And Cagney, who never got angry, suddenly had the unholy urge to wrap his hands around her throat. What the hell was she thinking?

He parked his truck a block away, forcing his muscles to relax as he climbed down. His eyes returned to their normal steely gray, his shoulders relaxed as he limped to the wall.

Half a block away, he could see her clearly in the blazing glow of the three lanterns, and he felt his flat stomach clench. She was wearing her painting outfit again. That loose blue skirt hanging low enough on her hips to reveal her lean, paint-dusted stomach. And her tied white T-shirt outlined her full breasts, already clinging to her with the sweat of her exertions. Her black hair was down, flowing around her as something wild and alive, mixing and melding with the bright array of paints, until he would have thought she'd want to tie it back.

But she didn't seem to be noticing her hair, or his slow approach. Instead she was focused on the huge, arrogant peacock emerging under her brush with reckless, vehement energy.

She painted like a woman possessed, and he wondered what drove those lean arms of hers so that she could paint with such furious passion at nearly three in the morning.

He stopped just inside the glow of the lanterns. "Marina," he said quietly.

Her brush stilled, and he saw the sudden trembling of her hand. Maybe she saw it, too, because she quickly resumed her rapid feathering of bronzed gold across the peacock's array.

Cagney remained patient, his eyes settling into the calm relentlessness that had so often driven his older brother Garret crazy.

"I need to talk to you," he said levelly.

Once more the brush stilled, and this time he could see the struggle within her. With another burst of restlessness, the brush took off again.

"Well, I don't want to talk," she said, never taking her eyes off her work. "Words have never helped. I just want to paint."

Behind her, Cagney frowned, both at the strangeness of her words and at the dark, almost savage current that threaded through them.

"You don't have a choice," he replied at last. "I'm here on business."

She swore, a low, lean word of frustration and near pain. Her brush came down, and after a long moment, she finally turned. He was shocked by the wildness he saw in her face. And he was unprepared for the thin desperation hovering beneath it, shadowing her violet eyes.

"What do you want, Sheriff?" She sounded angry.

"You have no business being out here," he told her abruptly.

She didn't say anything, but her chin came up a notch in dogged defiance.

"If you had any sense in your head, you'd be afraid," he continued, then frowned as another thought struck him. Unless Daniels was right and she was the murderess. Then she would know she had nothing to fear. He took four steps toward her, his eyes pinning hers as he came closer and closer. He could see the sheen of sweat on her face and her chest. He could see the rapid beating of her pulse on her neck and hear her quick, shallow breaths.

"Why are you here, Marina?" He towered above her.

Her gaze didn't falter, but took on the grim determination of a cornered animal. Her lips thinned to a stubborn line.

"I would think that's obvious," she answered curtly. She had to concentrate not to fidget or flinch under the unwavering intensity of his gaze. The wildness, the desperation, still flowed through her blood. The fear hovered too near the surface, and she hated the fear, hated the fact that she jumped at every shadow and creak in her house. In all her life, she'd known only one way to fight the demons of her mind. With color, with light, with her art. So she'd come here, painting like a madwoman, waiting for the tranquillity that had yet to arrive.

"Why are *you* here?" she retorted evenly, her chin not relenting an inch.

"I came here to question a suspect," Cage said just as evenly, his own lips thinning. He had the grim pleasure of seeing her falter for a minute.

"I take it that's me," she said at last.

He nodded, his steely gaze still searching hers for any signs of weakness.

"Well, you'd better start asking," she said suddenly. "It's nearly three, and I have plenty of work to get done." So he now thought she was a suspect; the idea hurt, but she ignored the pain. Why should she think he would believe in her after just one wildly passionate kiss? She'd known Bradley for two years and that hadn't stopped him from virtually running from her the minute he'd found out the truth.

"Who is Kristi Davis?"

"Who?" She frowned at him, distracted by genuine puzzlement.

"Kristi Davis," he repeated patiently.

She shook her head. "I don't know anyone of that name. May I go back to painting now?"

"The night of June 5 at nine-thirty, what were you doing?"

"Getting ready for bed, of course."

"Any witnesses?"

Her eyes darkened with anger at the insinuations of that statement. "No," she replied flippantly. "I only kiss sheriffs before going to bed, and one wasn't available that evening. Tough break for us both."

His body responded to that last statement despite her sarcasm. Once more he could remember the feel of her legs wrapped around his waist, her mouth hot and hungry beneath his own.

"And at ten-thirty?" he asked tersely.

"For God's sake, I was asleep! I'm always asleep from ten to twelve. You know that, so stop wasting my time." Then abruptly her eyes narrowed. "Why, Cagney? Why these questions now, and why these times? What do you know that you're not telling me?"

He ignored her questions. "You said you started painting at twelve that night. Did anyone see you? Does anyone ever come and watch?"

Furious and impatient now, she shook her head. "Of course not. You came right before six, the first person who's ever interrupted. You took me home and I slept till eight, and was in the office by nine. All according to schedule because I happen to like my schedule. What I don't like is answering a bunch of questions at three in the morning from a man who should already know the answers!"

There was a trace of hurt in the last sentence, and she immediately bit down on her lip before she gave anything else away.

"What are you doing here?" Cagney asked again, his voice deceptively quiet. "There's been a vicious murder just four blocks from here, and all over Maddensfield people are suddenly locking their doors and windows. But you're standing out here at three a.m., all alone with no one around to even hear you scream."

Her face paled, and this time her gaze faltered. Suddenly the wildness was gone, the desperation had vanished. Until all that remained was the fear. She wrapped her arms around herself, an unconscious gesture that tugged at him.

"Tell me why you are afraid, Marina. Tell me what drives you to paint at three in the morning."

She just shook her head, her eyes darting to the darkness just beyond the lanterns, as if she could search all the shadows and see the evil lying there.

Cage stepped forward. Abruptly his large, callused hand cradled her chin, forcing her head up.

"Tell me," he commanded.

His gray eyes practically burned into hers. He stood so close, she could feel the whisper of his breath on her cheek, feel the heat and power radiating from his body. And she could remember the sensation of that long, lean body pressed hard against her own. She could remember the shamelessness of her words: *Take me anyway....*

Her cheeks colored, and she felt the burn of humiliated tears against her lashes. That she would have wanted this man so much, and want him still, when he didn't believe in her at all, when he could still look at her with gray eyes devoid of all emotion.

"Tell me about your leg," she retaliated sharply, her eyes defiant. "You want to know everything about me, well, then tell me something about yourself."

But he shook his head, his hand dropping. "This isn't personal," he replied, low and even. "This is about a murder committed just over four blocks from here. This is about the woman I grew up with, who was hacked up so badly I barely recognized her face.''

She winced, her face paling. Still she said nothing.

''But then,'' he continued relentlessly, almost cruelly, ''you don't seem that broken up about Cecille's death.''

He saw her tremble, saw her close her eyes from the impact of his words. But she didn't collapse and she didn't break down in a flood of tears. And somewhere in the back of his mind, he admired her strength. He had broken far stronger men with this approach in his lifetime. His skills at interrogation had always been unmatchable, those long, angry interactions with fist-happy Garret had taught him a thing or two.

Now he waited, letting the silence drag on and act as the most powerful tool. He'd berated her; he'd filled her with guilt. The silence should do the rest. But he didn't feel any satisfaction in it. There was no sense of accomplishment in breaking down a woman whom just hours before he'd held in his arms.

''I didn't kill Cecille,'' Marina whispered at last. She didn't look at him, didn't trust herself to look at him when she felt so raw and vulnerable. How did he know just where to strike, and how could he quiz her so unmercifully after having kissed her so passionately just hours before? She thought she might hate him, but she didn't have the energy left. Whatever might have been between them after the golden glow of the ball game and the fiery sparks of the late-evening kiss was gone.

''Who is Kristi Davis?'' Cagney pressed quietly.

She shook her head, eyes downcast. ''I don't know, Sheriff. I don't know who Kristi Davis is, and I don't know who killed Cecille. And I don't know why you are asking me all these questions. I don't know why you are doing this to me.'' Her voice cracked slightly, but she brought her chin up and looked at him with eyes that were still proud.

''Did you take a taxi to the Piedmont Triad International Airport at 9:30 p.m., June 5th?''

"No."

"Did you rent a car at 10:30 p.m. in the name of Kristi Davis and drive it back here?"

"No! I don't know how to drive—I told you that. And I don't know who Kristi Davis is and I don't even know how to get to the airport. Why are you asking me all this? Is it because I'm stupid enough to paint outside after the murder? Then book me for stupidity, book me for reckless endangerment. But I didn't kill Cecille."

"Then why did the woman on duty recall Kristi Davis as having long, black hair with a gray streak down the side?"

She gasped, her eyes widening with shock that appeared to be genuine.

"Cagney, it wasn't me," she insisted, her violet eyes clear and adamant upon his face. "I don't care what the woman said—it wasn't me. You know how I am, Cage—you've observed it enough times. I only sleep six hours a day, and when the time comes, I can barely keep my eyes open. I don't know what is going on, but I didn't do anything to hurt Cecille. I swear it."

The problem was, he did believe her. As he'd told Daniels, the story was too pat, pointing toward a woman who had a publicly known feud with Cecille and a widely known sleeping schedule. And looking at her eyes now, he couldn't believe anyone could fake shock that genuinely.

But he was still the sheriff, and he had no evidence to the contrary. She had no alibi, and she did have motive and opportunity. It was not a redeeming combination.

"I have to ask you again," he said quietly. "Why are you so afraid, Marina? And why are you out here when any sane person would be behind locked doors right now?"

She went rigid in front of him, and for the first time he saw something new in her eyes. Fear, yes. But not looking-over-your-shoulder-type fear. No, plain, definite fear of *him*. She turned away immediately, taking a step back until she almost brushed against the fresh paint of her peacock. He frowned, his cop's instinct kicking into overtime.

"Talk to me, Marina," he said forcefully. "I need to know."

She nodded, still not meeting his eyes, and from this close, he could see the rapid pounding of her pulse in her neck, the sheen of sweat across her brow. Her black hair swept forward to shield her face, but the thin, white streak stood out like a badge of guilt in the lantern light.

"I don't know what to tell you," she said at last, her voice muffled. That much was true. People always said they wanted to understand; people always said they wanted to be trusted. But the truth of the matter was, there were some things people just couldn't understand.

And suddenly, she was really and truly afraid. Not the dark, sinister fear that often hovered, unexplained, at the fringes of her mind. But the real gut-slamming fear that someone had killed Cecille, horribly, viciously, and that person was still out there.

What if the fear she'd been feeling lately wasn't just a product of her imagination, as it had been thirteen years ago? What if this time it was real?

"I don't know what I'm afraid of," she whispered suddenly, a faint shudder rippling through her. "I only know that lately, lately it's felt like someone's been watching me. Except that when I turn around, no one's there."

Cagney's frown deepened. "Did you feel this 'sensation' on the night of the murder?" he asked sharply.

She nodded.

"Out here in the lot?"

Once again she nodded.

"Then why are you here now, Marina?"

"Because it's worse at home," she said simply.

He felt his blood go cold, and in his mind he could see the cut-up body of Cecille Manning far too clearly.

"You should have told me sooner," he said tersely.

She shrugged. "What was there to tell, Cagney? I've never seen anything. I've never even heard anything. For all I know, I just have an overactive imagination." Self-mockery tinged the last part, but Cage didn't notice.

He still frowned at her, his gray eyes sharp. For a moment, she held her breath under that gaze, wondering if he would continue to press the point. Wondering what she'd tell him if he did. Bradley had certainly seemed to think being hospitalized for two years had turned her into a justifiable fruitcake. What would this man think? She wasn't sure she wanted to know.

Cagney finally looked away from her and she slowly released her pent-up breath.

"Except," Cage was musing, "now it seems clear that someone wants you framed for this murder. Who else have you been fighting with since you moved here, Marina?"

She shook her head. "I've only lived here two months, Cage. All I do is work and paint. It's not the most social existence in the world."

"What about Bennett Jensen?"

"I've exchanged a handful of words with the man," she told him honestly. "I just know he and Cecille were involved, and given that he's a married man, I don't approve. Especially after having met his wife. Evie Jensen definitely deserves better than that brute."

"Marina," Cage said at last, a small, frustrated sigh escaping his lips, "I don't like any of this." He stared out into the darkness, a frown crinkling his brow. Then he swung his gaze back to her, his face intense. "I'm going to keep you under watch at all times," he told her bluntly. He raised a hand as she opened her mouth to protest the invasion of her privacy. "You don't have a choice," he informed her levelly. "I'm willing to consider the idea that you're being framed, and I'm concerned that someone is indeed playing with us all. But I also have to consider that maybe you are involved. Until those questions are settled one way or another, you're not getting out of my sight."

Her lips thinned, and a part of her mind registered the irony. The man could kiss like the devil, but he still acted like the sheriff, and she was no more to him than a part of his job. Even knowing that, her stomach jumped with anticipation. With his steady presence around, maybe the shadows would seem farther away. Maybe she'd be able to sleep without the faceless nightmare returning.

"Fine," she said at last. "But unless you're arresting me, I have every intention of doing this my way. Which means I paint from midnight to six a.m. You're welcome to bring a chair."

Cage gave in with a nod. What the hell, it wasn't as if he was sleeping well these days anyway. Besides, though he would never admit it to her, he felt better knowing that he would be around. He didn't like seeing the fear in her eyes, and he refused to contemplate her ending up like Cecille Manning.

"Do you feel someone is watching you now?" he asked slowly.

She shook her head.

"Good," he said shortly, and for one small moment, he saw the trace of a smile on her lips. That one moment, they connected again, bound by a mutual concern. The thought eased some of the tightness in his leg and some of the guilt he felt at his earlier abrasiveness.

He knew, however, that moments like the one on her porch were long behind them and would not happen again.

Perfect, he told himself. He'd been a fool before, and now he was the sheriff. That was the way it was supposed to be. He turned his eyes back to the darkness beyond the lanterns, and as she began to paint, he held guard in the night.

Sometime around four he realized he was relaxed. The warm night air felt balmy against his skin, the sound of distant crickets soothed his ears and his rhythmic pacing had stretched out his leg to near-painless existence. It had been a long time since he'd truly appreciated a Maddensfield night.

When he'd been a kid, he used to lie out in the backyard and simply stare at the stars. Sometimes Liz would come and join him, and they would lie there together in total silence. He'd always liked those nights. By daylight, things often appeared harsh and urgent. But night descended like velvet, soft and slow and sensuous.

He spared one glance at Marina, still lost in fierce concentration on her peacock. Her skirt swayed with her movements, and he caught the tantalizing glimpse of curved calves and delicate ankles. He pivoted and paced the other way.

In D.C. he'd never just stared at the moon and stars. In D.C. the nights had been filled with a restless urgency, a harrowing danger. He could remember those first couple of years, when he'd served in narcotics. Nights then found him suited up, waiting outside a suspected drug house with muscles poised and adrenaline flaring. They'd kick down the door and the race would be on. Could they grab the perps before the drugs were flushed down a toilet or dumped in a grease pot on the stove? How many semiautomatic weapons were under the bed, just waiting? He could never quite forget all the screaming and yelling of a house filling with adrenaline-crazed, muscle-bound men.

And now he was here, pacing through a thick-molasses night, the smell of paint and the sound of crickets filling the air. It was all about murder, but nothing felt the same.

He pivoted and began walking in the other direction, peering out into the darkness. His gaze swiveled around to find Marina standing back from her peacock with a critical eye.

"It's very good," he said quietly.

She glanced up sharply, as if she'd somehow forgotten Cage was there. "He's getting there," she said. Only the base work was done, the bald colors of royal blue, green and gold swirling across the array of feathers. Now she would need to add the details, the texture, the patterns, that would make the bird truly come alive.

"Do you know what the wall will look like when it's all done?" Cagney asked curiously.

Marina shook her head. "I've never considered it in its entirety," she said honestly. "I think the sheer size of it still overwhelms me. So I take it bit by bit. I stand here, and I just see what I want to add, and then I add it.''

"You've never done anything else like it?''

She shook her head, turning long enough to see him frowning at her with frank curiosity from across the circle of light.

"What did you do in New York, then, with all those spare hours?''

"Worked,'' she said with a shrug. "There wasn't much else I could do. After all, you don't walk around New York City late at night. I used to keep enough fresh clothes in my office to last three or four days, simply changing and cleaning up in the locker room of the health club downstairs. I got a lot done, learned a lot, rose up the ladder, so to speak. But it was all just work.''

He nodded, filling in the bits and pieces from what he already knew of her. "So you came here, where you would feel free to do something else at night.''

She nodded, then flashed him a wan smile. "You have to admire the irony of it all—that I came here to get away from the danger.''

"Yes. I suppose you do.''

"And you?'' she said suddenly. "Why didn't you stay in the big city of D.C.?''

She could see him stiffen just slightly, his face growing more wary in the intimate circle of the lanterns. But she'd expected that. She already knew enough to understand that D.C. had everything to do with why he limped and why he never talked about it.

"Being a big-city cop wasn't who I wanted to be,'' he said at last, his voice carefully neutral. "There's something to be said for small-town life. Have you ever thought of having someone sit on the fountain there—'' he pointed at the mural ''—you know, reading or something?''

He was changing the subject, but she let him. At least they were talking once more. It was better than nothing.

She turned her gaze up to the fountain on the wall where he was looking. "I could do that," she said after a minute. "Or what about a young boy rubbing a lamp?"

He nodded, following her vision. "You read a lot of fairy tales growing up?"

"Fairy tales, myths, fables. Everything. My mother used to read me long stories every night before tucking me in. I loved it. And you?"

"I was a Western kind of kid," he admitted out loud. "Wyatt Earp, Doc Holliday, that kind of thing."

Immediately she perked up, turning to him with such a bright, admiring face he had to suck in his breath. "A cowboy," she declared. "Of course! That's exactly what the wall needs. A cowboy."

She whirled back around, leaving him with the sensation of a firefly darting away. He let her go, watching her examine the wall with new insight and fresh enthusiasm. He wasn't sure he could handle all that brightness focused upon himself. He wasn't sure he could stand the impact of her brilliant smile upon his stomach.

At five-thirty, Cage helped her close up the paint cans and they rode together in silence to her house. This time her porch light was blazing, but it only served to illuminate the spots where hours before she'd practically thrown herself at this man. She slid out of the truck without meeting his eyes.

"Thanks for the lift," she said as casually as possible. "I imagine you must be very tired by now."

He nodded. It was true enough. And just for a moment, his gaze slid to the porch, to her and then to the empty passenger's seat of the truck.

"Good night," he said, keeping his eyes on the steering wheel.

She nodded and walked to her porch. He watched as she let herself inside, waiting with tense muscles as she closed the door behind her. Five minutes went by, and she didn't reemerge. All must be well, and so he hunkered down lower in the front seat of his truck, tipping his hat forward to shield his eyes from the now-rising sun. Two hours of sleep.

He didn't know how she did it.

Fifteen minutes later, Marina peered out the bay windows of her living room to see his truck still parked in her driveway. Belatedly she understood the full implications of him watching her all the time. She stood there in her oversize T-shirt for a moment, trying to figure out what to do next.

She didn't want him around, she reminded herself. She could take care of herself. But then she remembered his grim look as he'd inspected her sliding-glass doors. She remembered the sensation of no longer being alone in her own house, and she remembered waking up with a scream choking her throat.

And that moment, she decided she didn't care if Cagney Guiness was the devil himself. When he was around, she felt better, and that was all that mattered. She grabbed her robe and pattered out to the driveway.

He sat up abruptly the minute she tapped on the window. She saw him frowning, his gray eyes growing alert as he quickly opened the door.

"What's wrong?" he demanded as he stepped down from the truck.

This close, she was forced to remember every long, lean line of his body. She remembered the power of those shoulders, the leanness of those hips. The muscled hardness of those legs supporting hers.

She clutched her thin robe closer with one hand and took a careful step back. "Everything is all right," she managed to say, keeping her voice level and professional. "I just thought..." She faltered for a minute, not wanting to admit the full extent of her fears. "I just figured that you might be more comfortable inside. On the couch, of course."

"The truck is fine," he said with a frown. She looked so jumpy all of a sudden, as if the tiniest shift in the wind might send her scrambling. He wasn't used to seeing her like this.

Once more her jaw opened; once more he saw her struggle with something.

"Oh, but it's no problem," she insisted, her voice slightly higher pitched than normal. "I mean, as long as you feel obligated to stay, you might as well take advantage of the couch. It pulls out, you know. I'm sure it's much better for your leg. Why, I could even make you a cup of coffee in the morning."

And abruptly he understood. She was afraid again, and she wanted him inside so she would feel better. The simple need tugged at him, and he had to fight the urge to take her into his arms. He was just the sheriff, dammit.

"The couch would be perfect," he said.

She nodded furiously, the relief too evident on her face, and he could tell she was aware of that, as well. It seemed to shame her, but she didn't change her mind as she led him into the house. Upstairs, she found an extra sheet and one blanket, moving quickly, deftly, while he watched from the hall.

Then she led him back downstairs and busily began to set up the bed. So much nervous energy, even after an entire evening of painting. For the first time he began to understand just how deep the fear must run, so that now, preparing to go to sleep in her own house, her fear was actually growing stronger.

Unconsciously he reached out toward her. She chose that moment to turn around, and he dropped his arm promptly to his side.

"I need to go to work tomorrow," she said. "Is that okay?"

"On a Sunday?"

She hesitated for a moment, her eyes suddenly faltering to find him standing so close. "Generally, there's a lot to be done. And now, well, with Cecille gone, there's a lot of confusion." She paused for a moment, then rushed on. "I get up at eight, so I'll shower and change first. Then I'll brew some coffee and wake you up, if that's all right."

He nodded silently, his steady gaze flickering down to the gap in the top of her royal-blue robe, then back up to meet the shadows in her eyes. It looked like she wore a T-shirt under that robe. He would bet she slept in just that T-shirt, her long legs beautifully exposed to tangle in sheets and drive a man half-mad.

"That sounds fine," he willed himself to say.

She nodded, pausing once more. Then he saw her nod to herself and force her shoulders back.

"Good night, Cagney."

"Good night, Marina."

A last quick nod, then she turned and went back upstairs. And once again he was struck by the impression of a woman preparing for war.

The frown remained on his brow long after he had eased down onto the fold-out bed and attuned his ears to all the creaks and groans of an old house. But minute lapsed into minute, and he didn't hear anything from upstairs. With a long, careful sigh, he allowed himself to relax against the bed, falling into the light half sleep of an on-duty sheriff.

But Marina didn't cry out during the night. This time, with Cage Guiness keeping guard from her sofa, she slept the deep, dreamless slumber of exhaustion.

Chapter 7

She hadn't quite expected the impact he would have on her.

Coming down the stairs in the morning, her long, dark hair still damp from the shower, she paused in the landing, her eyes drawn to the sleeping figure on her sofa. He was still fully dressed, his boots and hat placed on the floor with meticulous precision amid the randomly tossed sofa pillows. A lone sheet covered his lean hips, but she could still see the blue of his denim jeans through the thin cover. There was nothing provocative in the way he lay, just a man on his back, hands clasped under his head. She could even see his sheriff's star lying bronzed and pointed against the dark blue of his button-up shirt.

So why did her heart suddenly constrict in her throat? Why did her feet, which normally pounded across her hardwood floors in a rush, suddenly land as soft and gentle as a kitten's? She didn't want to disturb him. She wanted him to sleep a little longer, looking comfortable and male on her fluffy, gray sofa bed.

Worse, she wanted to creep over gently and slide under the cool sheet to join him. What would it be like to feel his body once more pressed against hers? Would he wake slowly like a lazy panther, rolling over to take her into his strong, lean arms? And what would those eyes be like—soft and fuzzy with sleep as they found her own? She'd bet he might grin again, that easy, slow grin she'd seen at the barbecue. But then the grin would fade and his eyes would darken as he bent his head to find her lips....

She pattered hastily into the kitchen, not daring to look at him again. She took the coffee beans out of her freezer, her hands shaking.

Why couldn't she get him out her mind?

She wasn't the kind of woman who suddenly fell for men. She worked. All her life, she'd simply worked. The doctors had encouraged her to draw when she'd first come home from the hospital. Very therapeutic, they'd told her parents. And Jim and Nancy, so worried about their only daughter, had bought her every art book, paint, pastel and pen set known to mankind. Imagine everyone's surprise when she'd been good at it.

So she'd become an artist, and she did love it. She loved the colors, the texture, the patterns. She loved the power that seemed to flow from her hands, the ability to create beauty when a part of her threatened to drown her with its darkness. She'd developed her sleeping schedule, and its peculiarity only added to her artistic mystique. Her parents had stopped worrying so much, and years faded into years without the horrible terror returning again.

She'd gone away to Wellesley, consoling her parents with twice-weekly phone calls. Four years later, she'd returned to New York, vibrant and talented and in control. No more nightmares, no more unknown fears that choked her throat late at night. She'd landed a plum job, her parents relaxed and life seemed to fall into place.

Her father had actually introduced her to Bradley, the son of one of his financial associates. She couldn't even recall her first impression of him. Now she could only remember his face that last afternoon, the way the color had fled, his jaw slacking open, his eyes growing round. The way he'd looked at her as if she'd suddenly sprouted two horns and a tail after two years of intimate acquaintance. He'd left the table of the French restaurant in a rush, some inane excuse fluttering limply from his mouth. He'd called her two days later. He was disappointed, he said. She should have trusted him before, he said. This just changed everything. He didn't think they were right together anymore.

She hadn't said anything, just nodded like an idiot while the tears rolled down her cheeks. And deep within her heart, she'd felt the darkness within burn in triumph. She was imperfect; she was not whole.

Loco, loony, bats in the belfry, lights on but nobody's home...

Two years of carefully cultivating the relationship, one simple step at a time, taking it slow and easy so as not to tax herself. And it was all lost in a single afternoon over almond croissants and café au lait.

She didn't tell her parents for another week. They'd been so proud of her and Bradley, the perfect little yuppie couple. Bradley the sophisticated financial wizard, her, the artist already winning national ad awards.

Maybe they'd thought she'd fall apart, but the morning of the third day, Marina discovered something else, instead. She'd become strong. She wasn't the pale little twelve-year-old girl who jumped at shadows and screamed at nightmares. She was a grown woman with a fantastic career and amazing talent. She didn't need her parents to protect her, and she certainly didn't need Bradley to believe in her.

She'd learned the hard way how to believe in herself.

A wry smile crept over her face. What would her parents say now if they knew their daughter had practically thrown herself at a man she'd known only three days? What would they say to see her living in a rundown house and painting an abandoned wall all night long?

But then abruptly Marina's smile faltered, and she stared at the cracked sink before her with something akin to despair. And what would they think to know a murder had been committed just three nights ago? What would they think of the fact that their daughter was the prime suspect? And what would they do if they knew that for the first time since she was fourteen the nightmare had returned?

"Sorry for oversleeping."

She turned too quickly, Cage's voice startling her as the bag of coffee beans flew out of her hand. For one moment, Cagney saw something dark and uncertain pass through her eyes, then she was bending to pick up the bag before all the beans slid out.

"I'm sorry," he said, hunkering down to assist. "I didn't mean to scare you."

"It's all right," she said hastily, not meeting his eyes.

This close, he could smell the warm spice of her perfume mingling with the fresh tang of soap and shampoo. As he leaned forward to rescue a few wayward beans, he felt the silky touch of her long, damp hair slide across his arm. His body tightened, and he had to shift slightly to ease the pressure against his jeans.

His gray eyes were carefully dispassionate as they both stood.

"Did you sleep okay?" he asked softly.

"Fine, thank you." Her voice sounded stilted, and she still couldn't quite bring herself to look at him. He stood too close, and she could remember with graphic detail her earlier thoughts. She couldn't recall ever feeling as shaky as she did now. As if her nerve endings were on fire. As if she would sell her soul for the touch of his hand on her arm, the feel of his lips exploring her own.

"You can put the coffee beans in the sink," she said breathlessly. She turned quickly and reached for the coffee grinder. The noise offered her cover, and she ground the beans into virtual dust waiting for her equilibrium to be restored. He's the sheriff, Marina. He thinks you may have killed Cecille. If he knew everything, he'd throw you in jail right this minute.

"I think they're done," he drawled behind her.

Abruptly she popped off the button, her cheeks flushing. "Of course," she said. "This just helps draw out the flavor."

She grabbed the coffeepot with a clatter and busied herself with the next step. Behind her, Cagney watched her restless movements with a frown furrowing his brow.

She looked herself this morning. She wore a brightly colored dress with rose, blue and lavender flowers flourishing amid a jade-green sea. The sleeveless dress flowed down her figure, beautifully tailored to highlight her narrow waist, her graceful hips. The loose folds of the skirt swirled around her brown legs. He could see the wink of a silver anklet, and it drew his eyes to her narrow ankles and shapely calves for far too long. He forced his gaze up, only to follow a line of tiny black pearl buttons up her back to the shiny cascade of her hair. Buttons like that could drive a man crazy. They made him want to free them one by one, until he could peel back the silky fabric to expose smooth, dusky skin. He wondered if tiny flecks of paint were still splattered on her stomach. He wondered how that skin would feel against his hand.

"Coffee," she said cheerily.

She was holding out a bright orange mug to him. He stared at it blankly for a minute, until he realized it was shaped like a tropical fish. He accepted it, the brush of her fingers against his own tightening his stomach.

"Do you collect mugs?" he asked neutrally enough.

She nodded. "Cream or sugar?"

"I'm fine, thanks."

She took both, inhaling the rich coffee aroma with such a look of satisfaction his hand began to shake. His jaw clenched, and he forced his mind to attention with near brutality.

"We can sit at the table if you'd like," she offered. He nodded, following her to the small antique table in front of the sliding-glass door. Outside, the June sun blazed down on the tiny backyard. The fence around the yard was a harsh, wintered gray. Holes winked back in several places. He shook his head. He wanted to put bars around the entire place.

"I haven't done much with the backyard," Marina said next to him, following his gaze. "I'm just not home much during the day."

"What time do you leave work at night?" he asked.

She shrugged. "Eight at the earliest. Generally more like nine. I come home, grab a little something to eat, putter awhile, and then generally it's time for bed. My real personal time isn't until after midnight, and as you can tell, my weekends aren't really much different. I don't think my neighbors would like me hammering a new fence at two a.m."

"Have you spoken with any of them?"

She shook her head. "Not really. As I said, I'm not home much during the day."

"We really should do something about your sliding-glass door," he said abruptly.

She nodded slowly, and he felt a spurt of guilt at the shadow he saw pass through her eyes.

"Cagney," she said after a minute, her clear violet eyes rising up to find his. "Cagney, do you think I killed Cecille?"

He was still, his gray eyes betraying nothing as her gaze plundered them. "I don't know," he said at last. "But I'm willing to keep my options open."

She nodded, pushing away the tinge of hurt that tightened her chest. He was being honest, she should be grateful for that. But then, she didn't want him to be honest. She wanted him to believe in her. Just once, she wanted someone to believe.

"I'll take you to work," Cage said, draining the last of his coffee. He wondered if she knew how open her face was. He wondered if she knew just how low that hurt in her eyes made him feel. He held out his hand for her cow mug, then carried both cups over to the sink.

"You make great coffee," he said gruffly, searching for an air of normalcy. It was too intimate, waking up on a woman's couch and drinking coffee with her in her kitchen. He was supposed to be a sheriff on duty, not a slumber-party guest.

"Would...would you like to take a shower or anything?" she asked behind him.

His hands stilled on the sink faucet. No, that would be far worse. To stand in her shower, using her soap, drying off with her towels. A man should only have to take so much.

"It's okay," he said. "I'll clean up at my place later."

"You aren't going to stay with me at work?"

He shook his head. "No, I have to catch up with Daniels. My deputy, Davey, can handle the day shift."

She wondered why the thought of him leaving her should bother her. She should be grateful to get away from his presence. But when he turned around, she lost her train of thought again.

He looked so huge in her kitchen. So lean and powerful and male amid the small counters and porcelain sink. She could see the way his blue shirt stretched across his shoulders, shifting as he dried his hand on her pale-blue kitchen towel. And his jeans encased narrow flanks and long, well-formed legs.

She could taste him on her lips once more.

His hands stilled in the towel, his eyes growing suddenly dark as he watched the hunger bloom in her eyes. Her gaze fell to his lips, and he felt it like a physical touch, the spark spiraling down to explode in his loins. His body went hard, the desire going from low-burn to three-alarm fire in less than a second.

So help him, God, he wanted her. He wanted her hard; he wanted her long. He wanted her on the kitchen floor, her legs locked around him while he rung his name from her lips like a prayer. He wanted to plunge into her body, lose himself in the liquid heat. He wanted her nails in his back, her teeth in his shoulder. He wanted her gasping and needy and exhausted. He wanted to make her scream with the intensity. And he wanted to throw back his head and cry out his release like a wild beast coming home.

His jaw clenched, his face went white with strain and the veins on his neck stood out. He wouldn't, he shouldn't, he couldn't.

He did.

He gave in, tossing the dish towel on the counter and grabbing her with one long stride. She came against him hard, her arms already tangling around his neck as her lips opened for his. His tongue plunged into her mouth, and she welcomed it with a primal groan of satisfaction. His hands found her breasts, rubbing the soft mounds as she pressed her hips against him. Two fingers tightened around her nipple, squeezing with delicate pressure until she almost screamed with the fierceness of the desire. She bit his lower lip, tart and reckless as his hips surged against her own.

She wanted him, needed him with an intensity she didn't understand and was beyond questioning. When his hand came around to the row of buttons down her back, she sighed her approval, her hands searching for the hem of his shirt. His fingers fumbled with the buttons, while his tongue plunged once more inside her mouth. She pressed against him, relishing the feel of muscled hardness against her burning breasts. She tugged at his shirt, then in a burst of impatience stepped back enough to rip it off over his head. For one long moment, they just stared at each other, molten steel burning into black desire. He pulled her back against him hard.

This time her lips found his pounding pulse at the base of his throat. She tasted the salty tang of his skin, pressed against the sheen of sweat covering his bare, muscled chest. His skin was pale compared with her dusky complexion. It was smooth and hard and rippled as he groaned. Her hands closed over his biceps, feeling the muscles bunch with sleek power under her touch. She thought she might die from the heat.

Her lips dropped lower, until she came to the round nub of his male nipple. Lightly her tongue flickered across the nub, licking like a well-satisfied cat. She heard him suck in his breath, felt his hand cup her cheek, holding her close. She took the nipple between her teeth and sucked hard.

With a growl, he pulled her up and captured her sweet mouth. His large hands folded around the back of her dress, but this time they didn't fool with tiny buttons. This time they grabbed the material and tore it, the tiny black buttons raining down like pearls around their feet.

Immediately his mouth left hers and she could feel the cool breeze of fresh air against her skin as he pulled the top of her dress down her arms. Then his lips were there, burning her skin like a trail of fire from her throat to her breasts. His hands found the clasp of her bra, the black lacy wisp tumbling quickly to the floor. Then his mouth was on her breast, drawing in the nipple as she whispered his name like a plea.

"Yes. Do that. Just like that. Oh, please, Cagney. Please!"

He complied with every request, relishing the feel of her breast in his mouth, her back arched against his hand. He could feel her hands tangling in his hair, drawing him closer, urging him on. She tasted warm and sweet and willing. She felt soft and generous and giving. She was pure in her passion, total in her submission and absolute in her trust. His strong hands could bruise her skin or wring her neck. Yet she gave herself over to them completely.

Trusting him. Needing him.

And once again, through the red-hot fury of their passion, he felt the pain. It slashed through his belly like a knife, slicing through the ardor, hacking off the desire. Until suddenly he felt the guilt like a giant, cold stone, settling low in his stomach.

With a tortured groan, he pulled himself away. And before Marina could move or react, calm, gray-eyed Cagney steadied his hands on the countertop and kicked her cupboard with such brutal fierceness the wood split. The pain that shot up his left leg was at once fiery hot and icy cold. He bit his lip in agony and felt his face pale. On the counter, his arms trembled.

"I'll replace the cupboard door," he murmured hoarsely. He couldn't turn, couldn't force himself to look at her. He knew the stark pain he would find in her eyes, and he wanted to kick himself a thousand times for doing that to her. How could he be so weak? Why couldn't he just walk away?

He was the sheriff, dammit. She was a potential murder suspect. And he couldn't keep his damn hands off her. He was a fool. A giant, damn fool.

He kept his eyes on sliding-glass door and told himself the stinging came only from the bright June sun. Behind him, he could hear the rustle of her pulling her dress back up.

"I'm . . . I'm sorry," she said after a minute.

The words were soft, a mere whisper in the wind, and they tore at him like fine-grained sandpaper. He wished she would yell at him. He wished she would curse him and call him a rotten bastard. He wished she would turn away from him and never look at him with softness again.

"It's not your fault," he said harshly. "I ought to know better, that's all."

The words stung, but she blinked back the tears. The whole situation was ludicrous, she thought soggily. Here they were, standing in the kitchen with little pearl buttons all around them. He had no shirt on, she was half-undressed and neither could look the other in the eye. And both had probably never felt quite so alone.

"I'm not normally like this," she said after a minute. "I've never acted like this before in my life."

"Yeah," he said with a sigh. "Me, neither. But it doesn't mean a damn thing."

He heard her drag in her breath like a wounded cry, and it only completed the pain searing his leg. He hated feeling like this. He hated the stone coldness in his stomach, the desire that even now throbbed through his body like an ancient pain. And he hated the need to draw her into his arms and rest her head upon his shoulder.

"Marina, it would be easier if you hated me," he said grimly, his eyes still out the window.

"I'm afraid I'm not any good at that," she told him quietly. She hesitated, watching the muscle tighten in his jaw. "Cagney," she said after a bit. "Cagney, this is getting to be ridiculous." The words were hard to find, but she forced herself to find them anyway. His withdrawal hurt her, wounded her pride. But she could see that it hurt him, as well, and that lent her courage. "Look," she began, taking a small, hesitant step forward. "We're both adults," she managed to say reasonably enough. "We're both attracted to each other. In other circumstances, I'm sure it wouldn't be this intense, I guess. But...well...you are the sheriff, and I am who I am. So I suppose we're back to your starting proposition of this will never happen again. We...we could at least be civil."

He turned, his gaze stark, his smile self-mocking. "How civil can I be when every time I look at you I taste you on my lips?"

Her breath left her, her eyes growing round. "Maybe neighborly?" she whispered.

He was almost going to say something else, then abruptly he shut his mouth and ran a tired hand through his rumpled black hair. "You're right," he said levelly. "We're both adults."

He drew himself up, unconsciously rubbing his left leg. "I'll replace the cabinet by nightfall," he said.

"Don't worry about it. The whole thing will be replaced sooner or later."

"I'll take care of it," he said again, his gaze level as he looked at her. She held her dress up over her breasts with one hand, her shoulders and arms bare, her lips swollen and freshly kissed. His body remained hard, wanting. The guilt remained cold. "Why don't you go up and change?" he said quietly. "I'll take you to work."

"That probably would be best."

Upstairs, her hand still trembled as she peeled off the remnant of her dress. Her breasts felt swollen and painful from the raw desire, her throat thick. She could still hear the sound of his foot slamming through her cabinet. She could still see the pain that had slashed like ice through his gray, gray eyes.

She didn't understand why he affected her the way he did. She didn't understand why just looking at him made her stomach tighten and her heart accelerate. As if carried away by madness, both seemed helpless under the spell. But that didn't change reality.

He had no real interest in her. Once the madness passed, he could look at her with eyes so cold it made her wince. She remembered last night all too well. He could be brutal, and he could be relentless. Those eyes of his saw everything.

And what about her? She was living a half-truth, terrified he might find out the rest. She berated him about his leg, then hoarded her own secrets like a miser. And she could still see Bradley's face in her mind....

She winced and took out a pink summer dress from the closet. She didn't want to go through that again, even for a gray-eyed man who made her feel safe. Because she knew of demons he would never be able to slay. She knew. She definitely knew.

It made sense when she smoothed the dress over her hips. She agreed with it completely as she pulled on a pair of matching, low-slung pumps. She looked tailored and polished when she was done, the square collar and fitted skirt an entirely different picture from the last dress. The outfit was too formal to wear to work on a Sunday, but she decided she didn't give a damn.

She looked in control.

Until, of course, she made it all the way downstairs and saw Cagney standing in the living room. Until she saw him turn at her approach, then go rigid with the pain that slashed through his leg.

At that moment, she wanted to damn the control to hell. At that moment, she wanted to run to him and take his face in her hands and force him to let her in.

"You ready to go?" he asked dispassionately from the living room.

"Yes."

"Fine, then, let's go."

He motioned to the door, and for a minute she stood still out of sheer perversity. Then slowly she walked down the final two steps. "You should have a doctor look at your leg."

"It's fine."

"You're limping like a three-legged cat."

"It's fine."

"I take it back, then. Your leg merely matches your temperament."

"Sweet and good-natured," he said as he opened the door for her. "Are you going to yap all the way to work?"

"I just might."

"Fine, then. Want to hold these for me?"

He said it so smoothly she felt no premonition. She held out her hand like a child, then watched dumbly as he poured eight tiny, black pearl buttons into her palm.

She didn't say a thing on the way to work. And neither did he.

He was pacing, the motion no longer soothing but sending stabbing shots of pain through him with each and every step. He didn't care anymore. The pain in his leg was better than the pounding in his head and the tension in his neck. He glared at Daniels one more time, then did a sharp pivot that almost sent him reeling.

"Sit down," Daniels barked yet again, the irritation clear on his face, too. "For crying out loud, you're making me nervous."

"No sexual assault?" Cagney repeated for nearly the fourth time in the past thirty minutes.

"No sexual assault."

"Signs of struggle, skin under the fingernails? Anything?"

"Fingernails freshly manicured."

"Freshly manicured?"

"Lab boys think the killer went under them with a metal fingernail file. You know, just to be safe."

"God, we are dealing with a monster."

"Hell hath no fury like a woman scorned."

Once again Cagney frowned, his pacing stalling for a split second, then resuming as Daniels groaned.

"I'm telling you for the last time, Guiness. Sit the hell down!"

Cagney simply ignored the man. He didn't care if his pacing made Daniels restless, he didn't care if his leg hurt like the blazes and he didn't care if his office had just reached one hundred and two million degrees. Daniels already looked as if he was going to pass out from heatstroke or kill Cagney from blind rage.

But Cage just didn't care. All he wanted to know was who murdered Cecille Manning, and did she have to be a woman?

"Female rented the car?" he asked yet again.

"Yes," Daniels told him. "Yes, yes and yes. A female rented the car, a female took the taxi to the airport to rent the car that killed the woman. Female, female, female."

"But how did she get back after dropping off the car?"

"Bus, train, walking, hitchhiking. I really don't know. But it was a woman. Once again, we're back with a woman."

"Maybe she had an accomplice. Maybe she was really renting a car for a man. Maybe that's the link we're missing, Daniels. Just because she rented the car doesn't mean she committed the murder."

"Maybe you have Cheez Whiz between your ears." In exasperation, Daniels stood. His heavy-set body was already soaked with sweat, and his face was an unhealthy shade of red. At this point, he hated Maddensfield for its heat and humidity alone. And he couldn't believe this man before him kept pacing, when any intelligent creature would be curled up asleep through this kind of heat. "Why can't it be a female, Guiness? Why can't you just accept the fact Marina Walden may have committed a murder? Just how closely are you watching that beautiful body anyway?"

For one moment, Cagney's raised foot stilled. He turned, his gray eyes cold, and stared at the man before him.

But Daniels, for all his bluster, did not back down. "You can give me the evil eye all you want," the older man said shrewdly. "I'm not telling you anything that isn't already running through the back of your mind. So why don't you share it with me, Guiness? Why can't she be the killer?"

"Because it's too simple," Cagney said levelly.

Daniels threw up his hands in the air, rolling his eyes heavenward. "Why can't it be simple?"

"Because it's never simple. We have a woman without even a shoplifting record and we're suddenly saying she's capable of committing a vicious murder? We're saying the motive is money, but if she's so smart, wouldn't she at least make it look like an accident? Perhaps a burglary gone awry. Anything. There's just something wrong about a stabbing. It's too savage for money. Too...personal."

"Maybe she's a closet sadist. Maybe she was just due to snap."

Cagney shook his head, the frustration setting in once more. "We're going in circles."

"Damn right we are."

"Doesn't that tell you something?" Cagney challenged. "If it was that obvious, would we really be floating around this much? I'm telling you, there's something we don't know yet. Something we're not seeing. It's like a magic trick, and we're just jumping the hoops.''

Daniels frowned. ''What do you mean by that?''

''Look,'' Cagney said. ''My oldest brother, Mitch, is an amateur magician. I've watched him practice enough times to understand the theory very well. The heart of all magic is really misinformation. You give the audience just enough information that they make all the wrong assumptions, which creates the illusion. I feel that's what's going on here. The killer is providing us with just enough information for us to make all the assumptions he needs to successfully pull off the real trick. We've got to back up and start over. For instance, a woman with black hair and a gray streak rented the car. Let's pretend for a minute it's not Marina. Let's pretend it's just a woman dressed as Marina. Then let's pretend the woman only rented the car. What does that leave us with?''

''Nothing,'' Daniels answered dryly.

Cagney frowned. ''Or something we don't understand yet. Like the fact that there wasn't just one person involved. There were two. Now, why would there be two?''

Daniels shook his head again, but Cagney could see the doubt beginning to crinkle his brow.

''Jeez,'' the older man finally said. ''I really don't like this case.''

Cagney had to agree. His eyes strayed to the clock. It was six already, and he and Daniels had hardly made any progress. They just kept going around and around, the pieces refusing to click into place.

''I've got to go pick up Marina,'' he said at last.

Daniels just snorted, patting at the sweat on his brow with an already soaked handkerchief. ''Don't you get all the grunt work?'' Cagney shot him a warning glance, and for a change, Daniels heeded it. ''When are you going to get the air-conditioning fixed?'' he griped, instead.

''As soon as it's October,'' Cagney assured him.

''I think I'm beginning to hate you.''

"Just as long as you can catch the killer. Tomorrow, ten a.m., I say we go visit Bennett Jensen at his mill."

"Fine. But I get to be bad cop this time." Daniels lumbered to the door, stopping at the frame for one long moment. "You know, Guiness, as long as we're pretending not to know anything, maybe we should stop thinking of Cecille Manning as the target for the moment. You said Marina feels she's being watched, and it certainly appears someone wants her accused of the crime. So maybe this doesn't have anything to do with Cecille. Maybe she was just one step in a larger plan, and who they're really after is Marina."

The words didn't do anything at all to reassure Cagney as he stood there alone in the stifling heat of his office. And they didn't soothe him later as he picked Marina up at Manning and Harding and drove in tense silence to her house.

And they certainly didn't offer comfort as Marina opened her front door, looked inside and screamed.

Chapter 8

He pushed past her with a burst of adrenaline, his hand automatically reaching to his right hip, where one year ago a gun would have rested. But he hadn't worn the gun since that lone afternoon thirteen months before, and now his hand merely clutched at his belt. He swore to himself, his muscles tensing with useless action as his sharp eyes swiveled around the entryway.

Immediately he could see what had disturbed Marina. Through the archway on the left, the cabinet doors of her old buffet hung open, nearly ripped from their hinges. And it appeared that each and every piece of china had been methodically pulled out and smashed against the floor.

His gaze pivoted to the living room: the pillows lay peacefully on the sofa, the paintings hung straight, the dried flowers stood tall in their decorative vase. Everything seemed fine. He could feel, however, a telltale draft circling through the room.

"Stay here," he said curtly.

He crept steadily through the living room, having to walk on his toes to keep the heels of his boots from echoing on the hardwood floor. He entered the kitchen, his back rounded and muscles tensed for immediate response. Once more nothing moved. His gaze came to rest on the sliding-glass door, now lifted off its tracks and laid on the grass. The screen door flapped in the wind. He stepped forward to grab it with one hand, looking closer at the ragged edge. Something sharp and serrated had been used to rip through the wiry mesh. Something like a hunting knife.

And in his mind, he once more saw Cecille's ragged body.

He heard a small gasp, and pivoted with a raised arm.

Marina stood behind the table, her eyes glued to the remains of the screen door. Her face had gone absolutely white.

"I told you to wait on the porch," he said tersely, hating to see that look of horror in her eyes. He wanted to draw her into his arms and press her head against his shoulder. He wanted to tell her everything was going to be all right.

"Wait here," he told her firmly, instead. "I have to check upstairs." She didn't respond, just stood there with her eyes on the screen door and her hand clasped over her mouth. He went to the staircase.

Upstairs nothing moved and nothing seemed to be disturbed. Jewelry lay in plain view on the top of her dresser. A CD player still stood in the corner of the construction area, a random stack of CDs next to it. For whatever reason, the intruder seemed to have had only one thing on his or her agenda. To smash Marina's china.

Cagney shook his head, not liking the feeling of dread that was creeping up his spine. None of this made sense. None of it. And he suddenly had the horrible feeling that just might be the point. He hurried back downstairs to find Marina.

She'd left the kitchen and now stood in her dining room, her glazed eyes focused on the shattered remains of her china. Bits of blue and pink patterns lay scattered across the hardwood floor and enmeshed in the border of her Oriental carpet. She didn't seem capable of moving.

"Are you all right?" Cagney asked, his voice suddenly sounding loud in the absolute silence.

She didn't respond, but slowly bent and picked up one of the larger fragments. She turned it around in her hand, but it seemed to him she wasn't really seeing it.

"Marina," he said again, his voice sharper now. "Snap out of it, Marina. It's only china. It can be replaced."

"Stoneware," she said suddenly, her voice faint. "It's really just stoneware. Enesco stoneware."

The name didn't mean anything to him, but he nodded. "Don't touch anything more, Marina. I want the lab boys to come look at this. There may be prints, anything. We need to know who did this."

She nodded dully, like a drugged person not totally conscious. "There won't be any prints," she said softly. "We both know there won't be any prints."

"Well, we have to try, sweetheart. It's all we've got left to do."

She said nothing, just remained standing amid the ruins of her beautiful stoneware while he went to find the phone.

It took a half-hour for two men from the SBI crime lab to arrive. One dusted the sliding-glass door for prints. The other placed the larger pieces of plates in plastic bags to go to the crime lab. Then he used a special vacuum to carefully suck up all the remaining bits and pieces. Later the vacuum would be emptied and the contents analyzed for everything from traces of dirt to stray hairs. Cagney didn't envy the guy's Monday task.

It was nearly nine by the time the two men packed their kits back up and left. By then the downstairs had grown hot from the sliding-glass door being open and all the lights left on. Cagney could feel his shirt sticking to him with the North Carolina heat and humidity, but sitting quietly in her front-room chair, Marina didn't seem to notice. She simply stared at the bright painting before her, as if the abstract mix of colors could tell her something Cagney couldn't.

He went to work on putting the sliding-glass door back on its tracks, taping up the screen door with duct tape.

"We can get you a new door in the morning," he said. She nodded, and he saw her eyes dart to the bay windows for a moment as if looking over her shoulder. She shivered.

He crossed into the living room, his boots loud against the floor. Before her, he hunkered down until he could meet her eyes, ignoring the protests of his leg.

"It's over with now," he told her calmly, his eyes steady, holding hers. "Someone broke in, but left without doing any serious damage. And tomorrow, we'll buy you such a sturdy sliding-glass door they'll never be able to break in again."

"Someone was in my house," she whispered, the shadows stark in her violet eyes. "Someone broke into my house."

He reached up and took her hand, feeling it like ice between his fingers. He cradled her hand between his two palms and looked at her steadily. "They're gone now, Marina. And I'm here, okay? I'm going to stay with you all night long. Everything's going to be fine."

She half nodded, but he could still see the uneasiness in her eyes. Once more they darted to the window, peering desperately out into the darkening night.

"Come on," Cagney said, abruptly changing his tone of voice. "You can't be comfortable in that dress. Why don't you find something else to wear, and I'll think of something for us to do? It'll take your mind off things."

His brusqueness seemed to work, and for the first time, a bit of fog left from her eyes. "Do you like to play games?" she asked, her voice stronger this time.

"Sure, sweetheart, anything you'd like."

Her chin came up. "I bet I can whoop your butt at backgammon."

He grinned, that wonderful lazy grin from the barbecue, and she felt the last of the dullness leave her mind. He was here, and his gray eyes were steady in the night. He was strong, and tonight she needed his strength.

"Wouldn't you just like to try?" he told her with clear challenge in his voice.

She sat up suddenly. "Board's in the pantry," she said crisply. "You set it up. I'll go change."

He nodded, relieved to see the color back in her cheeks, the determination back in her eyes. She looked like Marina again, and as he watched her rush upstairs, he was surprised by the fierceness that clutched his chest. He would take care of her tonight. He would protect her.

Because by God, he couldn't stand the thought of anything happening to her.

When she came back down, he had the board set up on the coffee table, a fan blowing pleasantly across the living room to help alleviate the heat. He glanced up at the sound of her approach, his gray eyes abruptly darkening before they dropped back down to the board. But she felt that response like a physical touch against her hot skin, and her nerve endings tingled to life.

She'd dressed comfortably, all right, in a pair of cut-off jeans that were short beyond short and a cropped tank top that left her midriff bare. She'd told herself it was only because of the heat, but that didn't explain why she'd dabbed on more perfume or brushed her long, black hair to fly wild and free down her back. Smudges of paint still decorated her stomach, with another couple of blue streaks on the backs of her arm. It would take too much scrubbing to get them off, and considering they would only return the next evening, she never bothered with the effort.

Now, as his eyes lingered for one moment on the light smatters, she thought she might never try to get rid of the paint again.

"We roll to see who goes first," Cagney said hoarsely. He was suddenly impatient for the fan to cycle back around again. Damn, was it his imagination or had it just grown a few degrees hotter in here? His body felt so hard he could barely sit.

How much of this did one man have to take?

"Perfect," Marina replied, settling down on the floor Indian-style.

As she leaned forward to throw the dice, he glimpsed a tantalizing view of her breasts that made him suddenly aware of what she was no longer wearing: a bra.

He was surely a man in hell.

He didn't play the first game well. His eyes seemed constantly distracted by the way she moved, and the pounding in his leg was nothing compared with the relentless ache in his loins. He didn't know whether to curse her or ignore her. So far, he wasn't doing a very good job of either.

"I win," she declared grandly less than fifteen minutes later. "I thought you said you were good at this."

"Bad luck," he told her dryly. "The heat makes it hard to think."

"Come, now," she told him. "You grew up here. I'd think you'd be used to it."

"So you'd think," he agreed. He pulled himself up, trying to keep his eyes off the bare expanse of her legs. For a blinding moment, he could remember the feel of those legs wrapped around his waist, straining against him. He nearly groaned. "I need a glass of water," he said abruptly. She went to rise, but he waved her down. "I think I can manage that on my own," he said. "Do you want anything?"

"There's lemonade in the refrigerator," she said. "I wouldn't mind a glass."

He headed for the kitchen despite the protests of his leg. He was limping much worse today, no doubt the result of his nice rearrangement of her cabinet. You'd think the pain would be enough to teach a man his lesson. Then why, every time he looked at her, did he want her all over again?

He'd never had a woman affect him the way she did, and dammit, he refused to give in. Because he knew what would happen. His jaw muscle clenched, his eyes growing nearly black as he yanked open the refrigerator door. He'd be on fire for her, then abruptly remember everything, every damn little thing. Like the way the gun had felt in his hand that last afternoon. The way it had jumped with such power in his grip, the smell of the gunpowder cracking the air. The look of surprise on QVee's face as the bullet struck and he went down on his front porch.

The sight of a child dying from his hand.

He poured two glasses of lemonade and hobbled back to the living room. She was no longer looking at the backgammon board and gloating when he entered. Instead she was once more peering out the bay windows. And even from here he could feel the fear running through her.

"Marina," he said softly.

She jerked around, the terror that flashed through her eyes cutting him to the bone.

"Here's your lemonade," he said calmly, as if nothing at all had happened. "Now, why don't you let me show you how this game is really played."

She nodded, and though she never said anything, the relief on her face was genuine. This time they both played in earnest. Her aggressive style put him on guard, while his smooth persistence kept the pressure on. In the end, a lucky pair of doubles sent him to victory.

"Rematch," she declared instantly. "It was rigged. I want a rematch."

"Poor sport."

"Determined sport. It's one–one. What do you say?"

He agreed, going along with the challenge and enthusiasm in her eyes. He almost would have believed it was purely for the game if he hadn't seen her eyes continual darting to the clock behind him. It was five minutes to ten, but for whatever reason, Marina didn't seem to like the idea of going to bed.

"Aren't you getting tired?" he drawled innocently.

Instantly her back tensed with the defensiveness. "No," she said immediately, her eyes once more dashing to the clock. Then abruptly she flushed, realizing she'd just given herself away. She shrugged, searching for an air of nonchalance. "Maybe it's just from the excitement of the day," she said weakly. "Come on. Championship game?"

"As long as you're prepared to lose," he told her with another slow grin.

This time they played even more fiercely. It was a good match, with someone always struggling to get a man out off the prison bar. Rather than a smooth progression, it was a series of ups and downs as they each fought to get their last couple of disks home. Cagney could see Marina flagging. She yawned more and more now, her biological clock relentless. It was fifteen minutes past ten, and the woman who only slept six hours a day was fast approaching exhaustion.

Still, she hung in there until the bitter end. When she had the good fortune to roll the last two numbers needed to put her final two men away, Cagney was sincerely happy for her.

"It was rigged," he announced promptly, but his smile belied his words. "You didn't tell me you were a backgammon junkie."

"Backgammon, bridge, chess, pinochle," she listed off. "My mother loves to play games. People believe she plays for the cultured, polite entertainment. They don't understand just what she'd do to them if she ever lost."

"My brother Jake's like that. Man's way too clever for his own good and can't walk away from a challenge. He once spent an afternoon convincing little Liz to trade him all her nickels for pennies—said pennies must be more valuable because they were the only ones that were copper. 'Course, being seven she went for it hook, line and sinker, and dutifully handed him all her nickels. You should have seen his face as he raked in seven years' worth of nickels. He wanted them badly, but knew the minute Garret came home he'd kick his butt for tricking Liz like that.

"So then he decided to trade me all the nickels for dimes—said nickels must be more valuable because they're bigger. Of course, now his goal was lay it at *my* feet—I'd be the one holding all the nickels, the incriminating evidence. Plus, he'd make a profit on the deal. You see what we were dealing with? I told you he was the smart one, and this was at age eleven.''

"So what did you do?" she breathed, leaning forward, her eyes animated with the suspense.

"Well, I started to wonder why Jake was being so nice and trading us invaluable coins for valuable coins. So I went and asked Mitch and he just shook his head, finally explaining to me just how badly I'd been fleeced. He got up to go haul Jake to the mat, but I told him I'd take care of it. So I got Liz, told her what had happened, and we confronted him together. Told him we were feeling generous and wanted to give him back both the pennies and the nickels in return for quarters—or we'd tell Garret what he'd spent his afternoon doing.

"Did I mention Garret became a Navy SEAL? Garret was a big kid, a fast kid. You didn't want to mess with Garret.''

Marina started to laugh, full and rich. Cagney grinned at her, reveling in the sound.

"So you guys ended up with a tidy profit?" she quizzed.

"Yes, ma'am."

"And started developing the criminal mind-set that's been so invaluable as a sheriff," she teased.

"Guilty as charged. And by God, I saved two of those quarters. I think that was the only time I actually beat Jake at his own game.''

He hesitated, then went on. "And what about you? I can picture you raising a little hell in your time.''

She smiled and shook her head. "No, I was the perfect little princess. I swear." She shrugged, still smiling, but a bit wistful. "There weren't a lot of children in my building, and well, I was different, you know? The sleeping schedule, the..." She trailed off. "Well, I was different," she said matter-of-factly, "and you know how kids can be about that.''

He looked at her with probing eyes. "You say that very reasonably."

She grinned, a dimple appearing in one cheek. "Hey, it cost my parents ten grand in therapy for me to sound so well adjusted."

As soon as the words were out, she wished she could call them back, but Cagney seemed to take the comment in stride.

"Well, it seems they got their money's worth."

She nodded, then caught herself yawning. Cage arched a knowing brow. "Come on, Cinderella," he told her. "Ball's over and you gotta get some sleep."

She nodded again, gazing at the stairs with trepidation. As if sensing her apprehension, he abruptly reached over and captured her hand. "I'll be right down here," he told her quietly, his gray eyes steady. "If you need anything, I'll be right here."

She smiled, in gratitude, in relief. For one moment, she squeezed his hand, her fingers slender and strong.

"Thank you, Cage."

"Just doing my job."

She nodded, but her violet eyes were soft. "Come on," he whispered and tipped his head toward the stairs. "Time to catch some sleep. You're wearing me out and I need the nap."

She laughed, climbing reluctantly to her feet. The fan swirled her hair around her, tickling her bare stomach, caressing her arms. She sighed, rolling her neck and shoulders. The motion pulled her tank top tight across her breasts, but she didn't notice until she glanced at Cage to see that his eyes had darkened.

"Oh," she said.

"Oh," he agreed dryly. "You know, sweetheart, I may have to come up with a dress code for you soon."

She shrugged a delicate shoulder. "Why, Sheriff," she said with her most innocent voice, "I have no idea what you mean."

"Uh-huh," he said wryly.

She smiled at him mischievously and arched a fine brow. "I'm just dressing for the heat," she murmured smugly, and before he could reply, she waltzed toward the stairs. She could feel his warm gaze on her back and it made her feel strong.

But then she looked up the stairs to the pool of blackness waiting on the landing. Her hand stilled on the banister, her face growing somber. She squared her shoulders and flipped on the light. Even then, so many shadows remained.

"Do you have everything you need?" she thought to ask, grasping at any excuse to linger.

But Cage just looked at her with unreadable eyes and nodded.

"There are more sheets in the pantry," she babbled. "And another fan, if you want."

"Good night, Marina."

She sighed and took another deep breath. "Good night," she repeated, the words firm. She marched upstairs to her tiny bedroom.

And already felt the first twinges of terror rippling up her spine.

He couldn't sleep. Even with the rhythmic sound of the tiny fan, his restless thoughts wouldn't leave him in peace. And it was too damn hot to sleep in a pair of jeans and a T-shirt. These June nights were meant for naked flesh sprawled amid cool spring sheets. He thought he might be suffocating, but didn't trust himself enough even to remove his shirt.

There was already enough raw sexual chemistry between the two of them to fuel an entire Fourth of July fireworks display. He didn't need to add any sparks by lying around her living room half-naked. No, he'd promised himself never again and he would stick to that even if she did challenge him with a pair of the shortest shorts any red-blooded man ever saw.

And then those smudges of paint on her stomach. What would it be like to run his hands along those spots, feeling her stomach muscles contract at his touch?

He groaned, rolling over onto his stomach and finding absolutely no relief. Instead he concentrated on the pain in his leg. It was bad enough tonight, not meant for the lumpy discomfort of a pullout bed. But even then, it didn't begin to compare with pains in other parts of him.

With a groan, he sat up and glared at the green glow of the VCR's digital clock—11:02. Damn, he hadn't gotten any real sleep in three days. He should be able to pass out cold by now. What the hell was the matter with him? And why was he torturing himself over a woman he couldn't have?

He kicked his way out of the bed, standing tall and letting the breeze of the fan feather over him. He needed a drink.

But just as he was about to patter into the kitchen, he heard a noise. Immediately his foot stilled, all muscles tensing as his face froze in concentration.

Upstairs, it came again. It sounded like a whimper.

Frowning, he walked quietly to the base of the staircase. He heard it again, the low, tortured sob of a frightened child. He didn't think anymore. He bounded up the stairs two at a time, heading straight for the bedroom.

The door was already wide open, and he could feel the breeze waft through her cracked window, attempting to cool the tiny room with the fresh night air. It took several minutes for his eyes to adjust to the near blackness, but then he saw Marina, rolled up in a tight ball amid the sheets.

Once more, he heard the whimper.

"Marina?" he whispered. Too late, he realized his mistake. Her eyes flew open, registered the shadowed man standing at the foot of her bed, and she screamed, a deep, terror-filled scream that raised the hairs on the back of his neck.

"It's Cagney," he said immediately, but it was too late. She was lost in her world of fear and he couldn't penetrate. She screamed again, a haunted sound that made his blood run cold. In three long strides he was on the bed.

With one hand he covered her mouth; with the other he pulled her against him.

"Shh," he whispered in her ear, feeling her trembles all the way down his body. "It's just me, sweetheart. It's just me. You were dreaming, that's all. It's over now. It's all over now."

She began to shake in earnest, her body collapsing against his with sobbing relief. He rocked her against him, his head resting against the silky tangle of her hair while he murmured soothing words of nonsense in her ear. He had never felt such absolute horror before, never heard a woman scream with such raw terror. He thought he might now have a few extra gray hairs on *his* head.

Minute passed into minute, and gradually her shuddering subsided. He released his grip on her mouth, stroking her arm, instead. She still didn't say anything.

He waited patiently, allowing her time to draw herself out of the nightmare and into the present. After another five minutes, he shifted her in his arms, rolling her over until her head could rest on his shoulder. She sighed, a soft, shuddering sigh of exhaustion. Slowly her legs uncurled, until, like a blossoming flower, she unfolded to lie completely against him.

The trust of that motion moved him.

"Are you all right?" he asked quietly. One hand still caressed her arm in smooth rhythm; his other hand wrapped protectively around her waist. He felt her nod against his shoulder and felt the dampness of tears penetrating his shirt.

His chest tightened. He held her closer, gripped by a fierceness he could no longer explain.

"What did you dream?" he prodded gently. "Do you remember?"

She shook her head. "I don't know," she whispered hoarsely. "I never know."

He frowned in the darkness, not understanding her words. "What do you mean?"

"I never see anything," she said. "I never see anything at all. I just know something horrible is happening. And there is nothing I can do. Nothing, absolutely nothing."

He lifted his hand to cup her cheek and felt the fresh flow of tears against his fingers. Silently he wiped them away with his callused thumb. He rested his cheek against the top of her head, holding her close.

"You've had this nightmare before?" he asked gently. He felt her go suddenly still, and his hand paused on her arm. Then slowly, carefully, he resumed the stroking. But he was abruptly aware of a new emotion surfacing between them—wariness.

"Yes," she said after a moment.

"But you never see anything? A face, a landmark? Anything?"

"No." The doctors had tried many things all those years before. They'd tried hypnosis; they'd tried sleep therapy. They'd even tried drugs. But they'd never learned anything. Only that she was afraid, deeply and horribly afraid of something no one had ever been able to understand, least of all her.

"How long have you been having this nightmare?" Cagney asked neutrally.

"A long time," she said hesitantly.

"Even before you moved here?"

"Yes."

Abruptly his thumb came under her chin, forcing her head up until she could see the gray steadiness of his eyes even in the shadowed darkness. "Is that why you sleep so little?" he asked levelly. "Is that why you keep such a strange schedule?"

Helplessly she nodded.

He sighed, letting her chin go to hold her more firmly against him. "There must be something we can do," he said.

She could hear the genuine concern in his voice, and it made her cry once more, the large, crocodile tears that made no sound in the darkness. She hated these half-truths, she thought with sudden passion. She hated hearing the concern in his voice and knowing she should tell him everything.

Like there was nothing he could do. Like she'd been seen by all the best doctors around and there was nothing anyone could do. Except let her fight the darkness on her own terms.

But she could still see Bradley's face when she had told him about the two-year hospitalization, about the nightmares no one could explain, about the extreme paranoia that would seize her suddenly and for no good reason. She could still see his jaw slacken and his eyes growing round with the horror. And now, pressed against Cage's lean strength in the darkness, she didn't want him to know everything. She didn't want him to look at her as Bradley had done.

She wanted to keep Cagney and the steadiness of his gaze. He made her feel safe, as if for the first time she wasn't fighting her battle completely on her own. He understood about demons, too.

She pressed her head against his shoulder and the tears flowed faster with the force of her emotion, the depth of her need, the overwhelming vulnerability of her desire.

Cagney felt the tears against his shoulder once more, knew she was crying, though she didn't make a sound. He'd never known anyone who could cry like that, and the very silence of the ache tightened his chest. God, he hated to feel this beautiful woman in so much pain. She was so strong, so vibrant, so alive to drown in all this darkness.

And he had no idea at all what to do.

So he just held her, stroking her arm and then her cheek while she cried silent tears against his shoulder. Eventually the tears dried themselves out, leaving her exhausted and sagging against him.

He shifted to get more comfortable, and immediately she stiffened.

"Don't go," she said suddenly.

He could hear the thread of panic in her voice, and he relaxed immediately. "Don't worry, sweetheart," he drawled softly. "I'll stay here."

"Thank you," she whispered.

The words made his eyes close with the fierceness once again. "Go to sleep," he told her gently. "I'll stand guard."

He felt the slight curve of her cheek, a smile in the darkness. Then she sighed, a long sigh of absolute exhaustion. Minutes later, he could hear the easy, steady breathing of sleep.

The last of the tension left him, and he relaxed fully into the deep softness of her bed. He was aware of her bare arm under his hand, the skin smooth as silk. Dimly he could make out the spaghetti straps of a camisole, the satiny material warm from the heat of her skin. Her long legs were also bare, now tangled seductively amid his own.

But he didn't mind; he didn't mind any of it at all. His body might ache with the relentless pain of unfulfilled hunger, but for the first time in a long time, it felt like the right kind of pain. Lying in the darkness with her head on his shoulder, her arm trustingly across his stomach, he felt like a whole man.

He felt complete.

He slept the deep slumber of his own exhaustion. He didn't even wake at one a.m. when her dark-violet eyes fluttered open. He didn't stir as she slowly untangled herself from his embrace and pattered to the bathroom. There she took two aspirin with a glass of tap water.

She didn't bother with clothes. The second story was already too hot for even her white satin camisole and tap pants. Instead she moved quietly into the construction area of the floor, turning on each and every light in turn.

Then, with her gray-eyed man asleep just a room away, she set up a spare canvas and began to paint.

Chapter 9

She glanced up from her desk the minute she heard his footsteps. Her eyes were strained from staring at the computer screen too long, and it took a moment for her to focus. But then all of a sudden, she became aware of Cagney's grim face and unsmiling gaze. He was no longer wearing one of his short-sleeved shirts with jeans, she realized. Now he was wearing dark-brown slacks with a tan, button-up shirt. Maddensfield sheriff insignias blazed from each sleeve, highlighting the star on his chest.

Her eyes went back up to his face, and even as she watched, he shut the door of her office behind him.

He knows, she thought abruptly, and felt her stomach suddenly drop out from her. A faint ringing filled her ears, and her head seemed strangely light. *He knows.*

He walked over to her desk once more, his eyes so piercing she felt like a small rabbit suddenly pinned by the circling hawk. On her desk, her hands began to shake, and she suddenly had the small, semihysterical thought *Where are the almond croissants?*

"So how has your morning been?" Cage said, his voice like unsheathed steel.

"Fine," she whispered. She still couldn't take her eyes away him. She could just look at the barely controlled anger in his eyes and feel her chest tighten with a nearly unbearable pain.

"Andersen found you a new screen door in Charlotte," he said curtly, leaning over her desk as each word fell like a velvet fist. "Are you happy to get a new sliding-glass door, Marina?"

She nodded, licking her lips nervously with the strain. "Who... who..." she managed at last, "will install it?"

"I took care of all that," Cage said brusquely.

This time, the fury was closer to the top, and she got the impression it wasn't directed as much at her but, for this bare instant, at himself.

"I took care of everything, Marina. I'd hate for you to have nightmares again."

The intensity of the words made her pale, and for just one moment, she had to close her eyes.

"Were you ever going to tell me, Marina?" he drawled suddenly. "Were you ever going to say anything?"

Eyes still shut, she shook her head—then jumped as his fist slammed against the top of her desk.

"Look at me, dammit," he growled. "The least you can do is look at me."

She opened her eyes, knowing every emotion she'd ever felt must be so open in her gaze. All the regret and guilt and, of course, the fear. He took one look at her gaze, and uttered a low, savage word she didn't think had ever crossed his lips before. He turned away from her, but not before she saw the brief slash of pain in his stormy, gray eyes.

The emotion floored her, and for the first time, she felt some of her equilibrium return. She had hurt him. By withholding the truth, she'd given him the impression that she hadn't trusted him. But then she hadn't, had she? She hadn't trusted anyone.

She licked her lips again, and forced her mind to function.

"How did you find out?" she said quietly, only the faintest tremor remaining in her voice.

"Daniels," Cage said curtly. His back was still to her, his eyes fastened on the painting before him as if maybe it could provide him with the same peace of mind it seemed to give to her. It didn't work.

"It doesn't change anything," she forced herself to say, her chin coming up. "I didn't bring it up because it isn't relevant."

He turned, watching her with cold eyes. "Sweetheart," he said slowly, "it changes everything."

"Why?" she challenged. Dammit, she'd crumpled before Bradley, but she didn't feel like crumpling again. She was strong, she wouldn't go down without a fight.

Before her, Cage walked once more toward her desk, his gray eyes intent. Carefully, he bent over, his face so near she could see his dark whiskers shadow his clenched jaw.

"Daniels has been wanting to question you for days, but *I* am the one who kept telling him no. I'm the one who kept saying, 'It's too pat, Daniels. It's too easy. We gotta keep our options open.' I believed that, Marina. I believed in the answers you'd given me. And then he walks into my office this morning, asking if I knew you'd spent two years in a mental institution. Now, just when were you going to work that into the conversation, Marina?" *Why hadn't you told me?*

Her chin stayed up, though her hands started trembling anew on the desk. "It's not relevant," she insisted. Then she abruptly leaned forward, as well, her eyes clear and compelling. "Come on, Cage. You've spent the past couple of days with me. What did you see? Did my head ever once turn around three hundred sixty degrees while I screamed in garbled tongues? Did you find a rabbit boiling in a pot on my stove? Did I ever threaten or attack you with malicious intent?"

Slowly he shook his head. "You were hospitalized for something," he remarked, but his eyes were alert all of a sudden.

"I was twelve, Cagney," she replied dryly. "Lord have mercy on my soul."

His face abruptly darkened with the frustration. "Well, if it's that simple, Marina, why didn't you tell me? Why the hell didn't you tell me?" *Especially last night.*

The words were never spoken, but they remained hanging in the air between them. Why hadn't she trusted him, when he'd held her that close and sought to send her nightmares away? Why hadn't she trusted him, when she'd curled up in his arms like a child and begged him not to leave her alone?

She suddenly didn't know what to say, and his gray eyes were hard to meet.

"Do you know anything about mental illness?" she asked, instead, her gaze dropping down to her desk, where she began to fidget with a paperweight. He was much too close; she could smell the soap on his skin, feel the heat of his gaze. "Anything at all?"

"Only schizophrenia," he replied. "Only that it leads to delusions of paranoia, can cause people to kill because voices told them to."

"In other words," she said simply, "what you've seen on TV."

"Son of Sam," he shot back evenly. "I don't think his victims would tell you he was a figment of Hollywood's imagination."

She nodded. "Yes. That's true." Her chin came up, and she met his gaze squarely. "So is that who you think I am, Cagney?" she whispered. "Some serial killer listening to the ranting commands of voices in my head?"

His jaw clenched with his stubbornness. "I don't know," he said at last. The hurt that slashed through her eyes, however, almost made him take the words back.

"You should call my doctor," she said. She stood up from her desk, turning away from him to face the windows. "Before you condemn me, you owe it to your intelligence to at least get the facts straight. Dr. Joseph Epstein. He has been the one who worked with me as a child. I still talk to him from time to time."

"And what will he tell me?" Cagney asked evenly. His eyes still searched her back, as if he could will her to turn around. He hated this feeling that she didn't trust him. He hated almost worse the feeling that he'd caused her pain. But his feelings didn't mean anything anymore.

"He will tell you that no one has been able to make head nor tail of my case," she told him levelly. She shrugged. "I was always a nervous child. I would jump at the tiniest sound, sleep under my bed with the lights on, the whole works. Then, when I was twelve, I began to have this nightmare. Always the same, always that I couldn't see anything. I would just wake up screaming, and my parents couldn't comfort me. No one could. I was terrified of them, of the doctors, of everyone, everything."

Her voice broke, and for a moment, Cagney could see the shudder rippling through her. Her arms wrapped themselves around her middle in that unconscious protective gesture that made him feel like a total lout.

"I don't remember much of those two years," she whispered finally. "Only that I was afraid, deeply and deathly afraid of everything around me. The doctors said they tried everything. I don't know. I don't remember anything but an overwhelming blackness.

"Finally they worked out a regimen of medication, and gradually I came out of it enough to realize what was going on. That the demons were all in my mind, and no one could fight them but me. So I started to fight back, started to force myself to sleep with the lights out, to meet new people without screaming for help. I forced myself to doubt my own mind, and double-check everything with cool rationality and the input from my five senses. And slowly but surely, I pulled out of it. When I was sixteen, I eased off the medication without the nightmares returning. These days, between my schedule, my work and my family, it really hasn't been a major issue.

"Sometimes, if I'm under too much stress, I might become more nervous, paranoid. I'll look over my shoulder more—it's harder to turn out the lights at night. I might wonder if someone is following me. But then, I've been dealing with this a long time, and I know by now it's all really in my mind. And I don't want to sink back into that blackness, Cagney. I don't want to drown once more in the mind-numbing fear that shuts everything else out. I won't. And not just because of routines, but because I have the willpower."

She turned then, and he could see once more the steady set of her chin, the steely determination of her violet eyes.

"I lost two years, Cage, to a horror you can't even begin to imagine. I refuse to lose any more."

There was such conviction in her voice, such solid resolve, that he couldn't find it in himself to doubt her. And all at once, he understood. The bright colors, the lush plants, the glowing lights. She was a woman at war with the darkness. And all her zest and vitality and enthusiasm were her trophies for winning her battles. He thought for a moment that she might be the strongest person he'd ever met. But that didn't ease the tightness in his chest. Why hadn't she told him? Why hadn't she at least let him in that much? And what in the world was he going to do about it now?

"So what is your condition?" he asked at last.

She shook her head. "They aren't sure. Originally, they gave me drugs to help regulate a chemical imbalance. But I went off them when I was sixteen without suffering any side effects. Also, the consistency of my nightmare, of the feelings of fear, seemed to indicate a traumatic experience versus an overabundance of brain chemicals. It might be simply stress-related. In any case, it's hard to make a sure diagnosis. I was adopted, so no one knows my true parents to look at family history. And no one knows anything about what happened the first two years of my life, before I was adopted. They tried hypnosis, but they said I didn't recall anything that made sense, only a series of noises that seemed to upset me."

Suddenly she paled, and her violet eyes grew wide.

"And one of them," she whispered, "one of them was the sound of breaking china."

Cage felt himself go rigid. Once more that feeling of dread hit him, as if something dark and evil were right before him but he couldn't quite see it yet. Detective instincts kicked in, and the adrenaline fairly buzzed in his ears.

"Tell me, Marina," he ordered curtly. "When we call your doctor, will we find any history of violence?"

She shook her head. "No. I wasn't violent. Just terrified."

"And who knows about this, Marina?"

She smiled, a dry smile that came out somewhat sad. "When I came back from the hospital," she said softly, "none of the other kids were allowed back over to our apartment. Their parents were afraid of me. They thought I was Sibyll, too." She paused, raising her deep-violet eyes to meet his. "I haven't told anyone about it since, Cage. My parents know, and I check in with my doctor periodically. Things have been going to smoothly for the past eight years. There's been no need for anything more."

Of course, there had been Bradley. But she didn't see a need to get into that. This man knew too many of her secrets already.

"'Thing's have been going smoothly for the past eight years,'" Cage mused. His eyes narrowed. "But you've been afraid again," he said. "How long has it been going on? And the nightmare—when did it first return?"

Her brow furrowed as she tried to pinpoint an exact time, but it was impossible. Finally, she gave in with a small shrug. "I don't know, really. I guess it returned about a month ago. At first just little feelings, as though I was being watched. But I just kept reminding myself it was all in my mind. Then, I don't know. The fear grew, and the murder happened, and suddenly I was no longer sure it was in my mind anymore."

Cagney nodded, and suddenly, he was the one who felt fear. Strange, how in the middle of a bright June day such a chill could creep up his spine. But he was a man of instinct, and his instincts told him everything was all wrong here.

She was afraid of the sound of breaking china, and just yesterday someone had broken into her house and done nothing except break her plates.

He would have been suspicious that she'd set it all up, except she'd been watched all day long by Davey, who'd stated with absolute certainty she'd never left Manning and Harding until Cagney had picked her up a little after six.

Then another thought nagged at the back of his mind. The woman who went to the airport to pick up the car. The woman with a gray streak in her hair. Who hadn't any obvious way of getting back. There must be two of them. But why two, and who?

His head began to pound, and once more the frustration rippled through him. There were too many unanswered questions. Too many things that pointed to this one woman before him, and too many things that said just the opposite. And among them was his own bias. The fact that he didn't want to believe it was her. The fact that he'd held her all night long and finally felt like a whole man after all these years.

He was a man who never got angry, never got emotional, and all of a sudden he was struck with the insane desire to kick in another cabinet for the second time in just as many days.

He ran his hand through his hair, and fought for the control that had always been his mainstay. Cagney the quiet one. Cagney who could stare down aggressive Garret until his older brother had practically gone insane with the rage. Cool, gray-eyed Cagney.

The dispassion settled deep in his blood, and he squared his shoulders steadily.

"I want you to come to the sheriff's office," he said levelly.

Marina looked startled, then abruptly her violet eyes grew angry. "So that's it, Cage? The woman was once hospitalized, therefore she must be a killer? Are you kidding?"

He shook his head. "You're not under arrest," he stated firmly. "But, Marina, your medical history aside, we still have circumstantial evidence, plus the fact that you have motive and opportunity."

"Cage—"

He held up his hand again. "Marina, I want to believe you," he admitted lowly. "But as a professional, I have to acknowledge I'm biased in this case. We have a lot of questions we need to ask you—like why the lab guys found Cecille's hair in the vacuum bag from your house."

"I worked with Cecille, Cage," Marina interrupted immediately. "I had her over for dinner twice."

But Cagney remained unmoving, "All the same, Marina, we have questions—and I don't think I should be the one to ask them. I think maybe—ethically—Daniels oughtta be the one to question you now. Will you please come with me down to the office?"

Her lips grew tight; she searched his eyes with her own, but his eyes were merely silver mirrors, giving away nothing.

"Just tell me, Cagney," she demanded quietly, "do you think I killed Cecille? Do you think I'm capable of murder?"

For a silent minute, he didn't say anything. His eyes remained unyielding, his stance rigid. When at last he spoke, his words were calm, and even, and cut her straight to the bone.

"I remain open to all possibilities," he said.

She winced, the pain and disappointment too strong for her to hide. Her lips curled up in a bitter smile, and just for a moment, the stubborn tilt of her chin wavered.

"Isn't it strange," she whispered finally, "that those words can hurt me so? Isn't it odd, that after only a matter of days, I care what you think at all?"

She turned away, which was just as well, because he didn't think he could take much more. If someone stuck a million pins in his chest, surely it would hurt worse than that look of disappointment in her eyes. And once more, he could remember her scream of horror just twelve hours ago. Once more, he could remember the way she had clung to him, the sound of her silent tears soaking his shirt. He remembered the way her head had lain so trustingly on his shoulder; he remembered how she had begged him not to go, then fallen asleep like a child in his arms.

"I will get my things," Marina said. Her voice was stronger, her determination settling in her spine. She could feel the fear swirling in the back of her mind, see her hand shake as she opened her bottom drawer and pulled out her bag. But she refused to give in. She'd walked a long road in a tortured land most people would never see. She was a warrior, seasoned by the darkness, honed by the fear.

He nodded but didn't say anything as he led her out to his sheriff's Blazer. When he offered his hand to help her step up, she refused it pointedly.

She ought to call her parents, she realized as they drove through town. She hadn't talked to them in a week now, mostly because they always knew when she was lying, and she didn't want to admit to them that things weren't going well. The minute they found out she'd had the nightmares again, they would both be on a plane down or, more likely, demand that she move back up to New York. She wanted to handle this on her own. Even now, she was determined to handle this on her own.

She hadn't done anything wrong. If anything, she was as much a victim as Cecille. Sooner or later, she'd get them all to realize that, as well.

They pulled into the station.

This time she got out on her own, feeling the tension stretch so tight between the two of them it practically twanged in the silence. She remembered now that one night at the wall when he'd interrogated her with full intensity. How she'd hated him then for destroying her so completely, for being so relentless. How she'd thought there would be nothing between them again.

Why hadn't she listened to her own good instincts? After twenty-seven years of conservative living, why did she have to be so impetuous now?

Cagney opened the door, and she stepped into the small office. Abruptly the talking stopped and two men glanced up. The first, a painfully young-looking man in a deputy's uniform gawked openly at her. The second, an old man with short-cropped gray and a leathery face, stared at her with round eyes.

She was about to ignore them both with rigid pride, when the older man did something that made her eyes suddenly widen with shock.

He crossed himself in full view of everyone present. "Sweet mother have mercy," Roy Sherman said soft and low. "Sarita Davis is alive."

"I'm telling you," Roy insisted for the third time, "it's the same guy. Look at the bodies. Stabbed repeatedly by a serrated hunting knife. Now, maybe in a big city that wouldn't be much. But Maddensfield's only had two unsolved murders. They both just *happen* to suffer from the same M.O. They both just *happen* to occur twenty-five years apart *to the day*. It's the same killer. Same, same, same."

They'd been going over this for an hour now, Roy, Cagney and Daniels. Cooped up in Cage's tiny office, the heat soaking them to the bone without doing anything to dampen their tempers. Marina remained outside with Andersen watching her like a hawk. Which was fairly comical, considering that promptly at two o'clock she'd put her head down on Davey's desk and gone to sleep.

"Two murders, twenty-five years apart," Daniels retorted, his meaty face red and his patience short. "That makes no sense. Who the hell kills only once every twenty-five years?"

"I don't know," Roy shot back. "If I'd known, I would have arrested the son of a bitch twenty-five years ago."

Cagney held up his hand, interrupting the third round of the same argument. "We are getting nowhere," he stated levelly, his gray eyes sharp and calm as they penetrated the two men sitting across from each other like dueling opponents. "One final time, Roy, let's go over the facts. Just the facts."

Roy grunted, doing his best to calm his grumpy temper as he looked at Cage.

"Twenty-five years ago," Roy began again, "to the day, Mike Johnson and me received a call about Sarita Davis's place. She hadn't shown up for work, and her boss couldn't get through to her by phone. That may sound strange to you now, but in those days, that was just as good a reason to stop by a place. Neighbors looked out for one another, you know. Especially for Sarita, having to live alone and raise a kid all by herself."

"The facts, Roy," Cagney stated again, his voice patient.

Roy shot him a narrow glance. "You want me to tell it," the old man said, "I tell it my way. You weren't there Cagney. You didn't see the body like we did. You...you didn't see what that beast had done."

Cagney nodded, keeping his eyes level. But he had seen Cecille Manning, and that had been bad enough for him, even after eight years of D.C. homicides.

"First we found the dog," Roy said. "A big ole German shepherd, purebred, you know. Strong, young dog. He'd been gutted, and left lying in the grass like a dead fish. The smell." Roy shook his head. "You don't ever want to smell anything like that. We found Sarita in the living room of the rancher. She'd put up a good fight, startin' in the bedroom. She'd tried to get to the phone, then the knives. Finally she threw her entire collection of china at the beast, crystal, lamps, everything."

For one minute, Roy grew silent. His face was suddenly haggard, and it seemed to Cage that the old man's wrinkles stood out prominently.

"Didn't do no good, though," Roy whispered. "The killer stabbed her to death in her own living room. I ain't ever seen nothin' like it. I hope I never will again."

"And the child?" Cagney prodded quietly. A deep somberness had filled the tiny office, and for a change, not even Daniels spoke.

"We found Kristi in the back bedroom. The door had been shut, and Sarita had been leading the killer away, you know. I can't quite tell you what it was like to find her. She just stood there in her crib, this tiny, year-and-half-old baby whose hair had suddenly gone gray. And she looked at us with the darkest eyes, not saying a word even as I picked her up. She didn't even cry. She just stared at me with vacant eyes."

Roy's voice broke, and he had to look away. Cage could see the older man blink back the moisture in his eyes, and he felt a telltale tightness in his own chest.

"We brought in the SBI," Roy said finally, his gaze flickering to Daniels. "They never did find anything. And Kristi was put up for adoption. After that, I never heard anything more."

"Until now," Daniels said impatiently. "And now you want us to believe that Cecille Manning was killed by the same person twenty-five years later. Hell, you're seventy-seven years old, Roy Sherman. How old do you think the killer is by now? Who the hell will believe in some geriatric serial killer who strikes every quarter of a century?"

Roy's eyes grew narrow, and for one moment, he looked as if he might snap the younger, heavier man in half. Cagney once more raised an intervening hand.

"Come on, Daniels," Cage said calmly. "Even you have to admit there's a connection. Roy's right. In that past twenty-five years Maddensfield has had only had three premeditated murders and one was solved ten years ago. That leaves us with two unsolved murders, where the victims were both young, single females who were brutally stabbed with a hunting knife."

Daniels opened his mouth to say something, but Cagney waved him down. "Then we have Marina herself. Pretty coincidental that the second murder should happen only two months after she returned to Maddensfield, especially considering the fact that she doesn't even know she was born here. Yet two months after her arrival another woman is dead, and she feels someone is watching her. Then there's the matter of the broken plates in her home. Someone broke in just to smash all her dishes? Then her name itself. Kristi Davis. The same name of the woman who rented the car used to transport Cecille Manning's body. That's too many connections, Daniels, and you know it. The question is, what do they all mean?"

Roy, looking properly vindicated, turned his gruff old eyes on Daniels. "You want a third opinion," he growled, "you can always double-check with Mike Johnson. He retired from the police force in Charlotte, you know. But he never forgot about Sarita Davis. You couldn't walk through that house and ever forget."

Daniels held up both hands in mock surrender, but his face wasn't happy. "Fine," he agreed curtly. "But I don't like any of it. For all we know, Marina staged all this just to throw us off her trail."

"She couldn't have broken into her own house," Cagney replied patiently. "Davey watched her all day."

"Maybe she has an accomplice," Daniels countered shrewdly, echoing Cagney's earlier thought. "Didn't you say there might be two people involved? How else could the killer return from the airport?"

Cagney nodded, looking uncomfortable as the thought struck too close to home. "But I was there," he said at last. "I saw her face, Daniels, and I'm telling you she was honestly terrified." And he'd been there to hear her nightmare just hours later, to hear the raw horror of her screams. He glanced out his door window, seeing her still asleep with her head on the desk. He wondered what she would do when she woke up and learned the truth. He wondered if having her nightmares solved after all these years would bring her peace or only make the horror real.

Suddenly he turned to Daniels. "That's what we're missing," he said abruptly.

Daniels and Roy both looked up sharply. "What do you mean?" Daniels quizzed with his customary frown.

"You're assuming she knows what happened all those years ago," Cagney said. "But she doesn't. And they tried to find out. She said the doctors even did hypnosis, but she couldn't tell them anything. *Because she didn't see anything.* Roy said she was shut up in the room the whole time. She never saw the killer—she never saw the body. She knows nothing about the crime but certain sounds that scare her. *Like the sound of breaking china.* I'm telling you, Daniels, the killer is playing her. He knows who she is just as surely as Roy does—"

"She's the spitting image of her mother," Roy said, "and then there's the gray streak. Maddensfield's a small town and word of the murder got around fast. Everyone knew baby Kristi's hair had gone partially gray. Hell, I recognized her in five seconds, and I didn't even know she was adopted."

Cagney nodded. "Obviously, the murderer figured it out, too, and now he's playing her right into the madness. He didn't get her twenty-five years ago, so he's going to get her now. Except this time, he's having fun with it."

"What about Cecille Manning?" Daniels interrupted.

But Cagney shook his head. "It has nothing to do with her," he said as one by one the lights started to go on. "The whole time it's Marina the killer has wanted. All of this has merely been part of the game, the blood lust. Maybe the killer knows she was hospitalized as a child and is trying to drive her back over the brink."

Daniels grunted, but for a change the red-faced man was listening. He turned sharply to Roy.

"Who were your suspects twenty-five years ago?" Daniels demanded.

Roy shook his head. "Never got very far. We searched for drifters, drilled some of the locals. There'd been some talk that Lloyd Jensen had been 'seeing' Sarita, but he was with his wife the night of the murder. Everyone was accounted for. We had no witnesses, no murder weapon. Hell, we didn't even have a motive."

"You got the records?"

Once more, Roy shook his head. "They all burned up in the fire. On the other hand, the state assisted with the case. You gotta have some records someplace."

Daniels gave a short bark of laughter. "Hell, with our system, that's like looking for a needle in the haystack. I'll see what I can do, though. It's the best chance we have."

Daniels eyes also drifted to Marina, still sleeping on the desk. "I want her looked into, though," he said suddenly. "You say she didn't know anything about her real parents or living here or anything. I want that confirmed. Awfully strange, if you ask me, moving all of a sudden from New York to a small town where her real mother was murdered. Awfully strange."

"Sometimes," Cagney said, "the truth is stranger than fiction."

"Yeah, well, I don't want strangeness or fiction. Just the facts. A twenty-five-year-old murder. I just don't like it. What are you going to do about her—" Daniels jerked his head toward the window "—in the meantime?"

"Twenty-four-hour surveillance," Cagney replied immediately. "If the killer broke into her home, he's only getting closer. I don't want to leave her alone for a minute." Suddenly he frowned. "We have to stop doing that, you know," he said quietly, gazing at both men with steady eyes. "We keep saying 'he' for the killer. But it was a woman who rented the car in Kristi Davis's name. Maybe that's where you went wrong twenty-five years ago."

Roy nodded, then gave a small shudder. "Shoot, just the idea of a woman being capable of such madness..." He shivered again. "God, I don't like any of this."

Cagney agreed, and after another round of who was to do what, the meeting broke. Daniels left, still frowning as he walked by Marina sleeping on the desk. Cagney glanced at his watch. It was only 3:30, meaning she was due to sleep for another half-hour.

He had a feeling things were only going to get worse from here. And looking at her, he didn't like that idea. He'd wronged her by not trusting her right away. He hadn't liked the fact that she hadn't told him the truth. Oh, hell, he hadn't liked it at all. But he still should have listened to her more closely back in his office. Maybe, just once, he should have stopped second-guessing himself and gone with his instinct.

But then, he hadn't stopped second-guessing himself since the day he'd pulled the trigger and a fourteen-year-old kid had fallen at his feet.

He turned back to Roy, and quietly the two men talked while the clock ticked away. Until exactly at four, Cagney turned to peer out his doorway and saw Marina raise her head to meet his guarded gaze with her dark-violet eyes.

Chapter 10

Roy and Marina spoke in low tones in her living room while Cagney prowled the house. He tested out the new sliding-glass door, with its heavy metal frame, nonlift door and special back lock. He also checked the locks on the upstairs windows and examined the bolt lock on her front door. Mostly he paced out the ache in his leg and tried to pretend he didn't hear Marina's voice in the living room.

But every now and then, he would hear her whisper crack with the pain, and a muscle would tighten in his jaw. He walked back upstairs to investigate the construction site, trying to give her some privacy. Given their little interaction that morning, she probably wasn't comfortable with him around.

At eight-thirty, Roy rose, his blue eyes suspiciously bright. Marina walked him to the door, then abruptly, threw her arms around his sturdy frame. He held her for a minute, and even from midstairs, Cagney could see the old man's tears fall on her black hair. Roy patted her awkwardly on her back and disappeared out the door.

Marina stood there a minute more, a long shudder going through her. She closed the door quietly.

When she turned, she met Cagney's eyes for a fraction of an instant before walking pointedly back into her living room. Feeling like a truant schoolboy, Cagney followed.

"Will you be staying all night?" she asked from the couch. She refused to look at him, focusing instead on the plant sitting next to the couch. Absently she began to prune away the stray, brown leaves.

"Yes," Cagney said, facing the fireplace so he wouldn't have to stare straight at her.

"All right," she said quietly, the idea at once making her feel relieved and tense. There was a gap between them again. She'd wanted him to believe in her; he'd wanted her to trust him. What a tangled web they'd weaved.

"Marina," Cagney said after a moment, his gaze settling on her long, thick hair. He opened his mouth to speak, the confusion rising up in his throat. He wanted to apologize; he wanted to let her know that he had never really thought she could be the killer. He was just doing his job, his damn, bloody job. But no words would come out; no syllables offered consolation for the tightness in his chest. He closed his mouth and looked away from her abruptly. "So what will you do now?" he asked finally.

"What do you mean?"

"You know what caused your nightmare. You know about your...mother, why you were adopted. Doesn't that change things?"

Her hand stilled on the plant, her shoulders slumping ever so slightly. "I...I don't know," she said at last, the words barely a whisper. "I don't know what to make of any of it. What to feel."

She didn't say anything more, and Cagney simply stood there, sensing her pain and feeling inadequate to help her. The silence stretched on until he had to grit his teeth against it.

"When I was little," she said suddenly, "I used to feel so guilty. I mean, my adoptive parents had taken me in and given me a home, expecting a darling, perfect child. But I wasn't darling, and I wasn't perfect. Instead I screamed at imaginary shadows and cried late at night from nightmares. I shied away from other kids and saw terrors in everything around me. They had to hospitalize me.

"But you know, Cagney, they never complained. They never turned away from me. They never gave up on me. They found me the best doctors—they even visited me every day in the hospital when I could only look at them with wild, terrified eyes. They never blamed me, and they never once said, 'If only we'd gotten a normal child.' They were there for me. When everyone else turned away, they were still always there."

Once again she began to pick at her plant, and it was everything Cagney could do not to go to her.

"I still remember," she said quietly, "waking up in the middle of the night, crying and panicked. And my mom would come into my room and pick me up and hold me in her arms. Sometimes she would stay all night long, rocking me in the rocking chair and stroking my hair. When other kids wouldn't come over, she would just look at me quite briskly and say, 'We'll just have to have fun all by ourselves.' Then she'd bring out the board games and play with me. First Chutes and Ladders, Candyland and dominoes. Then chess and backgammon. Finally, when I was old enough, I would join her with her friends and we played bridge and hearts and pinochle. My mom is an amazing woman.

"When I graduated from Wellesley, we all cried. Not because *I* had made it, but because *we* had made it. All of us, together. My parents were my parents in every sense of the word. I could not ask for anyone better, anyone to love me more."

"They're still your parents," Cage said quietly.

"Exactly," she told him, tearing off another dead leaf. "I feel like I ought to call and tell them that I found out about this extraordinary woman. She came from Spanish nobility, but grew up here in North Carolina poverty. And she brought a child into this world without a husband, and did everything she could to give that child a life, no matter what the townspeople might have thought. Until one night, she fought a killer until her dying breath, leading him away from her baby. Sacrificing her own life so that her daughter might live. And she was my birth mother, and I wish…I wish I could have known her."

Her voice cracked, and Cage took an automatic step forward before he caught himself. He wanted to go to her; he wanted to pull her into his arms and rest her head against his shoulder. He wanted to stroke her long, dark hair and murmur words of comfort while she cried her silent tears against his shirt. He wanted to be there for her, but after this morning, he wasn't sure she would want that.

With a soft sigh, Marina swallowed the lump in her throat and summoned a watery smile. "I really hate to cry so much," she told Cagney. She rose off the sofa, finding a tissue and blowing her nose. She took a deep breath and squared her shoulders. "If you think about it," she said steadily, "this should be a relief. I no longer have to wonder if I was unwanted as a baby, if I was abandoned without the slightest twinge of regret. No one knows who my father was, but my birth mother loved me as child. Loved me so much—" Her voice cracked again and her eyes closed. "Loved me so much she died trying to save me," she finished in a whisper. "I wish I could have known her. I wish I had a picture."

This time Cage did step forward; he couldn't help himself. Slowly, his gray eyes unreadable, he touched her cheek. "Roy says you look just like her," he said gently, and gave her a small smile. "So if you ever want to see Sarita, you can just go look in the mirror."

She laughed, the sound a bit soggy but there. "Yeah, I suppose so." Her face grew pensive once more.

"What should I tell my parents?" she asked him quietly. "I want them to know, but I don't want to hurt them. I don't want them to think this changes who they are in my life. I mean, I wish I had known Sarita. But I didn't. And I do know Jim and Nancy Walden and they are the best parents a girl could have. I love them. I miss them." Her lips trembled again.

Tenderly, Cagney traced the full shape with his thumb, then felt her press her cheek against his palm. "You'll know what to say," he told her steadily. "You and your parents are very close. After everything you've been through, this is but a footnote."

She nodded finally, pulling back a little and wiping the last of the moisture from her cheeks. She squared her shoulders again. "Yeah. Yeah, you're right." She took another deep breath, then gazed at him with clear eyes. "So you're no longer angry with me?" she asked abruptly.

Surprised, he shook his head. "Why should I be angry?" he asked. After all, he'd been the one to turn on her.

"Because I didn't tell you the truth," she said, her head held high. "Because I didn't tell you everything."

Slowly he shook his head. "I was angry," he said quietly. "But then, I understand."

Unbidden, her eyes fell to his leg and the silence filled with unasked questions. Her violet gaze swept back up to his face, and he saw the challenge clearly. He knew everything about her. It was his turn now to reciprocate. His turn to trust her.

His jaw clenched, and for one long moment, he teetered on the brink of indecision. It wasn't as if it was some big secret. Everyone knew Cagney Guiness had grown into a man and become a big-city cop. And everyone knew that one afternoon Cagney Guiness had shot and killed a fourteen-year-old murder suspect. Everyone knew he'd killed a kid.

He turned away and limped toward the kitchen with a clenched jaw.

"Don't," Marina said harshly.

He froze in his tracks, slowly turning, while he felt the blood suddenly hammer in his head. Her eyes were furious.

"How can you just turn away like that?" she challenged fiercely. "I just poured my heart out to you. I just told you every aching emotion I've ever felt. And you can just turn and walk away? Are you made out of stone or something?"

Cagney didn't say anything, but his gray eyes turned to silver mirrors, betraying nothing. It only made her madder.

"Does it change things now that you know I have an illness?" she quizzed. "Do you suddenly think I can't take it? Do you suddenly think you can't talk to me anymore?"

He shook his head, a nearly imperceptible movement that did nothing to calm her. In three long strides she was before him, grabbing his hand before he had time to react. Furiously she placed his hand on her smoothly curved cheek.

"Feel that, Cage," she demanded hotly. "Does that feel like glass to you? Does that feel like the fragile skin of a woman who might shatter? Nothing's changed, you know, just because of two years that happened thirteen years ago. You don't have to treat me differently, and you don't have to stand there looking at me as if you want to come closer, while not moving at all. I can take it, damn you. I'm still me."

He wanted to tell her that wasn't why he was holding back; he wanted to tell her he didn't think less of her. But all he could think was how smooth and hot her skin felt against his palm. As if she might burn his hand, sear his soul with the intensity. He was the quiet, composed member of the family. At least he had been until he'd met her. Now the dull roar building in his ears had nothing to do with calmness, and the darkening of his eyes had nothing to do with dispassion.

She saw it, too, and her breath caught in her throat, her dark-violet eyes falling and lingering on his lips before they swept up to meet his gaze.

"Come on, Cagney," she challenged. "Kiss me. Kiss the crazy woman."

The raw bitterness in her words made him wince, but it also made him mad. He didn't think less of her, he didn't look at her as a headcase. He saw the strongest woman he'd ever met. He saw the only woman who had ever penetrated his control.

"You're not crazy," he whispered darkly. "I don't think less of you. In fact," he muttered hoarsely, "I want you."

He dragged her forward and captured her lips with his own. He could taste the salt of her tears, could taste the heat of her rage. But he could also taste the fire of her hunger, and as her arms wrapped tightly around his shoulders, he was no longer thinking of medical diagnosis, or shadows, or even his leg. He was relishing the moist depths of her mouth, the slick feel of her skin. He was fitting his hips against hers until he could nestle his growing hardness against her growing need.

He plundered her mouth, forcing her head back, delving into the deepest recesses. He wrapped his tongue around hers, sucking on it like a starving man, shivering with her answering groan. He licked the corners of her mouth, tortured her with a long, lingering exploration of every curve and indent. Then he thrust his tongue back in, finding her tongue, making her half-crazy with the desire.

Her hands slid under his shirt, sprawling across his smooth, muscled planes until he felt at once extremely masculine and totally on fire. Her strong fingers flicked over his nipples, and he groaned against her mouth. His head dipped and he found her earlobe, worrying it with his teeth while she sucked in her breath with the sharp stab of desire. She pressed her hips against his intimately, rubbing against his hardness.

She wanted this, needed this. Needed to believe he still saw her as a woman, that he still wanted her, desired her. She wanted to fill herself with the sensations, the raw passion, the electric desire. There was no room for pain or doubts or fear. There was just this man, his teeth succulent against her neck, his hands greedy upon her buttocks. She thought she might burst into flame.

She tore his shirt off over his head, and they barely broke stride. His hands had her flowered skirt, bunching it above her waist as he backed her up to the fireplace. Then his fingers had full access to her legs, stroking the long, luxurious lengths as his tongue plunged once more into her mouth. Slowly, surely, his right hand slipped between her legs. She shivered with the anticipation.

He felt her wetness, felt the damp seductiveness of her lacy panties against his palm. One finger outlined the elastic rim, and he heard her moan with the need. His hand delved underneath the delicate barrier to find her hot, moist folds. She stiffened instantly, so close to the edge he could already feel her scream of passion against his mouth.

His finger slid into her waiting warmth, finding her slick and tight and ready. She arched toward his penetration, her head falling back as the first wave of ecstasy hit her. He plunged his finger in again, his breathing harsh and shallow as he watched her eyes close with the overwhelming sensations. And again and again he thrust into her warmth, sending wave after wave crashing through her, until she collapsed against his chest in a mass of convulsing shivers, exhausted and satiated.

Carefully he lowered them both to the floor, letting his palm rest against her while she shivered with the aftermath, sweat coating her smooth, dusky skin. His body felt unbelievably hard, painful in its rigidity. He would not have changed it for the world.

His left hand came up and slowly began to stroke her hair.

"I didn't know I could feel like that," she whispered after a moment. "I didn't know anyone could make me explode."

His hips surged helplessly at her words, and he had to bite the inside of his cheeks to hold back the groan. He felt on fire. He thought he might die from the pain. But still he didn't move. It would be so easy, though. To roll her above him, to slide down his jeans until he could bury himself in that quivering flesh. To feel the warmth, the tightness. To thrust into her, to lose himself in her. He could please her again, watch her with glittering eyes while she found her own release, then pour himself inside her with fierce relief.

He twisted his hips slightly, putting more room between them. He barely trusted himself to move.

"Have . . . have there been others?" he asked tentatively. She'd always seemed so passionate he'd assumed she was experienced, as well. But now, listening to her amazement, he suddenly wasn't sure.

To his surprise, he felt a hot blush flood her cheeks. "Yes," she said at last. "At least, kind of. But he never." She seemed to lose the words completely. "He never made me feel like that."

The fierceness that gripped his chest was completely chauvinistic and primal. But that didn't stop him from clutching her a little tighter.

Slowly her hand opened on his bare chest, sliding down his slick muscles to wander the edge of his jeans. "Cagney," she murmured, "I want to please you, too. I want to feel you inside of me."

He closed his eyes, wondering if she knew what she was doing to him. Then her hand closed around his rigid length through the rough denim, and he nearly leaped from the floor with the desire. He had never wanted anyone this badly. He'd never wanted a woman until it hurt.

Very slowly, barely able to breathe, he reached down for her hand and placed it firmly back on his chest.

"It's okay," he managed to get out. "I'm just fine."

He didn't sound fine, though; he sounded like a man being gradually strangled by the force of his own needs. He could feel her frown against his chest, and he didn't have to look down to know her eyes were narrowing with puzzlement. He didn't release his grip on her wrist.

He understood the physical pain; he could bear the physical ache. It was certainly better than the deeper, darker pain he knew always lingered under the passion.

The sound of the .357 Magnum jumping in his hand. The look on QVee's fourteen-year-old face as the bullet struck home...

He winced, unable to completely shutter the sound. Instantly she was on one elbow, peering down at him.

"What is it, Cagney?" she whispered intensely. "What is it that you're keeping from me even as we lie together half-naked on my living-room floor? And how dare you do such a thing?"

He closed his eyes against her fierceness, his fist clenching and unclenching at his side. He could still feel her moisture on his fingers. If he brought his hand up, he would smell the warm, musky scent that was uniquely hers. Yet he still couldn't bring himself to say the words.

He didn't want to give that much of himself away.

And partly, deep down, he was afraid she wouldn't understand what that afternoon had really meant. She'd be like his partner, Melissa, his boss, and even his family: "Cage, you did what you had to do, Now, get on with it."

But in his mind, the afternoon hadn't ended, because it hadn't really been about QVee, the three-time murderer who'd opened fire on two detectives. It had been about what what QVee represented—the new kind of criminal who wore a child's face and didn't mind pulling the trigger because death was an abstract and didn't the Coyote in the cartoons always get up in the end?

And still no one knew who the new kind of cop should be. Which left Cage with the thought that not only had he killed a kid, but if he went back to D.C., he might end up shooting another.

And the thought of holding a gun again, of seeing that look of surprise on another fourteen-year-old face...

Cagney, the steady, composed, gray-eyed sheriff was really, deep down, a man who was afraid.

He rolled away from Marina, feeling her eyes on his back as he tried to stand too quickly and his leg cramped beneath him. His breath whooshed out in a low curse of blind pain, then he staggered to his feet.

Behind him, he heard the rustle of Marina's skirt.

"Suzanne told me you were too hard on yourself," she said sharply. "She didn't say you were a damn fool, as well."

"I'm sorry," he said at last, his voice curt to his own ears. "Forget about it."

"Forget about it?" she said incredulously behind him. She grabbed his arm as he was reaching for his shirt and forced him around. "I don't know about you, Cagney Guiness, but I don't fall onto my living room floor with just anyone. There is something between you and me, whether you like it or not. I've tried to walk away—you've tried to walk away. But when we touch each other... let's face it, there are nuclear blasts that have given off less heat. And if you'd stop being so bullheaded for just one moment, you'd see it, too."

He just looked at her hand lying on his arm, his gray eyes so steely another person would have taken a clear step back. But Marina didn't retreat, instead her eyes grew nearly black with the anger. Once more she searched his face with her intense gaze. Once more he looked at her like a man carved from stone.

She swore, something low and graphic that he'd never heard from her lips before. Her violet eyes grew even harder and more determined on his face.

Finally, he was the one who gave in with a small shake of his head. "Marina, it doesn't matter. It happened over a year ago and I don't want to talk about it. Can't you just leave it at that?"

Slowly, firmly, she shook her head.

His jaw clenched stubbornly. "Well, you'll just have to, sweetheart, 'cause I'm not much for words."

"You're shutting me out," she said in a low voice.

"It's nothing personal."

"How can you say that with a straight face?"

He closed his eyes and the frustration stabbed through him. "I'm thirsty," he said abruptly. "Would you'd like some lemonade?"

"I'd like the truth."

"Okay, how about ice tea?"

"You are so damn stubborn!"

"Ice water?"

She swore again, her violet eyes dangerous. "Lemonade," she said finally.

He nodded and turned toward the kitchen.

"This isn't over with yet," she called out behind him.

He had a feeling she was right.

"Jeez, Cage, you nearly scared me to death!" Suzanne Montgomery stood stock-still on her back porch, her hand still clasped over her heart. She'd just walked out her screen door, wearing a yellow oversize man's shirt and old brown trousers that were covered with various smudges of dirt. A floppy straw hat protected her hair but didn't quite hide the smear of dirt across her patrician nose. In her hand, she held a pail and a garden trowel. "Whatever happened to knocking?" she drawled as she sought to resume breathing.

Cagney didn't say anything, simply rocked in the old porch swing, his gray eyes sweeping over her unusually disheveled appearance.

"Strawberries?" he asked levelly.

"Last batch before I begin to make my jam," she explained. Her hazel eyes narrowed on him, a lifetime of friendship enabling her to read his face at a glance. "But then, you didn't suddenly appear on my patio at nine-thirty in the morning to discuss my garden, did you, Cage?"

Slowly he shook his head, his eyes unreadable.

Suzanne set down the pail and her garden trowel. With quick, efficient movement she pulled off her gloves. "Ice tea?"

"If it's no trouble."

"Oh tell me something about a man that isn't trouble," Suzanne called over her shoulder as the screen door banged shut behind her. In mere minutes she was back on the porch with two tall glasses of cool ice tea with mint sprigs.

"It's about that woman, isn't it?" Suzanne said as she handed Cagney his glass, then sat down comfortably on the porch steps. When they were growing up, Cagney often used to just appear on her back porch late at night. She would come down to find him, and they would often sit together in silence under the stars, pretending they couldn't hear her mother snoring in drunken oblivion. During the past year, he'd shown up a lot. But the visits had begun to fade again in the past couple of months. Funny, how she'd missed them. They'd always been the odd ones out, Cagney and her. And their friendship ran deep. Cage had seen her through times she didn't think she could have gotten through alone. "Marina Walden," Suzanne now mused. "She's quite beautiful, if I recall. So what did you do—go fall in love?"

Cagney frowned at her, then shook his head, only to find the motion faltering. "Of course not," he tried saying, his words cool.

Suzanne arched an elegant brow. "Oh, my goodness, Cage, you *have* gone and fallen in love. How delightful for you. It's about time one of us got it right."

"I haven't fallen in love," he said again, the words hedged with impatience now and a trifle defensive.

But Suzanne merely scoffed at him. "I saw how you looked at her, Cage Guiness. You haven't looked at a girl like that since little Mary Maples, and she decked you the first time you tried to steal a kiss. You wore that black eye like a badge of triumph for a good week and half, then started walking her home every day. You were insufferable."

"I'm hardly nine anymore."

"Exactly why it's time for you to look at someone else like that. So tell me, does she love you? Please say yes, Cagney. The only living I get to do anymore is completely vicarious."

"Speaking of someone who needs to fall in love," he said dryly.

"But we're not discussing me. We're discussing you and Marina Walden." Suddenly her hazel eyes narrowed shrewdly. "Have you told her about D.C.?"

Immediately Cagney stiffened, and she shook her head. "Now what are you even thinking, Cagney Guiness? It's been over a year. How long are you going to keep holding that over your head?"

"The kid's dead," he said flatly, his eyes falling expressionlessly on her lush, burgeoning rose garden. "It doesn't matter if it's been one week, one month or one year. Dead is dead."

"Yes," Suzanne agreed, "something I'm sure his victims are painfully aware of, as well."

"He was never convicted of the murders," Cagney mumbled without force. This was old ground between Suzanne and him.

Suzanne dismissed his statement with a wave of her hand. "He may have been just fourteen, Cagney, but the boy was also a drug-running gang member who'd killed three people. Don't make him a martyr just to hang around your neck. You did your job. We all know it. You're the one who won't let it go."

He gazed at his hands, seeing the ice-tea glass tremble in his grip. His jaw clenched, and the trembling stopped.

"I don't want to tell her," he said at last.

"Why not?"

"I don't know," he said quietly, his eyes finally meeting Suzanne's. "Maybe I just don't want to give that much of myself away. Maybe I don't want her to know everything."

Suzanne pursed her lips, shaking her head at him. "Sooner or later, you have to take the risk," she said gently. "You've punished yourself long enough, Cagney. Now give yourself a chance to live."

He merely sighed, peering once more out to the horizon as he took a deep sip of the ice tea. "All this from a woman who hasn't had a date since '81," he said ironically. "Aren't we the pair?"

Suzanne didn't take offense. She and Cagney had been friends too long; besides, her spinster status in the small town of Maddensfield was hardly a secret. Everyone accepted it, and maybe over time, she'd come to accept it, too.

"Have you heard from Garret lately?" she found herself asking. She picked a piece of lint off her old work pants with almost exaggerated casualness. But when she looked up, Cagney was shaking his head at her with exasperation.

"For crying out loud, Suzanne," he told her bluntly. "It's been a good fifteen years. Surely you're still not waiting for him."

"Of course not," she snapped primly. "I'm just asking, that's all."

Cage's expression said he clearly didn't believe her. He still remembered the way she'd mooned over his older brother—hell, all the girls had. But especially quiet Suzanne Montgomery, who'd come to school in threadbare clothes because her mother spent all the money on booze. And Garret used to punch out the first kid who ever said a word about it. Strange how, sitting on the front porch of the house Suzanne had grown up in, those days didn't seem so far away. He could still even remember Garret taunting him, trying to provoke his quiet little brother into an actual fight.

"We haven't seen Garret in four years," Cage said curtly. "Not since the night Liz's husband died, and then he just appeared in her bedroom at night, only to disappear by morning. We've gotten a few phone calls, postcards, but that's it. He didn't even make it to Mitch and Jessica's wedding. But then, Garret always could be a selfish bastard."

Suzanne didn't spare a glance for Cagney's last statement; she knew the waters that ran between the two brothers had never been peaceful. But then, she'd always considered it to be a sign of life's ironies that she should be attracted to the older, wilder one who had protected her on the playground, only to leave her crying out her sixteen-year-old eyes at a rainy bus stop. Why couldn't she have just fallen in love with Cagney, the steady and reliable one who'd taken her to the hospital all those years ago so she could watch her mother die from the alcoholism that had consumed her life? And it had been Cagney who had helped her hold the pieces together through those rough years of medical bankruptcy, Cagney who'd given her a strong shoulder to lean on those nights when she'd collapsed in exhausted tears from the strain.

But they had only ever been friends, and now, looking at him, she could be happy her friend had found love, even if she never would.

She rose, dusting off her pants as she gazed at him with decisive eyes.

"Stop hiding out on my porch, Cage," she told him dryly. "You know you've got a good thing. Don't blow it with a bunch of misplaced guilt. We need you here in Maddensfield, you know. You are a great sheriff, and I just know you'll be a wonderful Little League coach."

He studied her warily. "I already told you I don't want to have anything to do with kids," he said, but some of the vehemence was beginning to fade from his words.

Suzanne simply pretended she hadn't heard him.

"Scram," she told him casually. "Enough of this lolly-gagging around. I have berries to pick, and you have a woman to claim. You're in love with her, Cage. Accept it, marvel in it and get on with it."

"I don't even know myself anymore when I'm around her," he said with a self-directed frown.

Suzanne nodded, understanding after all these years without needing an explanation. "You've always had the Guiness backbone, Cagney. Sooner or later, you were bound to have the Guiness fire."

He continued to look pensive, but finally stood up from the swing. She took the empty glass from him, watching him place his black cowboy hat back on his head. When he glanced up, her eyes were serious.

"Cage," she said to him softly. "You have to tell her about D.C. You both deserve that much."

"Everyone thinks it's a lot simpler than it really is," he told her evenly.

She nodded. "That may be, but we only want the best for you. I'm sure she does, too."

"She's angry with me."

"Use a bit of that Guiness charm. No woman in her right mind can resist that grin. You'll be okay."

He half nodded, not fully convinced. He walked two steps down the porch, lost in his thoughts, before he remembered to turn once more.

"You're a good friend, Suzanne," he said levelly. "I'm glad you still accept uninvited guests on your porch. And I really do hope you stop mooning over Garret. He's never coming back, Suzanne. He said it when he left, and he meant it."

"I know," she assured him, but after all these years, they both understood the words were more ceremony than meaning. She was aware of what Garret had told his family all those years ago when he'd graduated from high school and left to join the navy. But she still remembered the bus stop. She remembered standing in the rain, her long, brown hair plastered to her back. She remembered her heart in her eyes, as she'd watched him heft that heavy duffel bag onto his muscled, eighteen-year-old shoulder. And she remembered him turning one last time with dark, glittering eyes. How that gaze had rested on her cheeks and the tears mixing with the rain. How, just for one moment, he'd reached out and wiped the moisture away with an unreadable expression. "Someday," he'd whispered. And then he'd turned, and boarded the Greyhound that had taken him to Charlotte and out of her life forever.

It would have been easier for her if he'd never said anything at all.

Now she roused herself back to the present and shut Garret Guiness out of her mind completely. She gave Cagney a delicate little shrug of dismissal, then set down the glasses in exchange for her garden pail. She had berries to pick and fresh strawberry jam to make for the church garden party.

When she looked back up, Cage was gone.

He drove straight from work to Manning and Harding. It was a little after seven, and time to relieve Davey from the day shift. Another day was done, and he and Daniels had made no progress after sifting through mounds of data. Phone records, inventories of possessions, appointment calendars. The police were enmeshed in Cecille's life, but no closer to the truth. All they knew was that Cecille called Bennett a lot both from home and the office. She'd also purchased a gun just two months ago, but kept it in her home rather than her purse. An unfortunate choice.

They had rescheduled their appointment to speak with both Bennett and Evie for tomorrow. Perhaps something would come up then.

Which left him just this night to get through, enduring the company of a beautiful woman who'd spent the rest of last night not speaking to him. His thoughts churned once more. Maybe Suzanne was right. Maybe it was time...

Marina opened the door of his truck, and the closed look on her face made him turn his eyes away. They didn't say anything during the ride to her house, and they didn't say anything as he pulled into her driveway. This time, Cagney went first after she unlocked the door, shouldering past her brusquely to peer into the house.

He snapped on the entryway lights before he saw it.

He turned quickly, moving to block her gaze with urgent instinct. But he wasn't fast enough. Her gaze automatically swiveled past his shoulders into her living room.

And the scream that rent the air made his blood run cold.

Chapter 11

He forced her head against his chest, absorbing her screams in his shoulder while he closed his own eyes and rested his head against her hair. He could feel her shiver with the horror, feel her body convulse with the savagery of the fear. And he stroked her back with long, gentle caresses, soothing her into quietness, while he tried to banish the sight from his mind, as well.

"First we found the dog. A big ole German shepherd, strong, young dog. He'd been gutted, and left lying in the grass like a dead fish."

Except this wasn't some beautiful German shepherd. It was just a mutt, some mangy, abandoned mutt that had probably been happy to answer an attentive whistle. A harmless, lonely old mutt, now disemboweled in Marina's living room.

Once more Cage closed his eyes, but against the darkness of his lids he could still see all the blood. He half dragged Marina into the dining room, keeping their backs to the horrible sight.

He eased his grip on her until she was at arm's length and he could peer into her face. Her eyes were dilated, the pupils huge and black and rimmed with a wildness he didn't like.

"Marina," he said levelly, "Marina I want you to listen to me. Are you listening to me?"

Very slowly, her breath still shallow and harsh, she nodded.

"I have to go check out the rest of the house, Marina. I have to make sure everything is safe. I want you to stay here. I want you to stand right here until I get back. Will you do that for me?"

She didn't move, just stared back at him with glassy-eyed fear. He gave her a slight shake, and her head rolled like a rag doll's. He could feel the panic beginning to creep into his own blood, but grimly forced it down. He had to remain in control, and he had to get her to snap out of this.

"Marina," he said sharply. "Marina, you'd better listen to me."

This time, she nodded faintly, her round eyes never leaving his.

"Stay here," he ordered.

Once more she made that small, nearly imperceptible nod that hardly reassured him. But he couldn't do either of them a bit of good until he had secured the premises. With reluctance, he let go of her shoulders, watching her carefully.

When she remained standing there, half-propped against the dining-room wall, he crept into the kitchen. Immediately his eyes fell upon the brand-new sliding-glass door. The killer hadn't been able to lift this one off the tracks, so he'd shattered it, instead. A good-sized rock rested in the middle of the floor, the passive accomplice. Once more the screen flapped in the breeze, cut through with relentless savagery.

Cage controlled his building anger. It was good that the sliding door had been shattered. A door that thick wouldn't have been easy to break, and certainly would have made a lot of noise. It was only seven in the evening. Surely the neighbors had heard or seen something.

He crossed into the living room, his gaze once more falling on the dog. He had to look away. He'd seen plenty of homicides in his lifetime, and Cecille Manning's body had been among the worst. But somehow, there was a sheer savageness to butchering a small, harmless dog, a ruthless pleasure that made his stomach churn. God, why hadn't he blocked Marina's view in time?

He made his way up the stairs.

The construction area, bathroom and her bedroom were all clear. He found he wasn't surprised. He hadn't really expected the killer to sit and wait. At this point, the killer seemed intent on doing his malicious deed and running. No, the killer wasn't ready to make his move yet; for now, he was enjoying the chase.

Cagney walked back downstairs and picked up the phone with the aid of a kitchen towel.

"Daniels?" he said after a minute. "This is Cagney. I'm at Marina's. Get over here now and bring the lab guys."

Then he hung up the phone and went back into the dining room—only to find Marina huddled in a ball in the corner, silent tears once more streaming down her haunted face.

Three hours later, the SBI men finished their examinations and removed the dog's remains from the living room under Daniels's watchful eyes. Marina slept upstairs in the relative safety of her bedroom, having been given a mild sedative by Doug Jacobs, Maddensfield's doctor since time immemorial. Dr. Jacobs had wanted to keep her in the hospital overnight, given her medical history, but Cagney had flatly refused.

He just didn't want her out of his sight. And he didn't want her waking up in some strange hospital room with nothing familiar around her and the memory of a butchered dog fresh in her mind. Dr. Jacobs had given him instructions for keeping her calm and rested, and Cagney had listened with an attentive ear. He would take care of her.

Tonight, all nights. It didn't matter anymore. His dispassion was gone, his detachment out the window. Now he roamed the house like a barely tamed panther, the gray vacuum of his existence replaced by a low burn that darkened his eyes and tightened his mouth. He was the hunter, and he wanted his prey.

"Mrs. Rodriguez said she heard the sound of breaking glass, sir," Davey reported curtly, his heels practically snapping together in attention as Cagney paused before him.

"Time?"

"Four-thirty?"

"Did she see anything?"

"No, sir. She said she didn't look over the fence. She thought it was just some kids causing trouble."

Cagney frowned, wondering if it was appropriate for the sheriff to want to hurt Mrs. Rodriguez. His fists were clenched at his side; he forced them to relax.

"Try the neighborhood children," he said at last, his voice still terse. "They're more likely to have checked things out. Someone had to have seen something."

"Yes, sir," Davey said. With a sharp whirl, the young deputy marched smartly out the door to pursue his newest task.

Cagney prowled over to where Daniels stood, the older man still staring at the blood-soaked floor with a look of disgust.

"We got ourselves a real winner this time," Daniels said gruffly. "A real psycho killer on the loose." Daniels shook his head. "The world just keeps getting sicker."

"Any breaks?"

"Just that the guy likes his hunting knife. No prints, but there is debris on the carpet from his boots. Lab rats may have something for us in the morning. Whether it's useful or not could be another story. Unfortunately, the ground's too hard from all this heat to give us any footprints."

Cagney swore, the word so fierce Daniels glanced up in surprise.

"Well, well. The saint has a temper." The dark look Cagney gave him would have made another man shut up, but Daniels simply crossed his arms in front of him.

"Actually," the state detective drawled. "It's good to see you coming back to life, because there's something else I've been meaning to mention to you."

Cagney narrowed his eyes warily. "What?"

Daniels nodded toward Cage's holsterless waist. "Nice belt, kid, but let's just say for a moment the killer had still been in the house. What were you going to stop him with, your incredible charm?"

Cagney stiffened, and for a long moment, he didn't say anything at all.

"Sooner or later," Daniels prodded quietly, "all riders must get back up on the horse. And now is as good as time as any, at least if you want to do yourself and that lovely lady upstairs any bit of good. This one's playing for keeps, Guiness. I don't want to walk into a living room one afternoon and find you looking like that dog."

"I didn't know you cared," Cagney replied tersely, his face unrelenting.

Daniels just shrugged. "I'm only telling you what you already know."

"I'll take care of it my way."

Daniels arched a bushy brow. "And just what might that be?" he said innocently. "Hide out in another small town where not even shoplifting has occurred for at least fifteen years?"

Cagney's face grew dark, his jaw clenching fiercely, until for one moment Daniels thought he may have actually pushed the man too far. But Daniels didn't back down, and he didn't try to step away. If Cagney hit him, it wouldn't necessarily be such a bad thing. The way he saw it, it was about time the sheriff showed some true signs of emotion.

Very slowly, Cage unclenched the fist at his side. Garret would have knocked the guy into last Tuesday by now. Jake would have cut him down with such sharp-edged words it would have taken the man days to realize just how deeply he'd been cut. Mitch never would have gotten himself in the situation to begin with. And Cagney... He relaxed his jaw; he loosened his stance. Then he turned and very steadily walked away.

You couldn't condemn a man for saying the truth.

He paused at the foot of the stairs. "Marina will be at my place tonight," he said evenly. "Andersen and Davey will be watching the house. If you've got the resources, I want someone at the wall, as well. We'll also need two people for day shift so Andersen and Davey can get some sleep. You and I have a lot of work to get done."

"Nine a.m., your office? Hell, is that air-conditioning fixed yet?"

"Nine a.m., wear short sleeves and bring a fan."

"Damn right I will. And the personnel won't be a problem. At the rate this killer is going, I'll soon be able to justify putting the entire North Carolina police force on his tail."

"Let's just hope it doesn't come to that," Cagney said. For one moment, his eyes darkened. When he spoke again, the words were like polished steel. "And Daniels, you were right about the gun."

Daniels merely grunted. "Well, you were right about the girl, so I guess that makes us even."

Cagney just headed up the stairs. When he came down minutes later, Marina was tucked in his arms, her violet eyes glazed against his shoulder. Daniels stepped immediately in front of the stain on the floor, and Cagney gave him a small nod of acknowledgment before disappearing out the door.

Daniels looked at the closed doorway a minute longer, then turned and hunkered back down to stare once more at the rug on the hardwood floor. His beefy face twisting into a scowl, he examined the fresh blood and wondered just how in the hell they were going to catch the bastard.

When Cagney carried Marina into his one-bedroom apartment, he knew a moment of awkwardness. His apartment wasn't meant for entertaining. It wasn't even meant for comfort. It was merely the place he slept, when and if he could. And compared with the bright, colorful beauty of her old home, his place resembled a prison cell.

Olive carpet, brown tweed sofa, chipped mahogany table, old gold-glass lamp. The living room looked just plain dismal, and the hot, mirthless air hardly helped. It even smelled like an apartment.

He sat her on the couch, played around with the ancient air conditioner, then went back out to his truck to retrieve the canvas and paint set he'd loaded up earlier. At least the half-finished picture added a touch of color. He set up the stand right in front of her, then looked at her once more with a concerned frown.

The color was just beginning to return to her cheeks, but her eyes were still dark and distant.

"Marina?" he said softly. She didn't glance up at him, her gaze clinging to the picture, instead. "You need to talk about it," he said shortly. "The doctor said it would be best if you acknowledged it, got it out in the open. You're safe here, you know. The darkness is far away, and I'm going to take care of you. Nothing bad can reach you here."

The doctor had told him he needed to establish an environment of safety and stability. Fine thing to tell a man who'd once had five goldfish die on him in just six days. But then, he thought he might be willing to try raising a barracuda if it would bring some light back to her eyes. Where was that fiery determination, that stubborn tilt of her chin?

He sat down at the edge of the old coffee table and looked at her more intensely.

"Come on, Marina," he cajoled. "Just yesterday you told me how strong you were. Just yesterday you put me in my place with that proud spirit of yours. Don't let some crackpot win now. You've come too far for that."

"My house," she said softly.

Cage leaned forward instantly. "What's that, sweetheart?"

She licked her lips, her eyes still on the painting. "That thing was in my house."

"I know, sweetheart. And I'm sorry. I'm so very sorry. But we've taken care of it now. We've got good boys watching your house. It'll be okay."

"I . . . I hate the fear," she managed to say through gritted teeth.

Cagney nodded, encouraged. "Fight it, love. Fight it for me."

Her eyes tore themselves away from the color-filled canvas to latch onto his face. "I don't fight it for you," she whispered fiercely. "I fight it for me."

"You really are the strongest person I've ever known," he told her suddenly, the words steady. "I can't imagine anyone ever being stronger."

She looked at him a minute longer, and abruptly, a long, dark shudder rippled through her. She closed her eyes, and when she opened them again, he could see that they were significantly clearer.

"May I have something to drink?" she asked simply.

"Of course," he said, rising immediately. "Root beer fine?"

She nodded, and minutes later he had an ice-cold glass for her. He sat down once more on the coffee table, while she took the glass with a slightly trembling hand. She drank for a long time.

"Do you remember what you saw?" he asked quietly when she at last brought the glass down. He hated to bring it up, but Dr. Jacobs had said it needed to be out in the open. If she could acknowledge it, talk about it, it would no longer be some half-realized fear floating around in her subconscious.

"There was a lot of blood and gore," she replied slowly, then swallowed thickly. "Please tell me it wasn't a person."

He instantly shook his head, leaving the coffee table to sit beside her. He sat there for just a few seconds before he decided he didn't care if he was supposed to or not, he pulled her onto his lap. She stiffened, then relaxed against him with a soft sigh that clenched his stomach. He wrapped his arms protectively around her, and he began to carefully stroke her beautiful, thick hair.

"It was a dog," he said at last, keeping the words straight and level. "Do you remember Roy talking about the dog twenty-five years ago?"

She nodded against his chest.

"Well, it seems our killer likes to play games, so once more we have a dog. But don't worry, sweetheart, the culprit is also getting sloppy. He attracted attention to himself this time, and we learned a little more. We'll get him."

She didn't move at all, remaining heavy and still in his arms.

"It's all real, then," she said at last. "This time it's real."

He nodded, and abruptly she sat up. He could see the frown on her brow, the strain around her eyes. One hand came up, and she absently rubbed her temple while her eyes sought out the glow of the window.

"You don't know what it's like to doubt your own mind," she said starkly, not looking at him. "You don't know what it's like to constantly be second-guessing yourself. 'It's not real—it's all in your head. At least maybe. Or could it be real and not in your head. Or maybe some of it's real and some is in your head.'" She rubbed her temple harder. "In a way, it was easier when I could just assume all fears were fictional. Now I don't know."

Cagney nodded, his eyes suddenly dark. He understood what she was saying better than she would ever know. How many times since the shooting had he refused to believe in himself? How many times had he looked at the locked trunk at the foot of his bed and wondered what he would do if he had a gun once more in his hand? Would he be able to fire it? Or would he simply see QVee falling down on the sagging porch and freeze like a Popsicle?

"It's okay to have doubts," he told her, not certain which of them he was reassuring.

She gave one more sigh, the last of the tension seeming to drain from her. "I suppose it is," she mused quietly. "I've made it this far at least. I imagine I can survive."

He nodded, unable to take his eyes away from her as once more her chin set in that delightfully upturned tilt. She stared at the dim glow of the shaded window a little longer, then abruptly she turned toward him.

Marina didn't say anything right away; instead she flattened her hand over his left breast and seemed intent on the feel of his heartbeat. Then she traced the line of his jaw, her soft skin rasping over his late-day whiskers. She pushed back his cowboy hat, playing with the straight silk of his dark hair, the way it waved around his face, then feathered along the collar of his shirt. He withstood it all, his breath held tight, as if exhaling would scare her away like a nervous rabbit.

Her thumb pressed against the warm curve of his lips.

"You feel real," she said at last, her voice clear in the silence. "Solid and warm and hard." Her hand drifted back down to his chest. "I can feel your heartbeat—it's like thunder in your chest. You have such a strong heart."

Her violet eyes came up, and intently they explored his own.

"When I first met you," she said abruptly, "it was your eyes I liked. They're clear and steady and calm. When you stood next to me in the lot, the darkness seemed to shrink away."

"And now?" he asked hoarsely.

She brought up his hand and curled it against his cheek. "Now I can't decide which part I like. Your hands are callused, you know. Rough, thick."

She traced his palm with her slim fingers, his large hand nearly engulfing hers, and his eyes were mesmerized by the sight.

"But they're gentle, too, and I like the feel of them against my skin. You have solid shoulders. Straight, broad. I can rest my head right here—" she pressed her hand against the curve of his chest "—and listen to the sound of your heartbeat while your arm curls around me. When you hold me like that, I feel so safe. Why hasn't anyone else ever made me feel safe like that?''

"I don't know," he whispered. He could barely talk his voice was so hoarse. He couldn't even move. His body had burst into flame at her first meandering touch, and now it was everything he could do to remember that she was getting over a major trauma. She was just looking for a little distraction, for something to take her mind off the fear. But when she leaned over and touched her lips to his neck, he thought he might die from the pain.

Next to him, on the couch, his hands balled into fists.

"Marina," he tried to get out.

"Shh," she told him softly. "Let me just do this for a little bit. Let me feel something other than all this darkness. Let me feel alive."

He shouldn't let her. There was only so much any man could take, especially a man who'd been denying himself for days now. But he could still remember the shadows in her eyes, and he knew he would suffer most anything if it would keep those shadows from returning.

He'd just never imagined such sweet torment.

She leaned forward, and very delicately, she kissed his eyelashes. It felt like a butterfly's kiss, and she rained the feather-light caresses down his cheek, ending at the corner of his mouth, while he held his breath in anticipation. Lightly her tongue came out and dipped into the corner. His lips parted, his breath escaping in a soft, tortured groan.

She outlined his mouth with her tongue, moving without haste. She seemed to contemplate every dip and curve, explore every nuance of his full, masculine lips. Then she kissed him thoroughly, her lips parting sweetly so she could enjoy the rich flavor of his mouth, the feel of his lips against her own, the taste of his tongue upon her own. And once more, it was not urgent or demanding. It was simply ample and sensual and filled with wonder. Like a child discovering a new kind of treat, she relished his mouth.

When her head finally came back up, his heart was nearly hammering through his chest.

"You won't make love to me, will you?" she asked quietly, her hands still resting on either side of his jaw.

Slowly, a condemned man, he shook his head.

"Why not?" she asked simply.

"It wouldn't be right," he told her hoarsely. "You're still in shock. You don't know what you want."

"And you would never take advantage of a woman, would you?"

"No."

She sighed, her gaze once more falling to his lips with unconcealed longing. "Maybe you should, Cagney. Maybe just this once, you should."

He had to close his eyes, but it didn't protect him. She merely picked up his balled fist from the couch and uncurled it finger by finger. She pressed a kiss into his palm, tasting the salty tang of his skin, then placed his hand on her full breast.

His eyes flew open, the gray depths an exquisite mixture of raw desire and aching pain. He wanted to move his hand away, he wanted to make this torture stop. But instead he found his thumb rubbing against her nipple, and didn't know if the sigh of pleasure came from her or from him. She arched against his hand, her eyes fluttering shut as his thumb and index finger closed around the sensitive nub and pinched delicately.

"Please don't stop, Cagney," she murmured. "Please, just this once, don't stop."

"It's not right," he said, but his fingers remained playing with her breast.

"I'm fine, Cagney," she assured him, her head still back with the pleasure. "My name is Marina Walden and I know exactly what I'm doing. I'm asking one Cagney Guiness to make love to me. I'm asking him to take off my dress and touch me with his hands. And I'm asking him to plunge into my body until I can taste the sweat on his shoulders and scream his name with satisfaction."

He felt his eyes glaze over with the passion, and at that moment, he didn't think the fires of hell could stop him from doing exactly what she said.

"Please tell me you never talked to anyone else like that," he groaned, already reaching for the zipper on the back of her dress.

Her head came forward, her violet eyes opening wide and clear. "Bradley would have keeled over where he stood," she said succinctly. "But Bradley can go to hell. I want you."

The zipper of her dress rasped in the silence as he undid it, and with burning eyes, he pulled the top of the dress down to her waist. She shivered as the cool, air-conditioned air hit her skin, her nipples hardening with the brief chill. His stormy, gray gaze settled on the rigid nubs, watching them with raw hunger as they puckered beneath the hot-pink lace of her fragile bra. He leaned forward and sucked on the right one through the thin protection.

She arched forward to meet his lips, groaning as his hot mouth tugged at her breast, sending shoots of desire spiraling toward her stomach. She buried her hands in his hair, knocking his hat on the floor so she could hold him close. She meant what she'd told him. She knew her own mind, and she knew she wanted him. He was everything strong and solid, everything real.

He made her feel powerful and wild and bold. He made her feel like a woman, not a flawed child wondering why the other kids didn't come over anymore. In his arms, she felt good and she felt right. In his arms, she saw warm colors and brilliant lights and lush enjoyment.

He sucked harder, and she sighed with the raw, pure pleasure of his mouth on her breast. She moved her hands to knead his corded neck and smooth over his broad shoulders. She found the sinewy strength of his arms, and shivered with the anticipation. Behind her back, she felt his hand release the thin clasp of her bra, and the lace fell free. In return, she pulled off his shirt, splaying her fingers across the sweat-slick contours of his muscled chest.

She bent down, nipping at his earlobe, then his throat. She kissed the muscled curve of his biceps, outlining it with her tongue, while she heard him gasp, breathless and sharp. He dragged her head back up and plunged his tongue into her mouth.

She tasted like fire to him, her body strong and well defined with its skimming planes and deep curves. Her spicy perfume tantalized his senses; her whimpers of pleasure assuaged his ears. His large hands curved around her delicately tapered ankles, following the lines up her bent legs until he could feel her heat just inches from his thumbs.

He wanted her with sudden savageness. He wanted to roll her to the floor and plunge into her slick body until he could find the relief that had eluded him for so long. He wanted to pour his tension inside her; he wanted to bury his head between her breasts and beg for the redemption that would never be his.

QVee standing on the porch, his face surly, his eyes dark. What were they bothering him for? He didn't kill the dude over on Ash Street. Hell, man, him and his brothers were hanging out at the 7-Eleven. Just ask anyone...

He kissed her harder, squinting his eyes shut as if that would block the pictures in his mind. He concentrated on her, and her wild beauty, her fierce passion. Her hand come down to the waistband of his jeans, and he wanted to groan with the desire. Slowly she outlined his hardness; slowly she caressed him through the denim. His head fell back against the couch, and he relinquished himself to the intense wonder of her touch, filling his hands with her breasts. She found the button of his jeans and popped it open. Her hand slipped inside his jeans and curled around him, hard.

QVee getting nervous, his shoulders hunching, his eyes darting. Suddenly reaching under his coat. Melissa's warning cry, the gun coming out, the sound of the shot. The instant pain in his leg, the fire, the burning...

He kissed her neck, her ear. His tongue darted inside to lick the tender shell of her earlobe, until she shivered against him and gasped his name. She began tugging on his pants in earnest now, and he obliged by raising his hips so together they could peel the heavy denim down. He finished dragging her dress over her head, his hands skimming along her bare, dusky skin. She felt so smooth and soft, like rare silk to the touch. And she shivered against him, pressing her breasts against his chest, while her moist heat settled against his hardness. She moved, a suggestive, sliding motion that took his breath away. He found her panties and ripped them down off her legs.

Eyes glittering, once more he smoothed his hands up her legs. Her eyes were on his, holding him captive with their violet depths. She didn't say anything; she just looked at the pain and fury and the passion on his face. And then once more, she slid her heat against his hardness.

His gun coming out, Melissa in a stance beside him. Another echo of gunfire through the silent afternoon air. The look of surprise of QVee's face, his young eyes dropping to his chest. The blood mushrooming there.

The fourteen-year-old gang member staggered to his knees, as Cagney collapsed on the ground in agony.

He grabbed her knees and parted her for his first renting thrust.

"I don't have protection," he said in one last moment of sanity. His blood roared in his ears; the pain twisted in his gut. And he was held captive by the clearest, fiercest violet eyes he'd ever seen.

"It's okay," she told him passionately. "I'm on the pill. So go ahead, Cagney, I want you. Take me. Use me, if that is what you need."

He growled, tortured, and steadied his hands on her hips, while his soul was torn in two. He lowered her onto his waiting shaft, gritting his teeth as he sank slowly into her. So moist and hot and tight.

My God, he had killed a kid, a fourteen-year-old kid! How had all his dreams of saving the world ever come to this?

He plunged into her, burying his length in her, feeling her cry his name. He reared back, only to plunge again, his hands strong on her hips, his neck corded with the effort. She rested her forehead against his shoulder, tasting the salt of his sweat. He drew back and thrust into her once more. She sank her teeth into his shoulder, and the pain made him wild.

Why hadn't he seen the shot coming sooner? Why hadn't he at least aimed lower? How could he have murdered a kid? What kind of man killed a child?

What had he done? What had he done?

She cried out with the first climax, and he felt it strip another layer of control away. He plunged faster, fiercer, driven by the pain and the passion. He was no longer the sheriff, no longer a man. The controls peeled away, leaving him wounded and bare and vulnerable. A being of intense passion, a being of unending pain.

He cried her name hoarsely, the last of the control leaving him as the sweat beaded and rolled down his face. No man left, just the hurt, just the fury.

Suddenly, brilliantly, the shock wave hit him. He bowed with the tension, his hips arching into hers, and he poured his relief into her willing body.

He buried his face against her neck, and while her body shuddered around him, he found his cheeks suddenly covered with tears.

Chapter 12

They both remained limp on the couch, their bodies glistening with sweat, their lungs heaving with the effort to breathe. Marina's head sagged against his shoulder, and she was aware of a heat too intense for the air conditioner to combat and the furious beating of Cagney's heart in her ear. Her muscles were too tired to move, her body a pure mix of utter satiation and exhaustion. She closed her eyes and felt another bead of sweat roll down her cheek.

"Do you think," she finally whispered, "that we'll ever use a bed?"

Cage didn't reply, and after a moment, she managed to force her hand up to cup his cheek. He turned his lips into her palm, letting his head rest against the simple support of her fingers; she took that as a good sign.

Something intense had happened to him as they'd made love. Something deep and painful that had moved her. She'd never realized the true depth of feeling behind his steady, gray eyes; she'd never realized the full explosiveness of his pent-up passion. Until their joining had stripped him bare, and she had seduced not just his body, but his soul.

If he turned away from her now, she wasn't sure she would be able to handle the pain. And yet, she still had no idea how to get him to open up without sex as a medium. She wanted him to talk to her; she wanted him to trust. She wanted him to tell her what caused such anguish in his eyes and tears on his cheeks.

She remained unmoving, intent on the feel of his hot chest pressed against her breasts, the sound of his slowing heartbeat in her ear. They both smelled like sweat and sex and passion. But it wasn't enough for the true intimacy she sought.

He shifted at last, his strong hands moving to where her legs still straddled his waist, joining them intimately. He smoothed down the bent shape of her legs, then suddenly lifted her up and off his lap. She almost cried out her protest at the loss, but he was standing before she had a chance.

"I'll get some sheets," he said without emotion. "It's probably coolest if we just sleep on the floor by the air conditioner."

She nodded, her violet eyes stark, but he didn't turn to see. He just walked naked into his bedroom, his limp suddenly seeming pronounced. For the first time, she could see the two round puckered scars of the bullet wound on his left thigh. One for the bullet entering, another for its exit. She shivered and forced her gaze up for his return.

Now he carried a flat-looking pillow and old cream sheets. He looked at them and seemed to frown, and she would have given anything to know his thoughts.

But he simply threw the folded sheets on the couch next to her, moving his coffee table with an unclothed casualness she envied. Now that they'd finally made love, at least physical closeness no longer seemed an issue with him. So why couldn't she say the same for the rest?

He disappeared back into the bedroom, then reappeared with a comforter, which he folded in half and laid out on the floor. Next he smoothed the bottom sheet over it, then tossed down the pillow.

"Not the most comfortable bed you'll ever have had," he said flatly. "But then, you don't sleep much anyway."

She simply nodded, staring at him with questioning eyes. He managed to avoid her gaze, yet he still held out his hand. Feeling suddenly vulnerable and exposed, she took it.

He was gentle as he pulled her down beside him. Tender even as he positioned her head once more upon his chest. His hand caressed her bare arm, then tangled in the long, dark luxury of her hair. She could feel him grow hard again against her knee, and was amazed by the answering restlessness deep in the pit of her stomach. The next thing she knew, she was on her back and his lips were once more upon her own.

It was slower this time, easier. The intensity of before had washed them both out, leaving only the aching aftermath of sudden uncertainty. They substituted soothing touches for the words they didn't know how to say, simple passion for the emotions they didn't trust themselves to feel. When he slid into her this time, her legs wrapping strong and sure around his waist, she had to close her eyes against the simple beauty, the pure rightness of his body moving within her own.

She urged him on with her hands, with her lips, wanting him to find release in her embrace, wanting him to find respite in her arms. And the climax that swept over them both was at once sweet and cool, the fresh breeze that followed a raging summer storm.

But the minute he pulled out of her and lay back down beside her, she felt the loss and it stung her eyes with its pain.

"It's eleven-thirty," he said softly. "We've gotten you off your schedule. You should sleep now."

She nodded against his shoulder, not trusting herself to speak. She was tired, and she did feel out of synch. She'd slept early due to the doctor's sedative and it had muddled her biological clock. It no longer seemed to know whether she was supposed to be sleeping or painting. She thought it at least matched the confusion in her head.

"Are we lovers now?" she asked quietly. She felt him go slightly still, then relax.

"Yes, I suppose so."

"And how does this system work?" she asked, forcing herself to probe steadily. "Will you simply be my lover until the desire fades, or once I'm out of danger, will that be the end?"

"This has nothing at all to do with the case," he said immediately. "If we were to look at the case, I shouldn't be sleeping with you at all."

"So we're lovers until you no longer want me."

He shifted uncomfortably. "Or until you no longer want me."

She couldn't see that happening, but she didn't say so. The words would give too much away, like the sudden mix of fierce need and aching vulnerability that was gripping her chest. She wanted to hold him closer. She wanted to melt against him until he could no longer let her go, and she could lie here forever, feeling safe and whole by his side.

"Have . . . have you had many lovers?" she managed to get out. She didn't want to know, but she needed to know. A woman should always know where she stood. Even if she couldn't stop the heartbreak, at least she could anticipate it.

Cage's breath seemed to still for a moment, and she could sense his unease like a palpable touch.

"A few," he said slowly. "Do you always ask so many questions after sex?"

"No," she replied, "but I do get hungry."

He relaxed a little, but the wariness was still there. "I could make peanut-butter-and-jelly sandwiches if you'd like."

She shook her head against his shoulder, curling her hand around his shoulder. She didn't want him to leave her side.

But she felt his hand quiet on her arm. He seemed to take a deep, bracing breath.

"Who's Bradley?" he asked softly.

"My fiancé," she answered simply. "At least that's what I thought he was. Then one day over croissants and café au lait, he apparently changed his mind."

Cage remained still, his senses one hundred percent tuned to what she had said. Silently he willed her to say more, to say anything to ease the sudden sick, uncomfortable emotion in his chest. He found he wanted to hurt Bradley, and he'd never even met the man. He made himself take a deep breath.

"We'd gone out for two years," Marina continued evenly. "And then I decided that to be honest, I really should tell him about my 'condition.' He always thought my eccentricities were part of my art. I guess I wanted him to know the truth. I wanted to see if he would love me still. Well, he didn't."

She said the words simply enough, but Cage could imagine the pain that had once lain behind them. After two years this Bradley person still hadn't been able to see the woman standing before his eyes.... Cage felt his arm tighten around her protectively. Bradley was a fool.

"Cagney," she whispered. For one moment, she lost her courage and had to squeeze her eyes shut. Then, grimly, she forced herself to go on. "Will you always be like this, so passionate in bed and so remote out of it?"

His whole body went rigid, and she could hear the breath escape from him like a low hiss. She closed her eyes and licked her lips.

"I'm not trying to coerce you," she said quietly. "If you don't want to tell me things, that's your choice. But you know so much about me Cage, and yet...yet everyone knows things about you that you won't even tell me. It doesn't feel right Cagney. It—"

She broke off before she embarrassed herself completely and admitted how much power he already had over her.

How much he could hurt her, how his deep need for isolation wounded her.

"You want to know about D.C.," he stated bluntly.

She nodded against him, wondering if her heart would thunder out of her chest with its nervousness. He was no longer warm and secure next to her. Now his body had hardened to stone with its wariness, his hand lying heavily on her shoulder.

"Would you tell me, Cagney?" she barely whispered. "Would you trust me, the way I trusted you?"

He almost hated her for those words. He hated the way the very softness of the request could tumble granite barriers as surely and swiftly as a two-foot-thick, solid-oak battering ram. He hated the hint of vulnerability in her voice, the fact that she wanted to know so much about him. But mostly he hated the fact that she had every right to expect the truth.

He took a deep breath and promised himself he'd keep it simple.

"I used to be a homicide detective in D.C. One afternoon, in the line of duty, I shot and killed a kid."

He heard her unguarded gasp, and it darkened his eyes. Let her be horrified; let her be shocked. It was a horrible, shocking thing to have killed a fourteen-year-old boy.

"And?" she said quietly against his shoulder.

"There's no real 'and' to it," he told her bluntly. "The fourteen-year-old kid was already under suspicion for two other homicides when my partner and I went to question him about a third. He opened fire, shooting me in the leg, and I returned fire. He died—I got a limp. The shooting was legit, my actions acceptable."

"So it was self-defense," she affirmed, relaxing again.

But Cagney wasn't listening anymore. He was abruptly untangling himself from her and sitting up with a force that left her feeling suddenly naked and cold.

"Self-defense," he growled.

He turned and pinned her with eyes that were shocking in their black anger. Marina caught her breath, not daring to utter a word.

"That is what everyone says. 'You did what you had to do, Cagney.' 'You were just doing your job, Cagney.' 'A man's job is a man's job, Cagney.' Dammit, a fourteen-year-old kid is dead and *I* pulled the trigger. *I pulled the trigger.* Now, what kind of job is that?"

"A tough one," she told him honestly.

He abruptly shook his head, gazing around his apartment with open frustration. "You don't understand. I don't know how to make anyone understand. Marina—yes, I had to shoot QVee. If I'm really honest with myself, I probably even had to kill him, because he would have fired again if I'd only wounded him. But—" He turned, looking at her with clear, tortured eyes. "That's not why I became a cop," he whispered. "I wanted to help, and I don't know how to help those kids. No one seems to know how to help those kids. So if I go back there, what do I do—just keep pulling the trigger?"

"But, Cagney," she protested, "you're just one person. You can't expect yourself to make up for the failings of economics and society and family."

"Then what's the point?" he challenged starkly. "What's the purpose of being a police officer if I'm no longer part of the solution but just a herder trying to control the problem? They told me I did my job when I killed him, Marina. What does that make me? A solution to society's failures, or an assassin?"

She gasped at the harshness of his words and the pain that laced them so exquisitely. She leaned forward to reach out to him, but the stony look he gave her stopped her cold. She felt that look like a dagger sliding slow and delicate between her ribs.

She forced herself not to back down.

"You're being too hard on yourself," she insisted levelly, her chin coming up as if to override his firmly set jaw. "You are a good police officer, Cagney Guiness. If it wasn't for you, I don't think I would have made it through the past few days. I believe in you, and I believe you're going to catch the person who...'' Her voice faltered for a moment, then gained strength as she clenched her fists. ''You're going to catch the person who killed Sarita, and who killed Cecille, and who probably right now is planning how to kill me. Maybe you can't help everyone, but you can help someone. You have to look at that. Because we do need you, Cage. In this day and age, there are just not enough heroes.''

For a fraction of instant, she thought she might have penetrated. She saw the gray depths of his eyes shift. The anger drained, and something else slashed across his eyes, something raw and hungry and powerful.

She willed herself to hold still, terrified that the minute she moved the stony anger would return full force.

''I need you,'' she found herself whispering, the words hoarse with unguarded truth. And suddenly she was afraid of how much of herself must be showing in her eyes. But she didn't know how to look away, and she didn't know how to back down. All her life she'd been the lonely woman fighting her own war in the dark trenches of her mind. Not until she'd met the steady gaze of this man had she ever really felt safe. And she loved him for that more than he'd ever know, and more than she would ever tell him.

Simply because he didn't want to know, and after having been alone for so long, she didn't know how to beg for someone to stay.

''I haven't held a gun since that day,'' he said abruptly, his voice raw. ''I can't look at one without remembering how it felt in my hands.''

''That's understandable,'' she murmured.

He shook his head. ''That's weak. Lots of other cops have shot people in the line of duty and they got on with their lives, their jobs. But not me. My hands shake just to think of holding the gun.'' He suddenly smiled, the motion twisted and self-mocking. ''So what do you think of your 'hero' now, Marina?''

"I believe in you," she told him honestly, her chin still high.

"And if the murderer breaks down that door armed with a gun, you think I can take him on bare-handed and win?" He shook his head. "You shouldn't believe in me, Marina. You shouldn't."

"When the time comes, you'll figure it out," she told him levelly. "Deep down, you're a very responsible man, Cagney, and you do your duty. You didn't walk away from this murder case. And you're the one who's been keeping guard in my house. You may think you're scared, but deep down, you're still capable, you're still strong."

"You see what you want to see."

She just watched him steadily, her clear, violet gaze slowly breaking him down. "I don't deserve you," he whispered hoarsely.

She smiled slowly and slanted him a tender, teasing look. "That's odd, because I deserve you."

He reached out, no longer able to stand the distance, and pulled her back into his arms. She went willingly, wrapping her arms around his neck, pressing her cheek against his heartbeat. She felt his cheek rest against her hair and she held him tight.

Carefully he leaned back to the floor, taking her with him. Then he tilted her head up and his lips found hers. Her naked body pressed against his and she showed him all the words she hadn't yet said.

Marina awoke abruptly, her eyes flying open as she was seized by a blind moment of panic. She remained still, her senses observing the hardness of the floor under her back, the smell of a strange apartment and the colorless feel of too many neutral tones. Then all of a sudden it came to her—Cagney's apartment. She was with Cagney.

She released her pent-up breath in a long sigh and allowed her heart to resume beating. Everything was fine now. Except where had Cagney gone?

Slowly turning her head, she finally saw him sitting on the edge of the sofa. He'd thrown his jeans back on, but his chest remained bare and golden in the light. His head was propped up by his elbows on the coffee table, and he seemed to be examining something with excruciating detail. Then again, from this angle, his eyes didn't appear to be open.

She sat up, and immediately his head jerked up. She gave him a small smile. "You should be sleeping, Cagney."

He smiled back reluctantly, but gestured to the pile of papers on his old brown coffee table. "Too much work to do." He leaned back, stretching a bit, then running his hand through his tousled hair. "Did you sleep okay?" he asked.

Marina nodded, absently rubbing her stiff neck, then rolling her shoulders. "About as good as camping," she declared. "But then, I don't think I've ever gone camping."

"New Yorkers don't camp?" Cagney said dryly.

"Well, more like Manhattanites, or maybe just my parents. I did go to two spas, though, and they were fantastic."

"Maybe sometime we'll go camping," Cagney finally said with a shrug. "The Blue Ridge Mountains are beautiful for that kind of thing."

Marina nodded, feeling her throat tighten unexpectedly at his words. She did want to go camping with this man. And she wanted to take him to meet her parents sometime, and maybe they could go hiking. There was so many things out there to do, and she wanted to know she could do them all with him. She wanted to know they had the time, they had the future.

She wrapped the sheet around her. "So what are you puzzling over there?" she asked simply.

"Phone records," Cage grunted. "But I've gone over and over them until my eyes burn and I still don't see a thing."

"Maybe there's nothing to see," Marina suggested.

He frowned. "I don't know yet," he said slowly. "Actually, I keep coming back to them because I'm half-certain something is here, but I never seem to find the time to really look at them closely. And now I'm merely falling asleep over them. Not a very efficient investigation method."

Marina stood, dragging the sheet with her as she wandered over to where he sat on the couch. She plopped down next to him, resting her head against his bare arm for a moment and breathing in the tangy scent of his skin. He felt warm and solid. She rubbed her head against his smooth, muscled skin for a moment, then leaned forward to glance at the phone records scattered across the coffee table.

"What are you searching for?" she asked, turning her gaze to meet his. He was watching her with a strange, tender expression in her eyes, and she lost her train of thought.

"Call patterns," he said abruptly, trying to keep a grip on his thoughts. She looked so sensuous and soft with sleep. And she moved with the casual grace of a kitten, pattering over here and curling up against him as if it were the most natural thing in the world. And he liked it. God, he liked the fierce satisfaction that gripped his chest.

"Call patterns?"

He forced his mind off the seductive tousle of her hair. "Yes," he said more firmly this time, picking up one of the sheets from the phone company. "First, I generally check for who has been called. Are there particular people who stand out—do these people make sense based on what we already know of the person's life? Then I like to check times. Any late-night calls or early-morning patterns that might tell us something. What were the last few calls made? To whom? Then you can always try to factor in what we know of the person's schedule the last couple of days. Any major things we know of that appeared to have sparked calls?"

Suddenly he frowned, and as Marina watched, sudden realization swept over his face.

"No," he muttered, nearly to himself, "it's not what activities sparked calls—it's what activities *didn't* cause phone calls."

Then, as Marina watched with bewildered eyes, he began to paw through the sheets of paper, until he apparently found the one he wanted. He breezed down it quickly, his index finger swift and sure. Then, with more mutterings, he tossed it aside to dig out another, which he also scrutinized.

He looked up to find her with an intense gaze. "Tell me, Marina," he said urgently. "The secretary, Martha, reported that Cecille called her at 10:30 that last night, trying to locate some files at work. But there's no record of that call either on the Madding and Harding records or at Cecille's home. But where else could she have been calling from?"

"Her car phone?" Marina suggested.

"Of course." Cagney reached for the third stack of records and efficiently whipped out a sheet the appropriate date. Once more he scanned down it, shaking his head. "Nothing. Nothing, nothing, nothing. But what does that mean?"

Marina could only look at him, not knowing enough about the case to understand. Once more he pinned her with his gaze. "What if it wasn't Cecille?" he thought out loud. "What if it was another woman claiming to be Cecille? Would she have been able to fool Martha?"

Marina frowned, then shrugged. "It's possible, I suppose. But Martha's been the receptionist for eight years now. She recognizes everyone from their voice, and well, Cecille wasn't just anyone. I'd be surprised if someone could fool her. Then again," Marina added with a small shrug, "it was fairly late at night."

"No, no, no," Cage said swiftly. "You're talking yourself in circles, which is exactly what Daniels and I do. The problem is we only have bits and pieces of the truth, and together they cause more confusion than resolution. Let's just take one idea for a moment and run with it. Let's say

Cecille did call Martha at 10:30 at night, but not from Manning and Harding. Where else could she call from?"

"Bennett's," Marina whispered finally, the distaste evident in her voice.

Looking at her, Cagney was forced to agree. But they didn't have access to Bennett's records, at least not at this point of the game. Then again, he and Daniels were going to talk to the man tomorrow. If they could come up with anything against him, any discrepancies, then they might be able to justify a search warrant, as well as request his records from the phone company. It was worth a shot.

On impulse, Cagney bent forward and kissed Marina hard on the lips. She responded by wrapping her arms around his neck, leaning into him eagerly. She tasted warm and passionate, pure and complete in his arms. He thought he might be able to take her a thousand times and still want her for the thousand and first.

The intensity of the thought scared him a little, and he found himself pulling back. "I should get some sleep," he whispered.

She looked at him with instant concern. "Yes," she said firmly. "You've hardly gotten any sleep lately, trying to maintain my schedule and your sheriff duties. A good night's sleep is exactly what the doctor ordered."

Immediately she stood, fussing over him with such unrestrained worry he wasn't sure he would be able to stand it. Worse was the feeling of disappointment when he realized she wouldn't be lying down beside him but would be working on her painting, instead.

He'd slept alone most of his life; why should this one night be any different? But he found himself rolling onto his side, where he could watch her focus on her canvas, now wearing his discarded shirt with only the top couple of buttons done. Her long tanned legs truly did go on forever.

He fell asleep with those legs imprinted on his mind, while another niggling thought suddenly burst in his mind. He recognized in that last moment of consciousness why

Cecille's ten-thirty call, in which she acted as if she was at work when she wasn't, bothered him so much.

It reminded him of someone who was trying to establish an alibi.

Chapter 13

"Oh, no," the secretary finished telling them politely. "Mr. Jensen isn't here right now. I believe he went downtown."

Cagney and Daniels exchanged glances. They'd had an appointment to meet the man. "And where might that be?" Cagney drawled politely.

The secretary looked less certain now. "I don't rightly know," she replied faintly.

Cagney arched a black eyebrow, sitting down comfortably on the edge of the desk while he tilted his Stetson back a little farther on his head. "Now, Betty," he began casually, "Detective Daniels and I are here on serious business. We're the law, and surely you want to cooperate with the law."

Betty appeared a little more hesitant now. Then slowly and surely, Cagney flashed the age-old Guiness grin. The rest of Betty's breath came out as a small little "Oh!"

"He likes to go the Lazy Q Tavern," she suddenly remembered.

"At ten a.m.?" Daniels quizzed with a frown.

Betty immediately looked uncomfortable, and Cagney shot Daniels a warning glance.

"I'm sure Bennett just likes their eggs, isn't that right, Betty?" Cagney said easily.

Betty nodded in agreement. "Oh, yes. He thinks their omelets are the best," she gushed.

Cagney nodded at her, standing now and straightening his hat on his head. "Thank you very much, ma'am. We do appreciate your help."

Abruptly Betty appeared uncertain once more, her blue eyes growing huge and vulnerable with earnest worry. "Is . . . is Mr. Jensen in trouble?"

"Of course not," Cagney assured her. "We just want to ask him a few questions, that's all. Won't take but a minute or two of his time."

The relief on Betty's face was nearly too much, and Cagney could sense, more then see, Daniels rolling his eyes behind his back. Cagney tipped his hat as a parting gesture, then herded Daniels out of the textile mill before his bluster could cause any more damage.

"For God's sake," Daniels said the minute they'd left the dust and noise of the knitting mill behind, "is there anyone that man doesn't have under his thumb? How old is Bennett anyway to be carrying on with twenty-year-olds like that?"

"A couple of years older than Mitch," Cagney mused, "so I guess early forties or so. Old enough to know better, I'm sure. Let's just find him at the Lazy Q."

"Eggs," Daniels muttered in disgust. "Bloody Marys are a hell of a lot more like it."

Cagney didn't doubt that, either, but he didn't say anything as they climbed into his sheriff's vehicle and headed back toward town. Ten a.m. and Bennett was already at a bar. What kind of troubles was the man trying to drown?

The Lazy Q wasn't hard to find. Maddensfield actually had seven drinking establishments, but the Lazy Q was by far the most rustic. Its wooden front porch looked like something out of a spaghetti Western, and its name appeared to have been branded into the splintered board hanging above the door. Definitely not a traditional Bennett establishment, Cagney thought, but one of the few taverns open before noon.

They pushed the swinging doors and walked in.

The bar was relatively quiet this early in the morning. The wooden tables boasted only a handful of men, mostly older-looking men with various remnants of breakfast before them. Cagney could hear snatches of conversation as he scanned the room.

"Getting too damn hot for a man to wear his own skin."

"And then the young bull said, 'Hell, that raging hunk of bovine flesh can have all my cows. I just want him to know I'm a bull!'"

He picked out Bennett sitting alone at the bar, his eyes glued to the TV monitor hanging from the ceiling. True to Daniels's prediction, a Bloody Mary rested in his hand. Cagney looked at Daniels, and together they approached the bar.

"Bennett," Cagney said calmly. The older man swiveled instantly, his sharp eyes taking in his new guests with unconcealed irritation. His white dress shirt was uncharacteristically wrinkled, and his face looked puffier than the last time Cagney had seen him. It appeared Bennett hadn't had a good past couple of days.

Daniels was wrinkling his nose at the smell of alcohol coming off the man. Good thing they caught him at ten, Cagney thought. By one, he doubted the man would still be standing.

"We need to ask you a few questions," Cage said evenly.

Bennett scowled at him. "I'm not drunk," he stated irritably, his words clear enough to support his point. "At least not yet. And I'm not causing anyone any trouble. Go harass someone else, Guiness."

"We had an appointment," Cage said levelly.

The man frowned, then scowled. "Oops, forgot about that," he said. He took a long drink from his Bloody Mary.

"We want to know about Cecille Manning," Daniels announced, diving right in.

Immediately Bennett stiffened, his bloodshot eyes growing wary and assessing. "What about Cecille?" he demanded bluntly. Bennett's grip tightened on his drink until Cagney could see the knuckles whiten. "People seemed to think you and Cecille had a relationship," Cage said smoothly, letting the implicit question hang in the silence.

"I don't really see where that's any of your business," Bennett retorted, taking another sip of his drink.

"The woman's dead," Daniels growled. "That makes it our business."

The glance Bennett shot Daniels was ugly, but then nervously he took in Cagney's calm, waiting stance. He relented with the unhappy look of a cornered snake.

"Yeah, so?" he said with a shrug. "Cecille was an adult. She knew what she was doing."

"And the night of June 5," Cagney said. "We understand you and Cecille went out to eat."

"Well, not out to eat per se. Though it did have a lot to do with satisfying hunger."

Cagney felt his jaw tighten at the bald insinuation, then forced himself to relax. God, Cecille, what had you been thinking to get involved with this man?

"What time did you two part?"

Bennett shrugged. "Ten, I guess. I don't know. That was days ago and I don't keep a log. We went out—I returned her to work around ten, I'd say. She was always going back to work."

"Anyone see you two together?"

"Well, I picked her up in the lobby. Everyone saw us then."

"But did anyone see you return?"

"It was ten, Guiness. No normal people are still at work at ten. Hell, you knew how ambitious Cecille was. All she ever cared about was that damn agency."

Was that a trace of hurt in Bennett's voice? Cagney couldn't quite force himself to believe it. He glanced over at Daniels, who was half scowling.

"So what did you do after ten?" Daniels demanded.

"Why, I went home to my wife," Bennett stated coolly. "At least, that's what I thought I was doing."

Immediately Cagney was on alert. "What do you mean, that's what you thought you were doing?"

Bennett's gaze narrowed, until suddenly it was calculating.

"Evie wasn't home when I got there. I waited up all night, and she didn't come home till eleven."

"Did she say where she'd been?"

"Said she had some thinking to do. That she needed to get away. 'Course, it must have been a lot of thinking for that little brain of hers, because she left again two days ago and I haven't seen her since."

"You don't seem that worried," Cage stated, though he was taking in Bennett's disheveled appearance with new insight. "You didn't even file a missing person's report."

Bennett just shrugged. "You know women, fickle and flighty, every single one of them. So she's got some burr under her skin. Sooner or later she'll be back. Cash only lasts so long."

Abruptly Bennett turned away from them both. He stared down at the thick, red mixture of his drink, then he took a long, harsh swallow. "Why the hell are you bothering me with this, Cagney?" he said finally, glancing up with squinted brown eyes. "We all know you have the real murderer right in hand."

Cagney felt himself go very still, and for one moment, he thought he might have misunderstood. "What do you mean, Bennett?" he found himself asking calmly, too calmly. Beside him, he could sense Daniels's hard gaze on his face.

"Marina Walden, of course. Cecille said she was as crazy as a loon when she hired her. Of course, I guess poor Cecille never realized she was a violent maniac until it was too late."

The room seemed to grow quiet in Cagney's mind, until all he could hear was the sound of his own pounding pulse in his ears. "I don't see how Miss Walden is any concern of yours," he said quietly, his gray eyes unreadable.

Bennett turned sharply, arching an eyebrow in mocking innocence. "Oh, I forgot," he said, clearly enough for the whole bar to hear, "you wouldn't want to know things like that. Tell me, is she as wild in bed as she looks?"

Cagney felt Daniels's hand suddenly rest on his arm, but he simply ignored it. His gaze never leaving Bennett's, he reached up and unpinned the bronze star from his chest. Very slowly, each move deliberate, he set the star down on the wooden countertop beside Bennett.

"Would you like to repeat that, Bennett?" he said, cool and firm in the silence.

Beside him, Daniels swore under his breath, but Cagney didn't register it beyond a brief fuzz in the background. His concentration was focused one hundred percent on the man in front of him.

Returning Cage's level stare, Bennett merely snickered. Everyone knew Cagney was the levelheaded one of the Guiness boys. Hell, no one would have dared say a wrong word in front of Garret; that was plain suicidal. And Jake was just too damn smart to be safe. But Cage was as calm as Garret was hot tempered. If Garret could punch a man into last week, Cagney stared him down into the ground. And Bennett wasn't afraid of a simple chilly look.

"I asked," he said loudly, "if she's as wild in bed as she looks."

"Good night, Bennett," Cagney said simply, then drew back his fist and slammed it cleanly into the other man's face. Bennett's head rocked back with the blow, and the air filled with the cartilage crunch of knuckles connecting with the flesh. Cagney knew one instant of primal satisfaction, and then Bennett was flailing back with a pure howl of outrage.

Cagney ducked the first blow, though the second caught him squarely in the shoulder. It threw his balance onto his weak leg, and for a moment he thought he might go down. Through sheer force of will, he regained his footing, blocking Bennett's next punch and clipping the other man once more with a clean uppercut.

Bennett crashed against a table but was up and yelling again before anyone could react. Cagney recognized the look in Bennett's eyes. It was pure blood lust, and at the moment, the new song was singing in his veins, as well. Bennett pounced again, but this time feinting to the left before his right fist came clearly across Cage's guard and caught him forcefully on the cheek. Cage thought his head might have exploded as he crashed back against two chairs. That didn't stop him, however, from coming back up for more.

He was just striding forward, when Daniel's arms wrapped solidly around him and dragged him back. Dimly he became aware of two men grabbing Bennett, as well.

"Enough," Daniels growled in the startled silence of the bar. "Grown men ought to know better."

He let Cagney go with a blistering glance, and for the first time, Cage became aware of the chaos around him. They'd broken a table, toppled some chairs. And he was suppose to be the sheriff, the calm, levelheaded sheriff.

Yet when he looked at Bennett's swelling eye and touched the bruise on his knuckles, he could only feel the satisfaction once more. He shook out his hand and forced himself to stand tall. He reached for his wallet and counted out a good chunk of change. He handed it to the wide-eyed bartender.

"This should cover the damage," he said evenly, his eyes never leaving Bennett's. He picked up his sheriff's star from the counter. "The fight was personal," he announced coolly in the silence. "Now, as the sheriff, I'm telling you that you have the right to press charges."

With a dark look, Bennett shook his head.

Cagney wasn't surprised; that just wasn't how things were handled in Maddensfield. He picked up his Stetson from the floor, dusted it briefly and set it on his head. "Then I consider the matter closed," he said firmly.

Once again, Bennett just nodded, though the glittering in his eyes was unmistakable. Cage turned, took five steps across the bar, then pivoted back to confront the shocked expressions of the other men. He rested his eyes once more on Bennett.

"Kristi Davis sends her regards," he said obliquely, and was rewarded by Bennett's instant stiffening, as pure wariness washed over the man's face.

Cage smiled, but not pleasantly, then walked out of the stunned bar into the blazing-hot day.

"You just don't do things halfway, do you?" Daniels was grumbling as they sat down back at the tiny sheriff's office. "First you're cold enough to freeze the devil himself, and now you're raising hell all over town."

Cage didn't reply. In the aftermath of the fight, he found himself at a loss to explain any of it. His life had been a steady, cool existence. Lately, however, his thoughts had been anything but calm. And when Bennett had said those things about Marina... He didn't think he'd ever felt so much rage boil up inside him. He'd wanted to hit the man, wanted the raw satisfaction of flesh connecting with flesh.

He found himself frowning, gazing down at the bruised mass of his knuckles and feeling the fiery burn of his cheek. If he even looked half as bad as he felt, it would be a miracle. No, clearly fighting was not the most efficient solution. But the realization still didn't completely dim the primal gratification seizing his chest. And for the first time, he almost understood Garret's wildness. Almost.

"We have to find Evie Jensen," he said levelly.

Daniels grunted, his eyes narrow and sharp. "Think she's the one?"

Cagney shrugged. "Hard to believe little Evie Jensen hurting a flea, but then, I can't think of anyone I've ever met being capable of that vicious a murder."

"She has motive, with Cecille and Bennett's affair."

"And opportunity," Cage agreed. "No alibi for that night or the past couple of days."

"Think she was the one who rented the car?"

"Could be. She has Marina's slim build, though she's slightly smaller. A wig, and I think she could pull it off. Though why she'd want to frame Marina, I have no idea."

"How old is Evie?"

"Midthirties, I think. Too young to have been involved with Sarita's murder. Hell, I doubt she remembers it. I know I don't."

"Maybe she just read about them," Daniels mused. "Maybe she put two and two together, came up with four and saw a way out."

"Out of what?" Cage asked bluntly. "On the one hand, we're saying she killed Cecille out of jealousy over Bennett, but then it appears she just left Bennett. Why the hell doesn't any of this make sense?"

"Maybe she thought her plan backfired," Daniels suggested, red faced and frowning. "After all, we didn't arrest Marina right away. Maybe it scared her."

"You ever meet Evie Jensen?" Cagney asked suddenly.

Daniels shook his head. "She married Bennett when she was eighteen. Whole town turned out for the wedding. Lloyd threw a bash like no one's ever seen since. She looked like a princess, sweet and demure and beautiful. But that was nearly twenty years ago, Daniels. She's lived with the world's most oppressive man ever since. You know she miscarried four times? Hell, last time I saw her a mild wind could have blown her over. The woman was a mouse, or perhaps worse, a shadow of a mouse. And now we're wondering if she could stab 130-pound Cecille Manning eighteen times."

Daniels shrugged. "You're the one who just broke up half a bar. Two days ago would you have ever seen yourself doing that?"

Cagney scowled. "That was different."

Daniels arched a brow. "It was because of a woman," he said succinctly. "You've been bitten by the bug, Guiness. And now your nice, peaceful days are over."

If possible, Cagney's scowl darkened. "It has nothing to do with personal feelings," he said stiffly. "Here in Maddensfield, we still protect the integrity of a woman's reputation."

Daniels merely snorted. "Save it for someone who's looking to buy a bridge. Point is, powerful emotions lead people to do powerful things. Maybe they could even drive a mouse to murder."

"Bennett knows Kristi Davis," Cagney said abruptly. "How do you think he figured it out?"

"Perhaps he remembers the name from before."

"Come on, Daniels. He would have been just sixteen or so, and Kristi Davis a one-and-a-half-year-old baby. There's no reason for him to remember that name across twenty-five years. Now, Roy recognized Marina right away, but then, he'd known the family personally, as well as being the sheriff to investigate the case. I'd say not many others could be able to make that connection. And one of the people who could is probably the murderer."

Suddenly Daniels straightened, his small eyes growing bright. "Think of what you're saying for a moment, Cagney. We have Evie, who had a reason to kill Cecille but probably no connection to Sarita's murder or Marina. Then we have Bennett, who seems to know Kristi Davis, but why would he kill Cecille? Yet think back to the beginning. We know there's a woman involved, because a woman had to rent the car. And we think someone else must have been involved, because how else did the woman get back after returning the car? Two people, Guiness. Evie and Bennett."

Cagney sat up, the wheels turning brightly in his mind. There were still holes there. Like why would Bennett work with his wife to kill his lover, and why did Evie leave him later? Unless Evie didn't leave. Maybe she'd helped Bennett kill Cecille by renting the car. Evie was well trained to do exactly as her husband told her. And maybe afterward, she'd been Bennett's liability. Maybe Evie hadn't left—maybe she was dead. It was a possibility. At least more of a possibility than they'd had before.

"I think we ought to push for a search warrant," he said slowly. "It'll be hard without any concrete evidence, but I'm sure you know a few strings you could pull."

Daniels nodded. "I'll check with the lab boys. They may have something we can offer up to make our case more solid. Hell, dust from the textile mill found in Marina's house, dirt from their front yard left in Marina's house. If they can give me any shred of evidence, I'll get the warrant."

"And I'll put out an APB on Evie," Cagney agreed. "There aren't many ways out of Maddensfield, and Evie's well-known. If she actually did run away, we'll find someone who knows something."

Daniels rose from the chair and stood briefly in front of the fan. "We're getting there," he said gruffly. "By God, we're finally getting there."

Cagney nodded, but his face remained tense. If they were making progress, why did his stomach still feel the cold slivers of dread? He pushed the feeling away. It was normal to feel anxiety at the end of the case, because by then the stakes were higher. The murderer, be it Evie and/or Bennett, was getting closer and closer to Marina.

He couldn't let the progress continue.

He would keep Marina Walden safe if he had to give his own life to do so.

He stood and followed Daniels out the door, then each headed for his own vehicle.

* * *

He drove back to his apartment because he needed to get cleaned up, he told himself. No matter that he kept an extra shirt in his office as well as a first-aid kit. He needed a shirt from his closet.

That Marina was holed up at his place had nothing to do with it. After all these years of solitude, he certainly wasn't taken with a woman now. They'd made love last night, and that was that. They were both adults, and adults had needs. Besides, it would be silly to argue that there was no chemistry between them. Marina had been right when she'd said they gave off more heat than a small nuclear explosion.

Physical desire was physical desire. Now that they had given in to the lust, surely their thirst would be slaked. And slowly but surely, the potent attraction would fade, until they turned from lovers to friends and moved on with their individual lives. He frowned. Funny, he had a hard time picturing that. He forced the image into his mind. That was the way things worked, and dammit, he was the one who wanted the boundaries.

He pulled into his driveway.

The unmarked state car sat across the street. He nodded toward the two men inside the brown sedan, then walked up the path to his apartment. The brick building was only two-stories high, and his apartment, being a one bedroom, was on the first floor. As he approached the door, he felt his eyes open wide.

The blinds had been pulled all the way up, giving him an unrestricted view of his tiny living room. Already he could see the thick green leaves of flourishing plants, and sitting right in the middle of the green frame was Marina, painting calmly at her canvas as if she didn't have a care in the world.

He was already scowling as he inserted his key into the lock and pushed open the door. She looked up at his entrance and smiled at him so brightly the harsh words of warning died in his throat. Then instantly her face wrapped into worry.

"What happened to you?" she exclaimed.

She stood immediately, giving him a great view of her bare midriff and long, dusky legs. She seemed to have acquired a new pair of shorts and a tank top.

"Is that blood on your shirt?"

"It's nothing," he said. He turned back to the naked window and his face crinkled into a scowl. "Now, what are you doing sitting in front of an open window like that? We're trying to hide you here, not announce your arrival."

In two long strides, he was pulling down the blinds, blinking as the room suddenly plunged into grayness, the sunlight snatched away. At once he was aware of the drabness of the room, of the unrelenting shadows, even though flowering plants now sprouted in every corner, a painting hung on the wall and a ridiculously bright afghan lay draped across the couch.

"And where did all this stuff come from?" he demanded. "You promised to sit tight while I was gone." He hated the full feeling of panic building in his stomach. What if someone had seen her? What if someone had followed her back here? What if he'd returned home only to find her sprawled dead on his apartment floor.

He couldn't lose her. *He just couldn't lose her!*

Marina twisted the paintbrush in her hand, but her chin came up stubbornly. "I had to get some things," she said levelly. "I had nothing to wear but that dress. And if I had to spend all day here, I figured I might as well add a few things." Her chin trembled a little, but her shoulders remained square. "You know I don't like the dark, Cage."

He half nodded, understanding her more than he wanted to right now.

He stalked off toward the bedroom, his limp ragged and unsteady.

"Did you at least take Barkley and Woods with you?" he said tersely as he ripped off his shirt.

She followed him into the bedroom, feeling his tension like a gathering thundercloud in the dark haze of his apartment. "I even made Barkley purchase the items while

I waited in the car with Woods," she said quietly. "Of course, I had to send him back twice for the shorts and shirt. He kept bringing out grays and blacks. Who would wear such things?"

Cagney's hand stilled on the dark-gray shirt he was about to pull out of his closet. Then with an oath he dragged it out anyway.

"I can't imagine his sin," he said ruthlessly as he began to pointedly pull on his own choice of colors. He was half-shocked when he suddenly found her hand on his chest, blocking his movements.

For a long moment, he just stared at her hand, noting the delicate, fragile fingers he knew to be strong, detecting the faint splatters of green and blue paint on her nails. He looked up, and found her violet eyes watching him intensely.

Slowly she stepped forward, until her body was only an inch from his. "You're angry with me," she whispered. "Why are you angry, Cagney?"

"I just don't want to see you get hurt," he said. Damn, but it was hard to think with her standing so close. He could smell her perfume, practically taste the sweet softness of her skin. He'd made love to her three times during the night, and now, only noon, he wanted her all over again.

She traced a light pattern against the bare expanse of his chest, causing him to suck in his breath. Her head came down slightly, her chin no longer sure. When her eyes swept up this time, he could see the luminescent hint of uncertainty.

"Maybe," she said quietly, "maybe you care about me?"

"Of course I care," he said. "I'm the sheriff."

For just one moment, he saw the disappointment slash across her face, and he had to steel himself against it as if it had been a physical blow. But he forced himself not to relent, and he forced himself not to pull her into his arms.

They were just lovers, he reminded himself stonily. It was all merely physical. He would not let it be more; he would not feel more. She might believe in him, but he knew better. She was actually the stronger one; he was the one truly imprisoned by fear.

Her hand fell away from his chest, and the loss of her touch wounded. The muscles in his face began to hurt from the effort to remain so impassive.

Slowly she touched the darkening bruise on his cheek. "So how does the other man look?" she said, her eyes unreadable.

"Worse," he said curtly.

"Resisting arrest?" she quizzed.

He remained mute, and suddenly she cocked a mocking eyebrow at him.

"Surely it wasn't personal, Cagney," she said throatily. "Surely the man of steel didn't let anything personal get under his skin."

He flinched as soon as her fingers brushed his lips. Abruptly he caught her shoulders, bent his head and seared her with a kiss.

"Happier?" he asked darkly.

She merely narrowed her gaze, then abruptly pulled his head back down. Her kiss was equally fierce, her lithe body pressing against his. She opened her mouth, welcoming him fully, demanding more, and the kiss escalated dangerously.

Just as suddenly she pulled back, her breathing ragged, her eyes dark. Cage struggled with his lungs and the overwhelming need to pull her back into his arms.

"It's more than just physical," she whispered, her eyes intent. "Sooner or later, I'm going to get you to admit that, Cage."

He opened his mouth as if to protest, but she silenced him by placing a finger on his lips. She stood on her tiptoes, and this time she kissed him softly. "Change your shirt, Cage. I'm going to finish my painting."

She turned and walked jauntily out of the room in her deep-purple shorts and cropped tank top. It took him a few minutes before he trusted himself not to call her back.

His lips still tingled; his body was still hard.

Maybe, just maybe, she had a point.

He finished buttoning his shirt with fingers that trembled slightly. Then, slowly, his eyes fell to the locked trunk at the foot of his bed.

Chapter 14

He didn't allow himself to think about it as he fumbled through his ring of keys to find the right one. The trick was, he told himself, simply not to make it a big deal. Sheriffs carried guns. Sheriffs needed guns to protect law-abiding citizens, like a certain beautiful violet-eyed woman, from harm. Ergo, this sheriff should retrieve his gun from his trunk.

It all sounded fine, until he opened up the lid.

A picture of Melissa remained taped to the top, wearing the blue suit from their earlier days. Her hand half covered her face, trying to ward off the camera, though she was laughing. They'd been partners for six years, and good friends, as well. Now he didn't remember the last time he'd talked to her. She'd tried to be there for him after the shooting. Her testimony and collaboration of the events had cleared his name in the routine investigation that had followed. But for the most part, he'd rejected her overtures of understanding. He'd been so sure she couldn't understand. So sure no one would.

Other cops had to kill in the line of duty. They got on with their lives. Remember that, Cage. Remember that.

He lowered his eyes to the bottom of the trunk. The air wafted up, stale and musty like an antique store. His old uniform was still folded neatly. Lying on top was the leather book holding his graduation diploma from the police academy. He used to take it out and marvel at it during secret, private moments.

He'd become a cop. At long last he was a cop.

Now he pushed it aside for the hard, black gun case resting beside his older holster. He'd turned in his police piece upon leaving the force. But he'd also personally owned a .357 Magnum. He pulled out the case and opened it.

It felt heavier in his hand than he remembered. Heavier, and more sinister than a simple tool should feel. He'd never ever been afraid of guns. Hell, his father had shown them all how to clean and load a rifle long before they were big enough to hold it. Henry had also taught them about safety switches, how to keep a barrel pointed away and how to never ever pull the trigger in jest. Guns were tools, not toys, and you didn't mess around with a tool.

He let the .357 Magnum simply rest in the palm of his hand, the four-inch barrel pointed at the outside wall. Damn, it felt heavy. Had this thing ever truly felt natural in his grip? Had he really ever whipped it out and pointed it as a natural extension of his arm?

Now he popped open the chamber and peered at the six empty spaces. He delved back into the trunk, reemerging with the .38 + P bullets he'd last favored. The bullets had been developed to give greater velocity and higher performance after the normal .357 Magnum cartridges were deemed inadequate in the sixties. Doped-up drug addicts were no longer dropping when hit, creating dangerous situations that seemed to demand more firepower. So guns had evolved, as well, until bullets were measured on their power, their ability to kill.

He forced his hand into motion, drawing out the first bullet from the set. His hand was shaking slightly, making

it difficult to slide the bullet into the chamber. Through
sheer force of will, he made himself continue until the gun
was fully loaded. Holding the black rubber custom grip
tighter than necessary, he clicked the chamber back into
place, sliding on the safety lock.

Then he slowly raised the gun, pointing it at the far wall
while he gazed down the fixed sight. Now his hand didn't
tremble at all, but the grimness settled on his shoulders like
a mantle of the heaviest steel.

He lowered the gun, sliding it back into his holster. It
needed some oil, but he didn't have any here. Probably
there was some at the office. He'd never asked, and both his
deputies, having made the mistake of bringing up guns
once, had never brought up the subject again.

He closed the lid of the trunk, locking it now out of habit
rather than need, and stood slowly. He slipped the belt
around his hips, feeling the weight of the gun riding low. It
felt awkward, heavy. Like the proverbial albatross, except
not around his neck. Hell, maybe that would be a better
place for it.

He squared his shoulders and walked into the living
room.

Marina was staring at the canvas in front of her. Not
painting, just staring. She looked up from seat on the floor
the minute he entered, and immediately her eyes rested on
his hips. For one moment, her gaze swept back up to peer
at his face, her violet eyes unreadable. This once, he was
grateful for the control of those wild eyes. If she'd looked
at him in pity, he didn't think he would have been able to
take it.

"Going out again?" she asked softly.

He nodded.

"Want an ice pack for your cheek?"

Unconsciously his fingers came up to rest lightly on his
throbbing face. He'd already forgotten about his injury, but
her words brought it back with a fiery vengeance. He must
surely look like hell.

"I think I'm all right," he said.

She appeared unconvinced, but her gaze swept back to her canvas.

"I called home today," she said abruptly. "I left some money for the call next to the phone."

He frowned, watching her intently. "You didn't have to do that," he said curtly.

She shrugged, not meeting his gaze. "I wanted to," she replied simply. "Besides, we talked for a while."

"And?"

Her gaze crept over for a moment, meeting his steady face halfway across the room, before her eyes scurried back to the safety of the canvas.

"They were upset. My mother cried. My father demanded I return to New York."

"You told them everything, then?"

Once more the shrug, but this one slightly more nervous. "Most things," she said slowly.

Suddenly her eyes fastened on his, the violet depths earnest.

"I told them about Cecille's murder, about the break-ins to my house. But I couldn't tell them about Sarita. Not yet, Cagney, not yet. Not when I'm still trying to figure what it means for myself. I've never lied to my parents before, never left anything out on purpose like that. Is it really so horrible?"

She hated the sound of pleading that had entered her voice, but she couldn't look away from him if she tried.

"You'll tell them when the time is right," Cage said firmly.

His gray eyes were once more the level slate gray she'd come to know so well. They calmed her, brought her strength.

"So are you returning to New York?" he asked softly.

Her chin came up. "Do you want me to go?"

"It would be safer," he said simply, then watched her scowl at his words.

"It would be running," she told him harshly. "And I don't run. I came here to build a life, and I'm going to build it if it kills me." Immediately she recognized what she'd just said, and her cheeks flushed a dull red. "Well, maybe that wasn't the best choice of words."

"I'll say," Cagney agreed. He watched her face for a long time, searching for the shadows, the nervous hints of fear. But all he saw was the determination in her chin, the proud set of her shoulders. She looked like a seasoned warrior on the eve of a battle, already understanding the evils of war, already anticipating the sweetness of the victory.

He could learn a lot from her.

"I need to get back to the office," he said at last. "There's a lot of work to get done."

Marina nodded."

Are you making progress?" she asked quietly.

"I think we may have something," he told her cautiously, not wanting to raise her hopes.

"Good," she said, though his words didn't quite ease the nervousness of her stomach. "But you should stay out of brawls, you know?"

"Deal," he agreed. Then, with one last twist of his lips, he walked out the door, the gun riding low on his hip.

"Cagney Guiness." The sharp voice pounced in his ear. "What is this I hear of you and barroom brawls?"

"Why, good afternoon to you, too, Suzanne," he drawled into the phone, leaning back from his desk. "I see the grapevine is working up to its normal efficiency."

Suzanne uttered an unladylike snort. "This has nothing to do with the grapevine, Cagney. The quiet Guiness son actually getting into a fight? If you're not careful you're going to find yourself on the front page of the morning paper. When did you start engaging in fistfights?"

"It just happened," he said vaguely, shutting his eyes at her words. He'd forgotten how small-town Maddensfield was. In a matter of minutes, he'd probably have his mother on the phone. Or worse yet, on his doorstep.

"I hear it had to with Marina Walden," Suzanne uttered shrewdly. "Now, why doesn't that surprise me?"

"Can't anyone around here mind their own business?" he half muttered.

"Of course not! This is Maddensfield. What we do is mind other people's business. Particularly when Cagney Guiness gets in a fight with Bennett Jensen. You know how many men over the years have wanted to land that blow? You'll be a living legend by morning, Cage. Woman will descend on you in hordes."

"I don't want women," he declared.

"No," she said innocently. "Just Marina Walden."

"Oh, for crying out loud." He exploded now. "Can't a man have some peace? Did you call me just to harass me about this, Suzanne? Because as a matter of fact, I've got a lot of work to do. Evie Jensen's missing and I need to find her."

Suddenly there was silence on the other end of the phone. It went on for so long, Cagney found himself forgetting his irritation and listening intently, instead. He leaned forward in his chair, all his attention riveted.

"Do you know where, Evie is, Suzanne?" he asked slowly.

"Depends on who wants to know," she said finally.

He understood immediately. "Oh this has nothing to do with Bennett," he assured her. "Daniels and I have a whole host of questions for her all by ourselves. Like where was she the night of June 5."

Once more there was silence, until the hairs on the back of his neck stood up with the tension.

"Evie was with me that night," Suzanne said quietly. "She'd had a fight with Bennett. He'd hit her pretty good, and well, she was trying to get up the courage to leave him."

Cagney's elbows rested on the desk hard, as he automatically reached for pad and paper to scribble notes. "You're saying she was with you all night? The whole time?"

"The whole night, Cage."

"What time did she arrive?"

"Oh, I don't know. Around seven or so."

"Did you stay up with her?"

"Yes. Until one or so. Then quite frankly we were both exhausted. You know I'm not one for late hours."

"And you're sure she didn't go anywhere in that time?"

"Cagney, the woman was distraught. She was bruised and crying and afraid. She said Bennett was getting meaner and meaner. She was terrified of the man."

He cursed, a low, curt word that immediately had her attention.

"I swear, Cage. Are you trying to turn into Garret?"

"No," he said, frowning as he saw all his earlier theories on the murder go up in smoke. "So tell me, did she truly leave him? Is that why she's no longer in town?"

"Oh, she left him, all right. I and a few of the other ladies from church helped her pack her bags Friday afternoon. We put her on a bus to a little resort in the mountains. She needs some time alone to think and figure out what she wants. Some time far away from that man."

"Suzanne, if I had to, could I talk to her?"

Suzanne sounded worried. "I don't know, Cage. I've actually spoken to her every day now, but I can tell she's quite upset. This has been a big step for Evie. I don't want you disturbing her more."

"I know, Suzanne," he assured her. "But this is important. I think Bennett had something to do with Cecille's murder. Actually, I thought she had something to do with it. I need to know more. Like why does Bennett know the name Kristi Davis?"

"What does Kristi Davis have to do with any of this?" Suzanne inquired sharply.

Cagney immediately sat up straight. "Why do you know the name?" he asked, suddenly tense.

"I know that's the name of Sarita's girl," Suzanne said vaguely. "The woman who was murdered all those years ago."

"And you actually remember the murder? Hell, Suzanne, you're only two years older than me and I don't remember the murder."

For the first time in his life, Cagney felt tension over the
none with Suzanne. She was hiding something, but Su-
nne didn't hide anything. She was as honest as they came.

"Tell me, Cagney," she said, the words slow and steady,
what do Sarita and Kristi have to do with all this?"

He hesitated only for a minute, then realized there was no
her way than to play out the trump card. "Marina is
risti Davis," he said bluntly. "She was adopted twenty-
ve years ago by a couple in New York."

"My God," Suzanne breathed. "My God."

"Suzanne, you'd better tell me what the hell is going on
I won't be held responsible for my actions."

There was a small pause as Suzanne shifted the phone
om one ear to the other. "Look, Cagney, I don't know
erything, and I'm not sure how this all fits in, but there's
reason I know the name Kristi Davis, and it actually isn't
om the murder. I heard it years later, and only afterward
d I find out about what happened to Sarita. You see, the
ght when Bennett and Evie got married, well, Lloyd re-
ly had too much to drink..."

"No," Cagney said softly. And suddenly he knew, too.
ngle-mother Sarita, father unknown.

"I'd never seen Lloyd as drunk as he was that night,"
izanne said. "Knocking back those whiskey sours one
ter another, as if tomorrow had no meaning. His son was
tting married, and he was like a man possessed. The next
ing I knew, he kept talking about his child, his little child
owing up and he wasn't there for it at all. I thought he
as regretting how much he'd worked while Bennett was a
by. We all know Lloyd lived at that mill. But then he kept
uttering how he'd bet she was beautiful, a real heart-
eaker like her mother. And he wondered if she had dolls,
d he wondered if she remembered him and Sarita at all."

"Oh, my God," Cagney whispered. "Who else knows
out this, Suzanne?"

"No one, I think. Lloyd didn't normally imbibe that
avily, and you can be sure I shut him up quick enough the
inute he started talking about those things. The last thing

I wanted to be was the receptacle of a drunk man's darkest
secrets. But he was in so much pain, Cagney. He came over
to my place the next morning, barely able to meet my eye
he was so scared. Can you imagine big, old Lloyd Jensen
afraid of anyone? He'd carried that secret for so long. And
he truly loved her, you know. He never acknowledged Sarita or their child publicly, because that would have killed
Sophie and Bennett, and he wasn't the kind of man to do
such a thing to his family. But I'm telling you, Sarita was
the love of his life. Her murder practically destroyed him,
and he couldn't even openly grieve. He went around in a
daze for weeks, drinking himself into a stupor every night.
By the time he snapped out of it, Kristi had been given up
for adoption, and he was afraid to claim her as his own.

"He told me he figured it was better for her to have a new
family. Sophie would have hated her for being the child of
the woman her husband loved, and Bennett was petty and
greedy, even back then. I think it ate at him, Cagney. She
was his little girl, and her world was torn apart and he
couldn't do anything about it. I don't think he ever for-
gave himself for that. He provided well for Sophie until her
death and he turned over his mill to Bennett. But the two
people he truly loved, he couldn't help at all."

Cagney closed his eyes, and the pictures that came to his
mind were too vivid for words. The last piece of the jigsaw
puzzle fell into place, and all of sudden, he could see everything, sharp and clear. "Why didn't you tell me this
sooner?" he half growled. "Why the hell didn't you mention this?"

Immediately Suzanne was outraged. "Lloyd Jensen
trusted me with that secret, Cage. And I agreed to keep it
long after he was dead and gone. That's a powerful story
there, and if Marina is indeed Kristi Davis, it could still hurt
a lot of people. The last I knew, you were investigating the
death of Cecille Manning. Why should I have started
bringing up Lloyd's old secrets over that?"

Cagney grimaced. Why, indeed? She never would have
known they were connected, because there was no reason

for them to be connected. Until you saw the broken china in Marina's home, listened to Roy's stories and then returned to discover a dead dog. Then the link was established, though at that point it had only been understood by the killer.

The killer, and now Cagney.

"I'm sorry, Suzanne," he said, feeling the adrenaline hit his blood full force. "It's not your fault. You had no reason—"

The door on his office flew open, and Davey streaked in, wide-eyed.

"Sheriff, sir! Daniels is on the phone. He's been trying to get through for the past ten minutes, sir. Barkley and Woods didn't call in, Sheriff. And he can't reach them by radio anymore."

"Gotta go," Cagney said tersely into the phone, and before Suzanne had time to so much as squeak a goodbye, he was slamming the phone down and standing. He grabbed his hat from the corner of the desk. "Wake up, Andersen," he said curtly, taking in Davey's still-damp hair from his recent rising. "Tell him to meet you at my apartment and to be prepared. It might not be pleasant. Radio in what you find. I'll call Daniels."

Davey nodded, his young face at once serious and sweaty. "And yourself, sir?" he barked.

Cagney settled his hat on his head. "I'm going to Marina's house," he said evenly, not questioning his instincts any longer. "As soon as you're done checking on Barkley and Woods, I want you to meet me there. And Davey, if they are dead, don't stand around waiting for the ambulance. Get to Marina's house as fast as you can drive and have the ambulance meet you there, where at least it might not be too late."

The very grimness of Cagney's voice made Davey pale, but the young man's shoulders remained straight. "Yes, sir. Will do, sir."

"Good, Davey. I know I can trust you."

For the first time, Davey's eyes fell to the holster around Cagney's hips, and the severity of Cagney Guiness carrying a gun seemed to shake him far worse than the gravity of Cage's voice. He turned sharply and marched out of the office while the sweat beaded and rolled down his young face.

Cagney didn't blame him. The fear ran cold in his veins, as well. But when he looked down at his hands, he found they were steady. Maybe some things were just like riding a bike. He sure as hell hoped so.

He'd never driven as fast as he drove to Marina's house now. He hit the railroad tracks with such speed the sheriff's Blazer was momentarily airborne. Then it came down with a dulling crash that threatened every bone in his body. He kept his foot flat on the gas, coming to a screeching halt three blocks away. He jumped down from the vehicle, not wanting to announce his presence with the roar of an engine, and ran the last three blocks through the throbbing ache in his leg.

From the outside of the house, nothing seemed wrong. No sudden lights blazed in the sun-drenched afternoon. No dark clouds or streaking lightning hinted at the violence building within. But he could feel it in the hot, still air. The rising tension, the steeping rage.

He felt the hairs on his arm rise, the shivers of hyperawareness tingle up his spine. He whispered along the side of the house, working his way to the screen door, knowing already what he would find.

A creature of habit. A creature addicted to his crime. He should have realized sooner why the killer was reenacting the twenty-five-year-old murder. Not because he was trying to drive Marina crazy, but because he needed the recreation for his own sickness. Murder was about power. And killers frequently returned to the scene of the crime to recapture that sensation of ultimate superiority. And there was one night, twenty-five years ago, when Bennett had last felt so all-powerful. The night the sixteen-year-old had destroyed his father's second family.

The formerly taped screen door flapped dully, the edges jagged and mangled in the sunlight. Cagney went to put a foot down, then jumped at the sound of a crashing plate.

He swung around the corner, gun pointed into the kitchen through the open sliding-glass door.

"Run, dammit," Bennett was screaming behind the counter, his face an unsightly red mottle. "Run, I said."

"No," Marina was shouting back, her eyes glued to the huge hunting knife waving in Bennett's hand. Its edge wasn't shiny and silvery but dulled with the black flecks of dried blood. "I don't understand what you want!"

Good girl, Cagney thought, admiring her control. Bennett liked the hunt; he needed the chase, the ability to prove his power by overcoming a running, struggling foe.

Bennett reached up, grabbing another plate from the kitchen cupboard, and shattered it on the floor. Helplessly Marina jumped, and Cagney could feel her growing agitation. He sighted Bennett down the barrel of his gun.

And just for a moment, saw the fourteen-year-old face of QVee Tops.

He forced the image away and held his hand steady.

"Bennett!" he called out sharply. Both Bennett and Marina turned simultaneously, but Cagney had overestimated the extent of Bennett's madness. In a split second of cool cunning, Bennett wrapped his hand in Marina's long hair and yanked her against his chest. Immediately the knife rested against her neck. It turned there, lingering almost lovingly against the faint blue pulse on her throat.

"Leave us alone," Bennett snarled. "This is old business and has nothing to do with you."

"It's over, Bennett," Cagney forced himself to say calmly. He could see the building wildness in Marina's eyes, and the sight of that blood-splattered blade against her throat was making his own nerves tense. He wanted to kill, the way he'd never wanted to kill. He wanted to destroy this creature threatening his woman.

QVee's eyes, rounding with the youthful brilliance of surprise as the blood suddenly mushroomed across his chest...

"Your father is dead," Cage said flatly, gritting his jaw against the images in his mind. "You already won, Bennett. You kept him from his lover and his daughter. You already won."

"No," Bennett raged. "It's not over. She's alive and she's here. I should have killed her when I had the chance. If it hadn't taken so long to get Sarita, if she hadn't made so much noise... I panicked, running away before the job was done. But this time, I plan on finishing it."

Marina paled at his words, and for a split second her violet eyes met Cagney's in an instant of stark comprehension. He willed himself to keep his attention on Bennett and the sharp blade still held so securely in his hand.

"You've already murdered Cecille," he said. "Wasn't that enough, Bennett?"

The older man practically spat on the floor. "Cecille was an ambitious fool. She thought she could blackmail me into leaving Evie. When she found out I'd never risk my mill in a divorce, she actually thought she was clever in coming up with a scheme to murder Evie, instead. But why in the world would I trade my quiet Evie for that scheming bitch? She didn't really want me, you know. She wanted my mill, and I'll never risk my mill. It's mine, all mine. I don't care what everyone says, 'Lloyd would've done this,' or 'Lloyd would've done that.' It's my damn mill now, and I deserve it. It's the only damn thing he ever gave me, and I was his son! His only son!" He scowled down at Marina, and the blade dug a little deeper against her skin.

"And you were nothing but a little brat who could barely stand up. You only had to gurgle words and he looked at you like you were a princess. All those nights, he told us he had to work late, when really he was sneaking down to visit you and your whore of a mother. I know, because I followed him once. I saw the way he'd bounce you on his knee and tickle your chin. You little conniving bitch."

He pressed in the blade, and blood snaked down its edge. Marina held rigidly still, too afraid even to breathe, while Cagney's finger clenched at the trigger.

QVee, slumping on the porch, his brown eyes wide with shock, with death...

He felt the sweat begin to trickle down his face.

"Sarita's dead," he found himself saying, the words remarkably level. "You killed her that night, Bennett. You killed her, the dog, everything Lloyd had something to do with. And little baby Kristi was taken far away, where your father could never bounce her on his knee. Even if she's back now, Lloyd's dead, so it doesn't matter. He still never got his daughter, and now you have your own family to worry about."

"Evie left me," Bennett said dully. "She doesn't care about me anymore. Like Cecille never cared, like my father never cared. No one ever, ever cared."

"But Marina cares," Cagney rattled off, thinking quickly. "She's your sister, Bennett, and she cares. Don't you, Marina?"

Marina almost nodded, her eyes wide, then quickly thought better of it. She managed to lick her lips and whisper the words around the tightness in her throat. "I always wanted a brother, Bennett," she said carefully. "I'm glad to know you're my brother now."

The words sounded stiff, but they were the best she could do under the circumstances. They were not good enough. The blade dug deeper into her throat.

"Liar," Bennett uttered in her ear. "You'd say anything now to get what you want. But I'm the one in control here."

He slid the blade along her throat, leaving a small trail of blood to emphasize his point. She couldn't help the whimper of pain that escaped.

And hearing it, Cagney wanted to throw down his gun and strangle the man with his bare hands, instead.

He found Marina's gaze and held it for a long minute, his eyes steady. He saw her relax almost imperceptibly, her face becoming composed, her eyes knowing. They were in this together. And together, come hell or high water, they would find a way out.

Then suddenly, the roar of sirens filled the air. Bennett jerked his head toward the living room, and Marina didn't wait for another opportunity. Seizing two self-defense classes' worth of knowledge, she rammed her sharp elbow into his gut and relaxed abruptly against his chest. Combined, the actions threw them off balance, and both of Bennett's hands flashed out on instinct to catch himself as he and Marina tottered to the floor. With a quick roll, Marina was out of the way.

Bennett came up with a howl of rage that drowned out even the sirens. He turned to Marina, but she was already behind the table. Then his eyes fell on Cagney, the man who had denied him everything. Like a thundering lion, he raised his knife and charged.

Cagney did not hesitate. He was no longer Cagney the D.C. detective, no longer Cagney who shot a kid. He was Cagney the man, protecting the woman he loved, fighting for the only shot at a real future he'd ever found.

He stood tall and, his eyes never wavering, pulled the trigger three quick times. And down like an animal went Bennett, plunging down to the linoleum floor, his body heavy as it hit. Abruptly the sirens stopped, and the air was filled with silence.

Cagney heard the sound of police cruiser doors slamming shut, then the sound of running feet. He didn't notice any of it. He stepped carefully into the kitchen, instead, his eyes glued to Marina's face. He held out his hands, and in a small rush she ran into his embrace.

He buried his face in the silky mass of her hair, breathing in the deep, mysterious scent of her perfume. Then he saw QVee's face one last time, and felt the first of the moisture fall into her hair. She held him tighter, crying her own anguish in his arms.

Together they weathered the storm.

Epilogue

It took hours to wrap up the paperwork from there. Marina had to describe how Bennett had broken into the apartment, his knife ready and his eyes wild. He'd forced her into the car and back over to her old house, where he'd become obsessed with the idea that she had to run. Her instinct had told her it was the wrong thing to do, like running before a coiled snake. He needed the movement, waiting for the first step so he could strike.

Davey and Andersen found Barkley and Woods slumped over in their vehicle. Woods had been caught by surprise and hit over the back of the head. Barkley had gotten his gun halfway out of the holster before being stabbed twice. He remained in critical condition at the hospital, though by midnight his vital signs had stabilized.

Cagney had called Suzanne, and while Marina went to the hospital to be checked over, Daniels drilled Suzanne on Lloyd's story. Cage had to write up and file a report on the evening's events. It was nearly two a.m. by the time the details were all accounted for and Cage was free to leave.

Suzanne agreed to call Evie, and left pensive with the weight of what to tell the fragile woman.

Cagney knew he was just exhausted, and there was only one person he really wanted to see. He rose and rolled his neck to relax the last of the strain, only to find Daniels watching him with calculating eyes.

"So you did it, Guiness," Daniels said bluntly.

"Did what?"

"Pulled the trigger, of course. So how does it feel?"

"A man's dead," Cagney said flatly. "That never feels great."

"Good, good. Just so long as you don't lose perspective."

There was another long pause, and suddenly Daniels nodded curtly. "That was a damn fine piece of police work, Guiness. I had my doubts in the beginning, but you came through. You are a sheriff of the highest caliber. And I'd tell that to anyone who asked."

Cagney accepted the praise with a simple nod, his gray eyes expressionless.

Daniels clapped him on the back. "So will you go back to D.C. now? God knows they can always use a good detective. Or I wouldn't mind recommending you to the state force here."

"I'm fine where I'm at," Cagney said quietly.

Daniels arched a brow. "Come on, Guiness. It was one thing when you were avoiding trouble. But that's not an issue anymore. Your talents are wasted here in this godforsaken town."

Cagney met the man with his level, piercing stare. "Maddensfield isn't godforsaken," he said coolly as he settled his black Stetson on his head. "It's home."

Abruptly Daniels grinned. He slapped Cage on the shoulder one last time. "I like you, Guiness. I really, really like you. Now, go find your woman. You're going to have to keep better tabs on her, you know. Now that you've taken to brawling over her honor and all."

"That's the first intelligent thing you've said," Cagney assured him, and headed straight for the door. He could still see Daniels laughing as he walked out into the warm, velvety night.

Marina was no longer at the hospital, he was informed. Her injuries had appeared minor, and she'd been released shortly, though Dr. Jacobs had recommended she call her personal physician in New York in the morning. She'd been through a serious trauma, and though she seemed fairly composed thus far, he wanted to make sure she was utilizing her support network.

With that information, Cagney knew exactly where she'd gone.

It was nearly three a.m. by the time he pulled his truck up at the abandoned lot. The posted lanterns glowed in the sultry night, illuminating the beautiful gypsy painting with such passion.

Her peacock was done, the arrogant creature strutting under the stallion's hooves with such disdain you almost had to admire the bird. But it wasn't the peacock that held Cagney's attention. It was the new creature she was painting in the middle of the brilliant market scene. Joining the fortune teller, fruit vendor and princess was a cowboy. And even from here, Cagney could see the outline of a bronze star on the cowboy's leather vest.

"You've gotten a lot done," he said quietly, stepping into the circle of lights. She nodded, not looking up from the deep red she was currently dabbing onto the cowboy's bandanna. Once more her movements were quick and fluid, as she completed the bandanna with a raw roughness that suited the dusty, untamed image.

She still wouldn't look up or stop painting, and after a minute, Cagney frowned. "Are you okay?" he asked softly.

For the first time, her brush stopped. "I don't know," she said at last, then began flitting over her work again. "I slept from ten to twelve. I didn't dream. Maybe that's a good sign."

"But?"

She shook her head again. "I don't know, Cage. So much has happened, I just don't know. Tell me, what did Cecille have to do with any of this? I just don't understand why she had to die, as well. There's been just so much violence."

Cagney nodded, understanding the undertones of her voice and wishing she would stop painting long enough for him to take her into his arms. Instead he could only step closer.

"Near as we can tell," he said steadily, his voice low and deep in the silence, "Cecille built her own trap without ever realizing it. She found out the truth about Bennett murdering Sarita all those years ago. I'm not sure how, but then, Cecille was always very resourceful. Now that she's dead, maybe we'll never know. It appears she thought to blackmail Bennett with the information, since he kept resisting leaving Evie. He was afraid of losing the mill in a divorce, and since Cecille wanted the mill, as well, she understood his reluctance.

"It seems—" Cagney had to pause. He'd known Cecille Manning all his life, and while she'd always been ambitious and scheming, it was hard for him to accept that she could have been this cold. "It appears she thought of a plan for her and Bennett to murder Evie. She needed a scapegoat, so she and Bennett agreed to frame you for the crime. I believe she must have bought a wig, then rented a car in your name. That's why she called Martha at 10:30 that night, pretending to be at work, though no record of the call shows up. She was trying to establish an alibi, because she was really calling from the car rental agency at the airport.

"Unfortunately for Cecille, she underestimated Bennett. He never planned on trading in Evie for her, but Cecille had become someone who knew too much. So he let her develop the plan, then he used the plan to kill her, instead…" His voice trailed off. He could still remember her body so clearly, and even if she'd been bent on murder, he still couldn't believe she deserved to die like that.

"Bennett's mistake," he said at last, "was leaving his car at the airport when he joined her to pick up the rental car. He thought he was doing the smart thing, providing himself with an untraceable way to return home after dropping off the car. He never realized that was exactly the problem. It *was* untraceable. Thus we were suspicious and began to think there had to be more than one person."

Marina simply nodded, mixing together some of the oil paints on her palette at her feet to form the exact shade she needed next. "And then he went after me from pure hatred. Because he hadn't killed me all those years ago."

There was a dullness to her words Cagney didn't like. He gave up on patience and stepped up behind her. He closed his hand over her brush, taking it out of her nerveless grasp, and forced her to turn around.

"Talk to me, Marina," he whispered. "Tell me all those thoughts swirling around in your head right now."

She looked at his bottomless eyes, her gaze at once dark and vulnerable. "I don't know," she repeated, her voice cracking. "It's hard for me to put all the pieces together. I'm an adopted child, Cagney, and like all adopted children, no matter how great my adopted parents were, I still always wondered what happened to my birth parents. And suddenly I learn not only about them, but that I had a brother. The only child really had a brother." She spread out her hands in front of herself, looking at him with sad eyes. "And they're all dead," she murmured. "My mother died by my brother's hand, and my father died lonely and separated from us both. And Bennett's dead, too, and I have to be grateful for that, because he destroyed my family and he wanted to destroy me, as well. So maybe in one way I'm ahead knowing the truth. But I'm behind, too, because the truth wasn't what I wanted it to be, and I don't have anything to show for it all. There's no one left."

"I know," he told her and drew her into his arms. She went willingly, resting her paint-streaked face against his damp shirt, wrapping her arms around his solid build. "But you don't have to come to terms with it tonight, Marina. You have the rest of your life to learn who your parents really were and to appreciate your adopted parents, as well. They still love you, and they'll be there for you through this, as they've been there for you through everything. I'm sure of it."

She nodded, but it didn't ease the tightness in her chest. Because maybe more than the pain of her unknown parents' loss, she was suddenly afraid of losing Cagney, too. This man gave her such strength. She could still remember the way his gaze had found hers as she'd stood there choking on the terror while the knife had pricked her throat. He'd looked at her, and the black panic had receded, as it had receded the very first night he'd found her painting in this lot. She needed his steadiness, the gray calmness of his eyes.

She loved him.

"Will you leave Maddensfield now?" she asked softly, the words half-muffled against his shirt. She breathed in the scent of his skin, warm and salty from the humid night. She never wanted to unwrap her arms from his waist.

He shook his head against her hair. It felt good to hold her after the long day. Good to feel her lean, soft body against him. She made him see colors, made him feel things he'd shut out for so long. He could already sense his body stirring. He wanted the reassurance of sinking into her, hearing her gasp his name, knowing she was his once more. He didn't think he would ever grow tired of the feel of her body next to his.

"Why?" she asked. "You faced your proverbial fears— you conquered the monster hiding in the closet. You can go back to being a detective now, rejoin the police force, you know."

"I like being the sheriff," he said simply. "You and Suzanne were both right. Maddensfield needs me, and I need Maddensfield. No place else has ever felt as right as here. And I think maybe I'm not cut out to be a big-city cop. It is a tough job. I have to admire those people. But maybe it wasn't the best thing for me after all. I grew up in a small town. I like things hands-on. I like to feel I'm really making a difference, that I really know the people."

"You could do a lot here," Marina whispered.

"So Suzanne's told me," he said dryly. He shrugged slightly, but his gray eyes were contemplative. "I do rather like the idea of coaching Little League again. And there's the Big Brother program and some antigang programs I might check out. I think if I looked into it, I could find some roles where I could really feel that I'm doing some good."

She nodded, holding him closer.

"What about you?" he asked suddenly, feeling the uneasiness creep into his stomach for the first time. "Will you return to New York now? Maybe this place has too many bad memories."

She was still for a bit in his arms, and he felt the uneasiness build into panic, until he was holding her tightly and feeling a sudden sting in his eyes.

"No," she said at last. "I like it here, in spite of everything. I like the people. And well, it has good memories, too."

Like going to the baseball game with him. Like the barbecue at his parents' house. Like rolling with him on the floor, feeling him move inside her. Maddensfield already felt like home, but maybe mostly because this man did, and she didn't want to lose him.

"Good," he said, the word sounding gruffer than he'd intended. He found himself playing with her long hair, stroking it with his fingers, feeling its heavy silk. He couldn't take it any longer, and bent her back to find her lips with his own.

The kiss was slow and hungry and bit sad. The need was raw around the edges, speaking of things he didn't know how to put into words, of a hunger than went straight to the core of his being. He wanted her as he'd never wanted anyone. And not for today or for tomorrow, but for forever, and he didn't know how to tell her that. She'd shown him so much about light, about hope. He wanted to rebuild. Once and for all, he wanted to leave the past behind. And he wanted her at his side to do it.

"Marina," he whispered finally, dragging up his head, his voice hoarse. "Marina, I don't want to be your lover."

She stilled in his arms, her violet eyes suddenly stricken. He rushed on before he lost his courage. "I want to be your husband, Marina. I want to grow old with you. I want to watch you paint at night every night for the rest of my life. I...I love you, Marina."

"Oh," she breathed softly. Then suddenly her arms were tight around him. "You fool," she murmured. "I've been trying to get you to say that for days. Of course I love you. How could I not love you?"

"Is that a yes?"

"That's a very *adamant* yes."

He grinned at her, that slow, sexy grin from the barbecue, and her heart melted again in her chest. "I love you, Cage."

"Care about me enough to leave painting for a few hours and come make love to me, instead?"

"Hmm. Choices, choices. All right."

"Tease."

"Love of my life."

"Let's go home."

* * * * *

COMING NEXT MONTH

#703 SURVIVE THE NIGHT—Marilyn Pappano
Heartbreakers

Framed! Escaped convict Dillon Boone had no choice but to do the unthinkable: take Ashley Benedict hostage. Her home provided a place to heal his wounds, while her arms promised love and acceptance…if only they could survive the night.

#704 DRIVEN TO DISTRACTION—Judith Duncan
Romantic Traditions

If anything, Maggie Burrows's life was pretty darn sedate. Then Toni Parnelli moved in next door—and immediately put the moves on Maggie. He was a younger man, determined to break all the rules—and more than determined to break down Maggie's reserve.

#705 A COWBOY'S HEART—Doreen Roberts

Sharon Douglass had loved and been left by her cowboy, and now their son wanted to follow in the footsteps of his rodeo-riding father…a father he didn't even know. Then Mac McAllister returned to Sharon's ranch expecting to save the day—but instead he got the shock of his life….

#706 BABY OF THE BRIDE—Kay David

Rachel St. James found herself the proud _almost_-mom of a beautiful baby girl—but with no husband in sight! Desperate for the adoption to go through, she proposed nick-of-time nuptials to friend Paul Delaney. Now the last thing the convenient groom wanted was for their marriage to end….

#707 BLACKWOOD'S WOMAN—Beverly Barton
The Protectors

Though Joanna Beaumont had learned the hard way about life's darker side, she still was every bit the romantic. Especially when it came to cynical J. T. Blackwood. His harsh demeanor beckoned her to heal his wounds—even as she welcomed his tender protection from the terror of her past.

#708 AN HONORABLE MAN—Margaret Watson

She'd ruined his life two years ago, and now Julia Carleton had the audacity to ask for his help. Well, ex-cop Luke McKinley would just have to say _no_. Only he couldn't. Not when his silence could mean harming innocent people…or the woman he'd fallen for, despite the odds.

MILLION DOLLAR SWEEPSTAKES

SWP-M96

It's time you joined...

THE BABY OF THE MONTH CLUB

Silhouette Desire proudly presents *Husband: Optional*, book four of RITA Award-winning author Marie Ferrarella's miniseries, THE BABY OF THE MONTH CLUB, coming your way in March 1996.

She wasn't fooling him. Jackson Cain knew the baby Mallory Flannigan had borne was his...no matter that she *claimed* a conveniently absentee lover was Joshua's true dad. And though Jackson had left her once to "find" his true feelings, nothing was going to keep him away from this ready-made family now....

Do You Take This Child? We certainly hope you do, because in April 1996 Silhouette Romance will feature this final book in Marie Ferrarella's wonderful miniseries, THE BABY OF THE MONTH CLUB, found only in— ▼ *Silhouette*®
™

Silhouette

SPECIAL EDITION ®

™

THE MACKADE BROTHERS

the exciting series by

NEW YORK TIMES BESTSELLING AUTHOR

Nora Roberts

The MacKade Brothers are back—looking for trouble,
and always finding it. Coming this March,
Silhouette Intimate Moments presents

THE HEART OF DEVIN MACKADE

(Intimate Moments #697)

If you liked THE RETURN OF RAFE MACKADE (Silhouette
Intimate Moments #631) and THE PRIDE OF JARED MACK-
ADE (Silhouette Special Edition #1000), you'll love Devin's
story! Then be on the lookout for the final book in the series,
THE FALL OF SHANE MACKADE (Silhouette Special Edition
#1022), coming in April from Silhouette Special Edition.

These sexy, trouble-loving
men heading out to you in
alternating books from
Silhouette Intimate Moments and
Silhouette Special Edition. Watch out for them!

Bestselling author

RACHEL LEE

takes her Conard County series to new heights with

A CONARD COUNTY Reckoning

This March, Rachel Lee brings readers a brand-new, longer-length, out-of-series title featuring the characters from her successful Conard County miniseries.

Janet Tate and Abel Pierce have both been betrayed and carry deep, bitter memories. Brought together by great passion, they must learn to trust again.

"Conard County is a wonderful place to visit! Rachel Lee has crafted warm, enchanting stories. These are wonderful books to curl up with and read. I highly recommend them."
—*New York Times* bestselling author
Heather Graham Pozzessere

Available in March, wherever Silhouette books are sold.

As seen on TV!
Free Gift Offer

With a Free Gift proof-of-purchase from any Silhouette® book, you can receive a beautiful cubic zirconia pendant.

This gorgeous marquise-shaped stone is a genuine cubic zirconia—accented by an 18" gold tone necklace.

(Approximate retail value $19.95)

Send for yours today...
compliments of ▼ *Silhouette*®
™

To receive your free gift, a cubic zirconia pendant, send us one original proof-of-purchase, photocopies not accepted, from the back of any Silhouette Romance™, Silhouette Desire®, Silhouette Special Edition®, Silhouette Intimate Moments® or Silhouette Shadows™ title available in February, March or April at your favorite retail outlet, together with the Free Gift Certificate, plus a check or money order for $1.75 U.S./$2.25 CAN. (do not send cash) to cover postage and handling, payable to Silhouette Free Gift Offer. We will send you the specified gift. Allow 6 to 8 weeks for delivery. Offer good until April 30, 1996 or while quantities last. Offer valid in the U.S. and Canada only.

Free Gift Certificate

Name: _____

Address: _____

City: _____ State/Province: _____ Zip/Postal Code: _____

Mail this certificate, one proof-of-purchase and a check or money order for postage and handling to: SILHOUETTE FREE GIFT OFFER 1996. In the U.S.: 3010 Walden Avenue, P.O. Box 9057, Buffalo NY 14269-9057. In Canada: P.O. Box 622, Fort Erie,

---

FREE GIFT OFFER   079-KBZ-R
ONE PROOF-OF-PURCHASE
To collect your fabulous FREE GIFT, a cubic zirconia pendant, you must include this original proof-of-purchase for each gift with the properly completed Free Gift Certificate.

079-KBZ-R

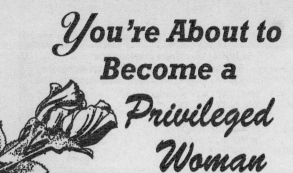

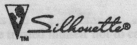